GAMMA QUEST

BOOK 1

LOST AND FOUND

MARVEL®

GAMMA QUEST

BOOK 1
LOST AND FOUND

Greg Cox

Illustrations by George Pérez

MARVEL®

BYRON PREISS MULTIMEDIA COMPANY, INC.
NEW YORK

BERKLEY BOULEVARD BOOKS, NEW YORK

Special thanks to Ginjer Buchanan, John Morgan, Ursula Ward, Mike Thomas, Steve Behling, and Dwight Jon Zimmerman.

X-MEN & THE AVENGERS: GAMMA QUEST
Book 1: LOST AND FOUND

A Berkley Boulevard Book
A Byron Preiss Multimedia Company, Inc. Book

PRINTING HISTORY
Berkley Boulevard paperback edition / July 1999

The Penguin Putnam Inc. World Wide Web site address is
http://www.penguinputnam.com

Check out the Ace Science Fiction/Fantasy newsletter,
and much more, at Club PPI!

ISBN: 0-425-16973-1

BERKLEY BOULEVARD
Berkley Boulevard Books are published by The Berkley Publishing Group,
a division of Penguin Putnam Inc.,
375 Hudson Street, New York, New York 10014.
BERKLEY BOULEVARD and its logo
are trademarks belonging to Penguin Putnam Inc.

PRINTED IN THE UNITED STATES OF AMERICA

10 9 8 7 6 5 4 3 2 1

To my parents,
for countless stops at 7-Eleven to pick up
my weekly comic book fix.
Thanks for going out of your way
to indulge my peculiar hobbies.

"The jaws of darkness do devour it up:
"So quick bright things come to confusion."
——William Shakespeare (1595)

"X-Men, Avengers . . . I will not pretend ours has
been a happy association."
——Ororo Munroe (1993)

ACKNOWLEDGMENTS

Thanks to Keith R.A. DeCandido, for agreeing that Iron Man and his Avenging comrades should meet the X-Men, and the Hulk, too. Thanks also to Marvel, for letting me play with their characters, and to all the various comics writers and artists whose decades of work have given me so much to build upon. And to Julie Bell, for the exciting and inspirational cover art; Sumi Lee, for tips on military hardware; and Marina Frants for yet more scuba advice.

Finally, as always, thanks to Karen and Alex, just because.

A

Chapter One

Waiting impatiently at a busy uptown intersection, Wanda Maximoff was tempted to throw a hex at the traffic lights. One little burst of probability-altering mutant power would change DON'T WALK to WALK easily enough, but that probably wasn't appropriate behavior for a card-carrying member of the Avengers. She could just see the headlines on the front page of the *Daily Bugle:* SCARLET WITCH CAUGHT JAYWALKING. MAYOR DENOUNCES NEW MUTANT MENACE TO PEDESTRIAN SAFETY.

Not that she was in uniform, of course. As near as she could tell, none of the assorted New Yorkers and tourists milling about at the crosswalk recognized her as a practicing super heroine; intent upon their own errands and itineraries, they paid little attention to the tall, auburn-haired woman standing in their midst.

Fine with me, she thought. For today's outing, which promised little in the way of super-powered conflict, she had foregone her distinctive "working clothes" in favor of strictly civilian attire. A stylish trenchcoat, belted at the waist, protected her from the chilly breeze blowing off Central Park while a pair of sensible brown boots insulated her feet from the sidewalk, the toe of one boot now tapping restlessly against the pavement. Reddish-brown curls tumbled past her shoulders. Large silver loops hung beneath her ears, matching the bracelets that jangled around her wrists. The hastily thrown together ensemble was more than suitable to her purposes, although, to be honest, her scalp always felt somewhat naked without the high-pointed headdress she usually wore into battle.

No melees today, Wanda reminded herself. As far as she was concerned, she was taking a personal day. Heinous super-villains and would-be world conquerors would just have to wait their turn; even an Avenger deserved a day off now and then.

The traffic signals changed of their own volition, and she crossed Central Park West, then headed north on Columbus Avenue. Although well into June, the day was overcast and surprisingly cool. Glancing up at the gray skies overhead, Wanda wondered fleetingly if she should have grabbed an umbrella before leaving the mansion. No matter, she decided, even as the first sprinkles of rain began to fall. She would be indoors soon enough.

The Manhattan Museum of Folk Art was located on the Upper West Side, across the park and a few blocks north from Avengers Mansion, her home for many years. Wanda paused for a moment outside the museum's unimposing concrete facade, inspecting the banners on display in the ground-floor windows that flanked its main entrance. As advertised in the Arts section of the *New York Times*, the building was proudly hosting an exhibition titled "Beyond Gepetto: A Century of Eastern European Puppetry."

Just what I came for, she thought.

The pelting raindrops and her own curiosity drove her past a pair of glass doors and into the lobby of the small museum, whose spare white walls and utilitarian design were presumably intended not to call attention away from the homespun art on display. Apparently, neither puppets in particular nor folk art in general were big draws these days; there were few other visitors in attendance. In fact, it looked like she had practically the entire museum to herself.

Just as well, Wanda reflected. *I don't mind a little privacy.*

After making a modest donation at the front desk, she followed a series of helpful signs, past displays of colorful quilts and whimsically-designed weather vanes, until she came to the exhibit that had lured her here.

Hand-carved wooden marionettes, painted in once-vibrant colors that had faded with the passage of decades, adorned the walls of a dead-end gallery near the back of the museum, where the curators no doubt hoped their presence would draw visitors past the institution's other exhibits. The marionettes' jointed legs dangled freely while whittled hands and arms pointed out informative blocks of text affixed to the walls between the puppets. Wanda declined to read the descriptive copy for now, preferring to focus first on the craftsmanship and imagination embodied by the puppets themselves.

As she admired their intricate detail and expressive, if exaggerated, features, she noted that the various artists had largely taken their subjects from the history and folklore of Russia and Eastern Europe: Baba Yaga, the Firebird, Peter and the Wolf, Rasputin, and so on. There was even a miniature puppet version of Dr. Doom, which would surely get its maker a stiff prison sentence if displayed anywhere within the borders of Latveria.

Not a bad likeness, Wanda judged, eyeing the forbidding metallic face beneath the doll-sized green hood, although she knew from personal experience that the real Victor Von Doom was infinitely more intimidating.

Inevitably, the sight of the puppets, so like the ones her adoptive father had made in the dimly-remembered days of her childhood, raised poignant memories in Wanda: memories of Django Maximoff, the kindly gypsy toymaker who had raised her and her brother Pietro after their mother's death during childbirth. Those had been among the happiest days of her far too turbulent life, until that fearful night an angry mob attacked the gypsy camp, separating her and Pietro from the only family they had ever known.

Torches in the night. Gaudily-painted wooden wagons going up in flames. The crackle of burning pitch. Thick smoke filling her lungs, choking her. Furious shouting and screams of terror. The darkness of the forest as they fled in panic, only to fall at last into the freezing river which swept them away. . . .

Wanda shuddered involuntarily. For years, she had repressed her recollections of those days, as her past slid into a morass of confusion and contradictions, but in recent years, as she uncovered more and more about the events that had shaped her youth, the memories had returned as well, sometimes springing forth from her unconscious mind with surprising force and clarity. Gazing now upon the handcrafted figure of the Wolf, its painted tongue hanging comically out of one side of its toothy jaws, it seemed to her that she could practically smell the smoke of the campfire, hear the horses whinny and the tambourines jangling, as she sat upon her now-dead papa's knee.

Her mind in the past, her body in the present, she reached out to touch the Wolf upon the wall. Was it just her imagination, or was the Wolf looking back at her, a feral gleam in its hungry, hand-painted eyes? Her fingertips hovered just out of reach of the hinged wooden jaws.

''Excuse me,'' a voice piped up behind Wanda, yanking her consciousness back to the here and now. She glanced back over her shoulder to discover a young woman, roughly college age or younger, standing behind her. "I'm sorry to bother you," the woman said hesitantly, "but . . . you *are* the Scarlet Witch, aren't you?"

"That's right," Wanda admitted. Engrossed in her memories, she had not even heard the other woman approach. Turning around to face the newcomer, she observed two more young people, about the same age, looking on from a few yards away while whispering furtively to each other.

Not quite as brave as their friend, Wanda guessed. Apparently, the museum was better attended than she had first thought. Art students, Wanda surmised, or maybe just broke college kids looking for a cheap diversion on a lazy Saturday morning.

"Wow," the boldest of the students exclaimed. She wore a faded Lila Cheney tee-shirt and a pair of kneeless black jeans. Tiny silver rings pierced the skin above one eye. "Would you mind?" she began, holding out a sketch pad and a felt-tipped pen. "I mean, could I have your autograph?"

"Why, certainly," Wanda said graciously, accepting the proffered pen and pad. Despite years spent in America, her voice still held a trace of a Balkan accent. "To whom shall I address it?"

"Janine," the fan answered, wide-eyed. Wanda greeted the interruption with good humor; she realized that, as an Avenger, she was definitely a public figure. Sometimes she wondered if, at the onset of her colorful career, she should have assumed a mask and secret identity like Tony Stark and Steve Rogers and some of her other colleagues. No, she decided once again—her life had been complicated enough without adding the difficulties of a dual identity to the mix.

TO JANINE, she wrote. WITH BEST WISHES, THE SCARLET WITCH. She had learned long ago that autograph seekers preferred the somewhat exotic alias to her legal signature.

All part of good public relations, she mused. Captain America would surely approve. She handed back the pad and writing implement even as, out of the corner of her eye, she thought she spotted a shadow moving on the adjacent wall.

What's that? she wondered, but when she looked to the side all she saw were the Rasputin and Baba Yaga puppets hanging as lifelessly as they had before. But wait—hadn't the scaly chicken legs dangling beneath the witch's mobile hut been positioned slightly differently the last time she had looked at them? Wanda tried to remember. . . .

"Thanks!" Janine enthused, eagerly reclaiming her prize and shooting a triumphant grin at her two lurking cohorts. Her jubilant eyes devoured the inscription. "This is so great! I've been a fan of yours for, like, forever. Even before you were one of the good guys."

Ouch, Wanda thought. Even though her beaming fan clearly meant well, the longtime heroine could have done without that reminder of her dubious days as one of the charter members of the Brotherhood of Evil Mutants. So much had happened to her since those distant nights around the gypsy campfire. Many hardwon victories to be proud of, true, but also too much tragedy and heartache.

Perhaps I was never intended to be happy, she thought ruefully, *but to defend the happiness of ordinary people like this girl.*

Then, without warning, the excitement in Janine's eyes turned to shock and fear. Her face went pale and her mouth fell open, while behind the young woman her two friends looked frightened as well. One of them screamed and dropped an armful of textbooks, his panicky shout echoing through the hushed atmosphere of the museum.

A severe overreaction to my notorious past, Wanda wondered momentarily, *or something else altogether?* She spun around just in time to see the puppets leaping impossibly from the wall, using their tiny legs to propel themselves straight at Wanda, attacking her. Closest to her, the wooden Wolf lunged for her throat.

Her reflexes trained by years of hand-to-hand combat against everything from Norse gods to the Lunatic Legion, she batted the fanged marionette away with the back of her hand, sending it skittering across the tile floor several yards away. But she could not stop its companion puppet, carved in the cherubic image of Peter the child huntsman, from landing heavily upon her shoulder and grabbing onto her reddish-brown tresses. The Peter puppet yanked her hair across her face, obscuring her vision while he tugged on its roots.

"Run!" Wanda shouted to Janine and other students. Suddenly, the museum was no place for civilians. She clutched at Peter, who was now straddling her neck piggyback-style, choking Wanda with her own hair, until she managed to pry him off her shoulders at the cost of two miniature handfuls of hair. Discarding the auburn curls, he snagged one of her silver earrings, ripping it from the tender lobe.

"Aiee!" the Scarlet Witch cried out. The pain distracted her, made it hard to call up her powers, but she hurled the marionette away with all the force she could muster, hoping the wooden simulacrum would shatter upon the hard, gray tiles.

No such luck. The oaken boy bounced twice upon the tiles, then sprung back onto his feet, joining Rasputin and Baba Yaga as they rushed across the floor at her. Unlike the playthings she recalled, these marionettes required neither strings nor visible puppeteer to give them animation. The gnarled head of the Russian witch protruded from the thatch roof of her doll-sized hut as it hurried forward atop oversized hen's legs, taking the lead from Rasputin and Peter. Malevolent cackling escaped, absurdly, from Baba Yaga's wooden lips. Painted yellow eyes leered above a jagged nose crowned by a bulging wart. The hut took a flying leap, the claws of the chicken's feet extended at Wanda's face.

You're giving us witches a bad name, she thought, ducking out of the way. Her hands came up to form a protective hex, but all at once the Firebird was flapping its gilded wings in her face, pecking at her eyes. At the same time, wooden jaws closed around her ankle, pointed teeth digging through her leather boot. *The Wolf,* she realized, trying to shake her leg free even as she snapped her face from side to side, striving to keep her eyes away from the Firebird's angry beak.

Who could be responsible for this? she wondered, her eyes tightly shut, grabbing unsuccessfully at the sound of the flapping wings. The Puppet Master? The Brothers Grimm? There was no time to even try to decipher the mystery. Between the Wolf gnawing on her leg and the Firebird jabbing at her face, she couldn't begin to think straight, let alone play detective.

The witch's hut rejoined the fray, clawing at Wanda's back, and she was grateful that she had chosen to wear the heavy coat instead of her somewhat skimpier gypsy garb. Despite her own peril, she feared for her comrades as well.

The others might be in danger, too, she realized. An attack on one Avenger often meant an assault on the entire team. *I need to alert Captain America and the rest.* There was a communication device in one of her coat pockets, but how could she get at it when she had to defend herself from these homicidal Pinocchios?

Her face turned downward, eyes squeezed shut, she forced herself to ignore the fangs and the claws and the beak and the flapping wings, putting aside the sharp, jabbing pains so that she could concentrate on a hex. Her fingers instinctively formed the right configuration, the gestures focusing her unique mutant ability to manipulate the laws of probability.

Even after countless efforts and exercises to hone her special gifts, she still had trouble describing what it felt like when she used her birthright. It was like breathing, in a way—you didn't think about it, you just did it. Wanda visualized the effect she desired, then let the power flow from somewhere deep inside her out to her fingertips, which tingled slightly as they released her mutant magic into the world.

The power manifested first as a shimmering sphere of crimson light that spread outward to enclose both the Scarlet Witch and her attackers. Within that sphere, mathematical probabilities shifted so that the most unlikely of possibilities became not just likely but an absolute certainty.

The Firebird's crystalline eyes blinked in surprise as an extremely improbable fluctuation in the air currents stole the wind from beneath its wings, causing it to drop like a stone, fortuitously slamming into the wooden Wolf at the very moment that, behind Wanda, Baba Yaga's ambulatory hut lost its balance and toppled forward. Her foot at last freed from the jaws of the Wolf, the Scarlet Witch deftly evaded the falling marionette so that it landed in a heap upon its fellow puppets.

The odds that three such happy accidents would combine to rid Wanda of her attackers simultaneously were ridiculously small, of course, except within the radius of her hex sphere.

That's better, she thought. The rose-colored radiance dissipated as she took a deep breath to collect her thoughts before the murderous marionettes regrouped. At last, she had a moment to try to figure out what was happening and why?

Who is behind this? She sensed no sorcerous energies at work, but some force had to have brought the seemingly harmless puppets to life. Telekinesis? Nanotechnology? Her mind grappled for a solution, even as she readied herself the puppets' next attack. There were too many possibilities, too many enemies old and new.

These might not even be marionettes at all, she surmised, *but cleverly disguised android assassins.*

Floodlights mounted into the ceiling called attention to the empty stretches of wall that the puppets had occupied only moments before.

Thank heavens I didn't go to the Natural History Museum instead. She could just imagine the dinosaur fossils and stuffed mammoths coming to life in place of the puppets.

Her fingers groped through her coat pockets in search of her Avengers I.D. card, which also doubled as a communications device, thanks to the ingenuity of Tony Stark.

If she hurried, she could still alert the team before the puppets came at her again. Manicured nails, painted in her trademark shade of red, tapped against the laminated surface of the card, and she had just started to draw it out of the pocket when she heard someone call out in alarm:

"Help! Keep away from me!"

The Scarlet Witch glanced back over her shoulder, where her cape usually was, and saw Janine cornered by puppet replicas of Rasputin and Ivan the Terrible. *Blast,* Wanda thought. The starstruck fan must have stayed behind to watch her heroine in action. Now, Rasputin and Ivan, brandishing miniature daggers, had backed the college student up against a glass display case on the opposite side of the gallery. Wanda wasn't sure what frightened the poor girl more: the puppets' hostile intent and weapons, or the fact that they were alive at all.

Just to complicate matters, a security guard, whom Wanda had seen posted in the lobby earlier, came running around the corner, only to come to an abrupt halt at the bizarre sight that greeted him. Pistol in hand, he froze, uncertain what to do.

Wanda sympathized with his confusion. *He was surely hired to protect the exhibits from the patrons, not the other way around!*

"Stay back," she warned him, flashing her I.D. "This is Avengers business. Let me handle it."

Not waiting to hear his response, she unleashed another hex at the puppets menacing Janine. The floodlights above the predatory marionettes suddenly exploded, showering Ivan and Rasputin with white-hot sparks that nevertheless missed Janine entirely.

Am I good or am I good? the Scarlet Witch thought, smiling with satisfaction as the puppets retreated frantically from the rain of sparks, whiffs of smoke rising from their wooden heads and shoulders. *But after all, they're only puppets,* she reminded herself. Maybe she didn't need any other Avengers after all.

"Get her out of here," she instructed the security guard, who hurried to comply. This time, Janine seemed perfectly willing to flee the scene. Keeping one eye on the smoldering forms of Ivan and Rasputin, not to mention the tangle of fallen puppets at her feet, Wanda breathed a sigh of relief as both guard and fan exited from sight. She still had no idea what force had animated the marionettes and until she did, she didn't want to have to worry about innocent bystanders.

I can take care of myself, no matter who is behind this. Ordinary humans are different.

An overwhelming blast of concussive force, striking her at the base of her neck, shattered her confidence and sent her reeling forward. Gray institutional tiles seemed to rush at her face as darkness encroached on the periphery of her vision, casting the stark white walls into shadow. Her I.D. card slipped from her fingers.

Of course, she recalled right before she blacked out. *That blasted Doom puppet . . . !*

A

Chapter Two

He crouched in the underbrush, sniffing the scent of his prey.

That way, he thought, nodding to himself. *Just like I figured.*

Most hunters might have never noticed the subtle deer path winding through the trees and bushes ahead of him, but Logan was the best there was at what he did.

The dense wilderness of the Adirondacks surrounded him. Towering pines and spruce trees branched out high above his head to form a verdant canopy that shielded the forest floor from the afternoon sun. A light breeze rustled through the branches, carrying with it a dozen separate aromas, each distinct and recognizable to Logan's keen sense of smell. Out of sight, but not beyond earshot, a mountain stream rushed through the woods somewhere ahead. Logan could practically taste the cold, clear water.

It doesn't get much better than this, he thought, a rare smile creasing his rugged yet ageless features. Twin peaks of bristling black hair rose from his scalp, looking like the vee-shaped points of the mask he often wore. Logan savored the primeval sanctity of the untamed wilderness, along with the sense of solitude. Here in the woods of upstate New York, it was easy to fool himself into thinking that he was the only two-legged mammal around for hundreds of miles.

Yeah, I needed this, he decided, breathing in the clean, intoxicating aroma of the trees and loam, so similar to that of the Canadian timberlands he had long ago called home. Even though he was no longer quite the loner he once was, thanks to Professor Charles Xavier and his X-Men, sometimes he still needed to put some distance between himself and other people, mutant or otherwise, and get back to his roots. *This is where I really belong. In the wild.*

His heightened senses revealed all the secrets of the woods to him. A whiff of wintergreen in the air announced the presence of a stand of yellow birch to the west, while his ears detected squirrels scurrying through the branches overhead. His fingers brushed against the scaly bark of a tall white pine, guessing the tree's approximate age from the feel of the bark. Probing gray eyes penetrated the shade, spotting the spoor of his prey as it led away to the north.

They were here less than an hour ago, he estimated. *I'm gaining on them.*

Rising from his crouch, Logan took off through the forest, moving with practiced speed and stealth. His well-worn cowboy boots trod softly upon a carpet of twigs, pine cones, and fallen needles, making little or no sound as he followed the trail. He had left his Wolverine uniform behind in Westchester; a red flannel shirt and faded Levi's were all he needed for this hunting expedition. Besides, he wouldn't want to give any stray hikers or forest rangers a heart attack by surprising them in his X-Men gear.

We're unpopular enough as is, he thought.

The deer path led uphill, toward the peak. Logan came upon the stream he had heard earlier, cutting its way through the sylvan landscape, and paused only long enough to take a couple of deep mouthfuls of the icy water, which was just as refreshing as he had imagined. *Like a cool beer on a hot day,* he decided. Licking the last drops of moisture from his lips, he waded across the stream, then headed up-country. If his prey had thought that the flowing water would throw him off the trail, they were in for a big surprise.

Scotch pine and aspen gave way to balsam and paper birch as he climbed the mountain, gaining elevation. Snow-white flowers bloomed from the occasional mountain ash growing along the trail, a sure sign of springtime. Logan sniffed the air again and nodded to himself. He was getting closer. Hunching over, his flared nostrils scouting ahead of him, he stalked forward even more quietly than before.

Easy does it, he counseled himself. The last thing he wanted to do was startle his prey as soon as he caught up with them. Retracted for the moment, his claws itched within their metal sheaths.

The timberland opened up before him, exposing an open meadow awash in golden sunshine. Sneaking up to the edge of the glade, Logan knelt behind a fallen log, its rotting carcass covered with moss and mushrooms, and peered with feral satisfaction at the sight of a family of deer—doe, fawn, and even, surprisingly, a buck—grazing upon the wild grass near the center of the clearing.

Gotcha! he thought, eyes narrowing. *Almost.*

Logan, sometimes known as Wolverine, ached to unsheathe his claws and pounce upon his prey with all the ferocity of his namesake, but more civilized habits prevailed. He seldom hunted to kill anymore, at least where dumb animals were concerned; it was sport enough to track a deer through miles of wilderness, until he came close enough to touch the skittish creature without being detected first. Not as satisfying, perhaps, as indulging his predatory instincts to the full, but enough of a challenge to make it interesting.

'*Sides,* he thought, *what'd Bambi and family ever do to me?* These days, he preferred to reserve his claws for those folks that really deserved them, like Magneto, for instance, or the Hellfire Club.

Officially, deer hunting season did not begin until winter, but the law didn't say anything about just tracking the animals. Logan liked it better this time of year, when he didn't have to worry about any trigger-happy weekend warriors tromping through the woods, shooting at anything that moved. *I've got the whole forest to myself, just the way I like it.*

This close, the musky scent of the deer was almost overwhelming. Logan started to creep around the lichen-wrapped log, then paused and sniffed once more. A scowl creased his feature; something wasn't right. The deer smelled like deer, all right, but the pungent odor was almost too pure, like someone had distilled the essence of deer musk and sprayed it on the trio of animals grazing a few yards away. Logan couldn't smell any evidence of fleas or ticks or even dried deer droppings; it was like all three deer had been raised, or at least painstakingly groomed, in a pristine laboratory environment, instead of the wilds of the Adirondacks.

There was something vaguely wrong about this perfect little domestic tableau—what was the buck doing here, hanging out with his family? Typically, adult male deer went their own way.

Maybe I'm just getting paranoid in my old age, Logan thought, *but I don't like the smell of this.* As far as he knew, nobody but nobody knew where he was right now, not even his fellow X-Men; still, he'd made plenty of enemies in his time, and he was too smart to underestimate any of them. There was always a chance that these harmless-looking deer were being used as bait in a trap. *Maybe I'll get a chance to use my claws after all,* he thought hopefully, looking forward to a good scrap.

Retreat was not an option. He had tracked this game too far to give up now. More importantly, if this was a trap he wanted to know who was behind it. A frontal assault, even into the jaws of danger, was better than looking back over your shoulder all the time, at least as far as Logan was concerned.

Let's get on with it, he decided.

Getting down on all fours, his nose only inches from the fragrant soil, he slipped around the overgrown log and into the tall grass. He crept through the clearing on his hands and knees, eating up the distance between him and the grazing deer. His senses and reflexes were geared up to razor-sharp intensity, yet he could detect nothing in the vicinity except a few birds and rodents here and there. If an ambush was in the works, he sure as blazes didn't know where it could come from; there was nothing here but the deer.

The fawn, its tawny fur still spotted with patches of white, was the closest to Logan. Balancing awkwardly on four spindly limbs, it nibbled on the grass within the protective shadow of its mother and father. So far, none of the animals appeared aware of Logan's approach, which was just the way he liked it. He came within reach of the baby deer, then stretched his fingers toward the fawn's flanks.

Here goes nothing, he thought, suspecting that the trap, if any, would be sprung once the deer reacted to his presence.

Before he even touched the unsuspecting animal, however, that unlikely father deer lunged at Logan, his head lowered so that an impressive rack of antlers came straight at the crouching mutant. The deep-throated roar of the attacking buck sounded in Logan's ears. He was only a heartbeat away from being gored.

"I knew it," he muttered. Something wasn't right about that buck.

Snikt. Matching sets of twelve-inch steel claws emerged from the backs of his hands as he swiped out at the oncoming antlers, responding instinctively to the threat. The sharpened edges of his claws sliced off the points of the antlers, sending the bony tips flying off into the scrub. The buck reared up on its hind legs, kicking out at Wolverine with its forward hooves. He threw himself backward, dodging the blow, and scrambled to his feet; mutant healing factor or not, he didn't feel like having his adamantium skull slammed by a two-hundred-pound deer.

What's this about? Logan speculated. Primal aggression from a protective papa or something more sinister? He glanced quickly to each side, but saw no sign of any human attackers—or inhuman, for that matter. Maybe, just maybe, all he had to deal with was some irate wildlife. That would be easy enough to handle. The only tricky part would be resisting the temptation to lash back with deadly force against an animal protecting his family. He clenched his fists, keeping the claws raised in front of him. There were three on each hand, all six poised to strike out at all comers. He had killed more than deer with those claws. . . .

Then, before his startled eyes, the buck's severed antlers *grew back* until they were even larger and more lethal-looking than before.

"That cinches it," Wolverine muttered. This was no

ordinary deer and the whole altercation was no isolated incident; hostile agencies were at work. And Bambi's father wasn't just bait, either. He was part of the ambush, maybe the most important part.

Lowering his head, the buck charged again at Wolverine, who braced himself for the attack, shining silver claws extended.

"Come and get me," he growled. "I smell venison on the menu."

A sudden impact, followed by agonizing pain, caught him by surprise as *another* set of antlers stabbed him in the back, tearing through the flannel shirt to gouge the skin and muscle below, the bony horns lodging deeply into his flesh, barely missing his spine.

"What the—?" he gasped, glancing backwards to see who or what had gored him.

Impossibly, it was none other than the fawn, now twice its previous size and equipped with antlers fully as large as its apparent father. Only yards away, the doe was also growing a rack of antlers, the bony tines extruding from the female deer's skull at an unnatural rate.

Kind of like Marrow, he thought instantly, the freakish sight forcibly reminding him of that disagreeable mutant rebel and the bony protuberances that spontaneously erupted through her skin. *But since when have there been mutant deer?*

Impaled upon the transformed fawn's horns, Wolverine tried to pull himself free, but the fawn reared up, dragging the hero's boots off the ground below, making it harder to get any kind of leverage. He gritted his teeth against the shock and pain of the antlers tearing through his flesh; his rapid healing factor couldn't repair the damage until he got the injured tissue away from the antlers. Meanwhile, bright arterial blood streamed down his back, soaking his shirt, while the original buck came stampeding toward him.

Jaw clenched as tightly as his fists, Wolverine yanked his entire upper body forward, ignoring the stabbing shrieks of pain racing through his nervous system. The convulsive effort ripped him free of the transformed fawn's antlers and he dropped onto the grass below—just in time to be gored in the chest by the onrushing buck.

A savage howl escaped his frothing lips as the points of the antlers dug into his ribcage. He slashed out wildly with his claws, but whatever wounds he inflicted on the buck's neck and shoulders closed almost as fast as he opened them; it was like slicing through some sort of living jelly.

An adaptoid? he guessed desperately. *A new kind of organic Sentinel?* The metallic scent of his own blood inflamed his senses, driving reason and intellect from his mind. He became an enraged animal, fighting to survive.

His preternatural healing factor kicked in, the gashes on Wolverine's back were already knitting up, staunching the flow of blood. But the lessening of the pain from those injuries was more than overpowered by the impact of two sets of hoofs pounding against the back of his head. While the buck stabbed him in the chest, both the doe and the fawn kicked at him from behind, their hoofs slamming again and again upon his skull. It felt like the Juggernaut was pounding on his head while Sabretooth clawed at his heart simultaneously.

It was too much even for his legendary endurance.

Funny, Wolverine thought, in one last burst of consciousness before darkness descended, *I thought I was hunting them. . . .*

Chapter Three

No one knew her real name, and the woman now known as Rogue preferred to keep it that way. Truth to tell, she rarely thought of herself as anyone *but* Rogue these days.

'Cept when I've got someone else's memories stuck in my head, she thought.

At the moment, thank goodness, her mind was her own, although she could barely hear herself think over the noisy chatter and confusion of the crowded West Village street fair in which she was presently immersed. Milling New Yorkers, ranging from college kids to senior citizens, and packed shoulder-to-shoulder, jostled and nudged their way past each other, between rows of covered booths hawking everything from hot Thai food to used books and LPs. Hucksters called out to passersby, pitching free massages, cheap phone cards, Peruvian sweaters and pottery, cold lemonade, baby clothes, comic books, keyrings, wallets, refrigerator magnets, strawberry crepes, antique movie posters, ice cream, blue jeans, and just about anything else Rogue could imagine. The booths lined both sides of Waverly Place between Broadway and Sixth Avenue, blocking her view of aging brownstones to the north and Washington Square Park to the south. The fair on Waverly, which had been closed off to traffic for the afternoon, had drawn a sizable crowd of shoppers and sightseers, including at least one mutant heroine from the suburbs.

Nothing like a little bargain-hunting to take one's mind off the super hero biz, Rogue thought, pausing to admire some reasonably priced turquoise jewelry; she was glad she had taken the train in from Westchester that morning. The sky, which had threatened rain earlier that morning, had cleared up, bathing the entire fair in sunshine. *Wolvie has the right idea going walkabout and all. It's not healthy to stay cooped up at the Institute all the time.* She had better things to do this afternoon than run through another training exercise in the Danger Room.

Too bad I couldn't talk Ororo into joining me, she thought, but the weather goddess had been too busy with her beloved garden to waste a day in the city. Still, it was nice to have some time on her own, especially after all the X-Men had gone through recently. Like that whole time-travel mess with Spider-Man last year, or that ugly business with Mr. Sinister . . .

"See anything you like?" the jewelry dealer asked her, leaning forward over his wares. Despite the Native American designs of the rings and necklaces, the dealer looked more Pakistani than Apache. He raised a glittering trinket from a velvet-lined wooden tray. "Earrings are only $15 a pair. Very cheap!"

It would take a diamond drill to pierce my *ears,* she thought, shaking her head. "No thanks. Ah'm just lookin'," she added with a smile, her melodious drawl betraying her origins somewhere below the Mason-Dixon line.

Rejoining the stream of pedestrians flowing by, she left the jewelry booth behind, blending in with the crowd, or so she thought. A couple of teenage boys, hanging out around a used-CD stand, looking for bootleg tapes of their favorite bands, whistled appreciatively as she walked past them.

Trust me, sugar, y'all don't want to be getting too close

to me. Rogue sighed ruefully, running a hand through the bleached white skunktail running down the middle of her long brown hair; one kiss from her lips would sure suck the swagger from those boys, all right, along with what passed for their minds. *Look, but don't touch, honey. The story of my life . . .*

Even though her mutant body was immune to extremes of heat and cold, she had on a long-sleeved sweater and gloves. Manhattan was way too cramped to do otherwise; she couldn't risk brushing any exposed skin against that of some poor stranger, not without taking a chance of absorbing all their memories and strength. *Not exactly the kind of souvenir I was hoping to pick on this little shopping trip,* she thought wryly.

Rogue was treating herself to some freshly roasted corn-on-the-cob, the melted butter dripping between the fingers of her glove, when she heard the angry shouting. At first she thought it was just another streetside salesman trying to attract the attention of the fairgoers, but there was a harsh edge to the yelling, very much at odds with the festive atmosphere of the fair, that caught her ear.

Some kind of trouble? she wondered, and began edging her way through the crowd toward the source of shouts. Maybe there was something she could do to help. . . .

Packed in with several dozen other people, including a young mother pushing a slow-moving stroller, it took her a couple of minutes to get close enough to the speaker to make out the words. As she did so, her expression darkening, an all too familiar rage awoke inside her.

"Wake up, America!" a man's voice bellowed. "Do you know *what* your children are? Don't sit back and let *mutants* take over our world. This is your fight, too! Fight the mutant menace! Join now!"

There were still plenty of firm yellow kernels left on the cob, but Rogue had lost her appetite. *Can't I ever get away from this garbage?* She chucked the half-eaten ear of corn into a dented metal trash bin, then followed the venomous rant to its point of origin: a portable booth staffed and sponsored, at least according to the banner running along its top, by the anti-mutant hate group who called themselves the Friends of Humanity.

Tee-shirts, pamphlets, buttons, bumper stickers, and posters adorned the booth and were also spread out on a tabletop facing the street. Rogue quickly scanned the slogans printed on the assorted paraphernalia, feeling her blood pressure rise with every malicious word she read:

MEN WERE CREATED EQUAL, NOT MUTANTS.
100 PERCENT HUMAN—AND PROUD OF IT.
REMEMBER THE ONSLAUGHT!
FIRST THE NEANDERTHALS,
NOW HOMO SAPIENS?
OPEN YOUR EYES—FOR HUMANITY'S SAKE.
SECOND PLACE NEVER COUNTS IN EVOLUTION.
SUPPORT THE MUTANT REGISTRATION ACT.

Phony wanted posters sported slightly doctored news photos of Magneto, Apocalypse, Sauron, and even some of her fellow X-Men, especially the less human-looking ones like the Beast and Nightcrawler. (Granted, it wasn't too hard to make Wolverine look scary.) Rogue was half-amused/half-disgusted to see a cartoonish artist's rendering of herself that made her look like a horror movie vampire, complete with fangs and pointed ears.

No fair, she thought. *I haven't looked like that since the last time I tussled with Sabretooth. Besides, my hips aren't nearly that big. . . .* On a deeper level, she felt torn between anger and nausea at the sight of the same old lies and insults being dished out once more. *You'd think people would be fed up with this stuff by now.*

The loudmouth manning the booth, a petition in one hand and a donation tin in the other, was hardly a prime specimen of ordinary humanity. Stuffed pretentiously into a three-piece suit that seemed one size too small for him, the man was red-faced and sweating, too full of simmering bigotry and resentment to possibly look at ease in his own skin.

"You there, miss," he said, making eye contact with Rogue. Thankfully, he didn't seem to be doing too much business right now; most everybody else looked more interested in snacking and shopping. "Would you like to support the Friends of Humanity?"

You're no friend of mine, she thought, fuming. She knew she should just walk away, leave this prejudiced peabrain to stew in his own stinking bile, but it was too late for that now. She strode toward the booth, clenching her fists. Why should she be the only one whose afternoon was spoiled?

"You ever met a mutant?" she challenged him. The press of the crowd squeezed her forward until she was squeezed against the edge of the table, her face only inches away from the so-called Friend of Humanity. She rested her palm on a stack of folded tee-shirts, not worried all that much about getting excess butter all over them. "You ever got to know one?"

"That's not necessary," the man said smugly, appearing all too happy to have an audience at last, even a hostile one. "I know everything I need to know." He put down his petition and waved a pamphlet in her face.

Heavy black letters advertised THE TRUTH ABOUT THE COMING GENE WAR. "The mutant menace is the greatest threat that humanity has ever faced. That's a matter of fact. Every time a mutant is born, humanity as we know it comes a little closer to extinction."

Right now that doesn't sound like such a bad idea, Rogue thought. "You ever think that mutants are no different than anybody else, 'cept for a coupla extra powers or somethin'?" She glared at him with furious green eyes, and wondered if any other mutants, unknown to her, had come to the fair today, only to have this kind of senseless animosity thrown in their faces. She could just imagine how devastating this clown's propaganda could be to some poor kid still coming to terms with his new abilities. *I've been an X-Man for years now, and a mutant for even longer, and it still gets to me.* "Some of the best people ah know are mutants."

"Then you're either naive or foolish," the FoH declared. His pig-like eyes narrowed suspiciously. "Or one of *them.*"

"And what if ah was?" she shot back, seeing a hint of fear chip away at the man's self-righteous demeanor. He stepped backward away from the table, his gaze darting from the woman in front of him to the vamp-like caricature of Rogue emblazoned on one of the tee-shirts up for sale.

At least, she acknowledged, giving the shocked hate merchant a conspiratorial wink, *they got the white streak in my hair right.*

"Get away from me!" the man said, his ruddy complexion going pale as recognition sunk in. He backed away from the table until he ran into the plastic tarp at the rear of the booth. "You don't dare hurt me. We have people everywhere. Friends in high places . . ."

Tell me about it, she thought. Sometimes it seemed like half the federal budget was going to bankroll new Sentinel projects and mutant eradication schemes. Rogue was tempted to tear the flimsy booth apart with her (sort of) bare hands, then take off into the sky, giving this two-legged varmint the shock of his useless life, but, no, that would just confirm all his worst fantasies about berserk mutant monsters on the loose. Instead, she contented herself with wadding up the "Rogue" tee-shirt in her fist and hurling the offending garment at the cowering FoH with just a fraction of her superhuman strength.

The last thing she expected was for the shirt to come flying back at her.

Flapping its fabric like the wings of an albino bat, the white tee-shirt reversed course in midair and rocketed straight at Rogue, wrapping itself around her face. She reached up to pull it away only to discover that the shirts on the table had come alive as well, swaddling both her hands so that she could barely move her fingers. Blinded and disoriented, she flailed out with her arms—and heard one of the metal posts supporting the booth crumple before the force of her blow.

"Ah don't believe this!" she tried to exclaim, but the fabric stretched across her face muffled her words. She felt more of the anti-mutant tee-shirts attack her all too literally, wrapping layer after layer of animated cotton and polyester around her head, cutting off her air.

I can't breathe! she realized.

Shouts and screams from the crowd penetrated the cocoon engulfing her head.

"Watch out! She's a mutant!" the Friend of Humanity hollered, like this was her fault or something.

One corner of the canopy over his booth sagged forward, bouncing harmlessly off the suffocating shroud of shirts that had thrown her into airless darkness. She tried to grab at the wrappings, but her hands might as well have been wearing padded boxing gloves for all the good they did her. She swung one arm down violently, hoping to shake off the clinging garments, but succeeded only in splitting the plywood tabletop right down the middle. Pamphlets and pins spilled onto the toes of her boots.

Careful there! she reminded herself, despite a growing sense of panic. Lashing out blindly like this, it would be too easy to injure some innocent fairgoer with her superstrength. *I need room to cut loose.*

Figuring the sky would be less crowded than the street, she flew straight upward, using her innate ability to defy gravity. Her abrupt take-off provoked another round of frightened gasps and shrieks from the teeming masses below. And still the obnoxious hate-monger manning the shattered booth wouldn't give it a rest.

"Mutant freak!" he called out. "They're everywhere, just like I said!"

I wish, Rogue thought. Frankly, she could use a little X-assistance right now. Although airborne, she still couldn't breathe, couldn't see. She wished desperately that Cyclops was close enough for her to grab onto; she wouldn't mind borrowing his high-powered eyebeams for just a second or two, so she could blast her blindfolds to smithereens. Instead all she could do was paw uselessly at the enveloping hood with swaddled hands, while her lungs cried out for oxygen.

Even Ms. Marvel couldn't survive without air, she thought, recalling the unlucky heroine from whom Rogue

33

had stolen her invulnerability and strength. *I'm blacking out. . . .*

Terrified pigeons, roosted atop and around Washington Square Arch, vacated the premises in a frantic flurry of wings, but Rogue was not awake to hear the panicky flapping. Unconscious, she plummeted to earth like a meteor, smashing through the top of the marble arch before carving out a crater, several feet deep, in the center of the park. The crater was still there, surrounded by smoking chunks of displaced pavement, when police arrived on the scene only minutes later. Shattered fragments of marble littered the ground beneath the broken monument, which now resembled two jagged pillars instead of an arch. Sculpted figures of George Washington, portrayed as both general and president, looked on in mute disapproval.

But Rogue was gone.

Chapter Four

"**A**vengers Assemble!"

The hallowed battlecry came readily to Iron Man's lips as he came within sight of Avengers Mansion. The crimson and golden sheen of his metallic armor glistened in the sunlight, reflecting the blue sky above him and the bustling city streets below, where excited pedestrians stopped in their tracks to stare and point at the armored Avenger as he soared by overhead. Micro-turbine jets in his boots propelled him over Fifth Avenue until he was directly above the venerable townhouse that had long served as headquarters for "Earth's Mightiest Heroes," as the tabloids loved to call the Avengers.

Beats "Earth's Lousiest Losers," he thought. As both a veteran super hero and, as billionaire Tony Stark, a successful businessman, he knew the value of good publicity. Even *Daily Bugle* publisher J. Jonah Jameson, that inveterate campaigner against costumed vigilantes, seldom had a bad word to say about the Avengers.

The mansion was only a short flight away from Stark's corporate offices in the Flatiron district; still, he wouldn't have begrudged the trip even if he had needed to fly across half the state to get here.

I've made my fair share of mistakes over the years, he reflected, *especially in my personal life, but one thing I can never regret is helping to found the Avengers.*

The team had done a lot of good for humanity, including saving the entire planet on more occasions than he could recall. Iron Man looked forward to meeting again with his fellow heroes, even as he wondered what sort of crisis had inspired Captain America to call the team together today. Cap's summons had not included any details.

Iron Man's boots touched down on the reinforced concrete heliport nestled amid the Gothic spires of the mansion. Moving with surprising ease for a man wrapped from head to toe in a state-of-the-art suit of combat armor, he approached a doorway a few yards away. Concealed security devices, designed by Stark himself, scanned Iron Man discreetly, confirming his identity before permitting him entry to the mansion. He descended a short flight of wooden stairs to the top floor, where he was greeted by a balding, middle-aged man clad in a conservative, impeccably pressed tuxedo.

"Good afternoon, sir," he said to Iron Man with an upper-class British accent, looking neither surprised nor intimidated by Iron Man's robotic appearance. "Welcome back."

"Thank you, Jarvis," Iron Man replied. The butler had been an indispensable fixture of the old Stark family mansion since before Tony donated the house to the Avengers. Iron Man couldn't imagine the mansion without him. "I hope I haven't kept everyone waiting."

"That seems unlikely, sir," Edwin Jarvis assured him. He glanced at his brass pocketwatch. "I believe the others are just now gathering in the meeting room."

Iron Man knew the way by heart, so he marched down a long, carpeted corridor lined with polished oak paneling and framed portraits of many of the Avengers' most famous alumni, such as Hercules, Wonder Man, Tigra, and the notorious Black Widow.

Wonder what Natasha is up to these days? he wondered as his eyes, peering out through two slits in his gilded faceplate, fell upon the latter portrait; he hadn't seen the Widow since that nasty clash with the Mandarin several weeks back. The thick olive carpeting absorbed the heavy tread of his iron boots until he came to a pair of sturdy double doors. His crimson gauntlet closed gently upon a crystal doorknob as he let himself in.

In contrast to the tasteful Old World elegance of the corridor outside, the meeting room looked like something out of a science-fiction movie. Banks of sophisticated computer circuitry and monitors covered the walls and ceiling, lighted control panels blinking on and off, while the room was dominated by a large chrome table, the top of which was emblazoned by a stylized capital "A." Egg-shaped metal chairs, designed to support the weight of even the Hulk if necessary, surrounded the futuristic round table. Iron Man's boots rang against the shining stainless-steel tiles beneath his feet as he crossed the room.

The chairs were all empty now, but not the room itself. Iron Man immediately recognized the imposing figure standing on the opposite side of the table, his athletic figure proudly wearing the red-white-and-blue colors of the nation he had served and protected for over fifty years. A single white star glittered upon his chest, surrounded by a shirt of bright blue chain mail. Vertical red and white stripes girded his waist while a symbolic eagle wing rose from each side of his blue cowl. Flared red gloves and boots completed the ensemble.

"Hello, Tony," Captain America said warmly. "Thanks for coming on such short notice."

"No problem," Iron Man said. The vocalizer in his mouthpiece distorted his voice, giving him a forbidding, mechanical tone. He took advantage of the mansion's privacy, protected by dozens of electronic countermeasures, by unlocking the metallic seals at the base of his helmet. Removing the headpiece, he placed it gently on the surface of the table, revealing handsome features distinguished by a trim black mustache and beard. A face often seen on the cover of *People* magazine looked vaguely out of place atop Iron Man's mechanized form.

That's better, Tony thought. He breathed a sigh of relief—despite all the improvements he'd made to the suit's ventilation and internal cooling systems, it still got a bit stuffy under the helmet. Besides, he had no secrets from Cap.

Captain America kept his own mask on, probably just from force of habit. Iron Man suspected that, after five decades of fighting for freedom, from the dark days of World War II through all the years since, Cap was more comfortable in uniform than out of it. His real name was Steve Rogers, Iron Man knew, but even his closest friends mostly thought of him as Cap. His proud stance and patriotic costume, from the A-for-America upon his brow right down to his bright red boots, had been an enduring national icon since before Tony Stark was even born. Cap's circular metal shield, similarly adorned with the Stars and Stripes, rested on the table as well, only a few feet away from Iron Man's helmet.

The tools of our trade, Iron Man thought.

He wiped the perspiration from his forehead and glanced around the room, wondering where the rest of the team was. As if in answer to his unspoken query, a spectral figure rose from the center of the table, passing through the solid tabletop, and the chromium floor below, like an insubstantial wraith.

Or Vision.

Translucent at first, so that Iron Man could spy a wall

of computer banks through the green-and-yellow body of the newcomer, the Vision emerged in his entirety a few inches above the Avengers insignia on the table, then drifted silently to one side and lowered himself into an empty chair. Once seated, he solidified quickly, effortlessly taking on mass and substance until he appeared just as tangible as Captain America and Iron Man. A voluminous yellow cape, that had previously floated about him like a phantasmal aura, settled upon his emerald shoulders.

"Forgive my delay," he said, his voice as cold and unfeeling as the grave, "but I was engaged in routine maintenance of my thermoscopic receptor."

Iron Man was not too startled by the Vision's eerie arrival. He had grown accustomed to the synthetic Avenger's tendency to pass through solid objects when convenient—a useful application of the Vision's unique ability to control his artificial body's density. It was just such an immaterial manifestation, he recalled, that had led their former colleague, the winsome Wasp, to christen the synthezoid "the Vision" in the first place.

A fitting name, he reflected.

If Iron Man, at least with his helmet in place, resembled a humanoid robot forged from gleaming steel, the Vision, in his solid state, looked more or less like a living mannequin sculpted out of plastic. A skintight sheet of green and yellow latex garbed his synthetic frame, except where his scarlet face peeked through, looking no more natural or organic than the statues in a wax museum. A polished golden gem resided in the center of his forehead, absorbing the solar energy that provided the Vision with his own artificial form of life. The mask-like face, slender and refined in its contours, was capable of expressing emotion, Iron Man knew, but seldom displayed that ability to any significant degree.

Especially since his marriage to Wanda broke up, Stark thought privately. These days, the Vision was even more icy and inhuman than he had been in years.

"Who else are we expecting?" Iron Man asked. He didn't want to rush things, but there was a stack of paperwork waiting back on his alter ego's desk. His executive assistant, Pepper Potts, could handle most of it if necessary, but Stark preferred to be a hands-on administrator whenever possible; he owed that to his numerous employees and stockholders. Avengers business took priority, though, as well it should. The fate of one company, even his own, hardly compared to the safety of the whole world.

"Just Wanda," Cap informed him. "Hawkeye and Thor are both pursuing solo missions, while Firestar and Justice are attending a New Warriors reunion. That leaves only the Scarlet Witch on the duty roster." He glanced at a digital chronometer mounted into the south wall, beneath a sizable viewscreen. The clock read 01:36:08 P.M. "I'm not sure what's keeping her. So far, she hasn't responded to any of my hails."

There was a moment of awkward silence as both Cap and Iron Man looked toward the seated Vision.

If anyone *might know where Wanda is . . .* the armored Avenger thought. The Vision and the Scarlet Witch had been deeply in love once, even happily married with two small children of their own. But several tragic reversals of fortune, including the loss of their twin sons, had taken its toll on their union. The Vision had even been completely disassembled and reconstructed at least once, losing much of his earlier personality in the process—or so it appeared. Iron Man didn't pretend to understand all that had happened to their relationship, but it was clearly no longer what it once was, and had not been for some time.

It can't be easy for them, he thought, *still living under the same roof, fighting beside each other as members of the same team.* Still, that was none of his business, even now.

Perhaps sensing his human teammates' discomfort, the Vision volunteered what he knew without being asked. "I believe Wanda expressed an interest in visiting an exhibition at a local museum, but I do not know when she expected to return."

Cap nodded solemnly, his chiseled jaw firmly set beneath his cowl. "Well, why don't we get started without her," he decided as chairman.

Iron Man agreed silently, taking a seat at the table. It was unlike Wanda to skip out on official Avengers business, but, given all the hardships she had endured over the last few years, he was inclined to cut her some slack. *We can always fill her in later if we have to.*

Cap walked over to the primary viewscreen and activated the widescreen monitor, which flared to life with a faint phosphor glow. "I received the following transmission at roughly 1300 hours. I think it speaks for itself."

A prerecorded image appeared on the screen, depicting the scowling visage of Nick Fury, director of the Strategic Hazard Intervention Espionage Logistic Directorate. Four times larger than life, Fury glared out from the monitor with his one good eye. A simple black eyepatch concealed the remains of his other eye, while what looked like a day's worth of stubble bristled along his jaw, which chomped down, as usual, on a cheap cigar. Only the gray at his temples hinted that the veteran spymaster had been around just as long as Captain America. Fury was a tough old warhorse, Iron Man knew; Stark had personally recommended Fury for his post at S.H.I.E.L.D., back when it was still called the Supreme Headquarters International Espionage and Law-enforcement Division.

"Listen up, heroes," Fury barked. His voice was as gravelly as a bad stretch of road. "S.H.I.E.L.D. has confirmed several UFO sightings in New York State, at least five in the last three hours. We're not talking swamp gas or weather balloons here; this looks like the real deal." His scowl deepened, as if the alleged alien spacecraft had arrived just to make his life difficult. He bit down hard on the base of his stogie. A puff of gray smoke rose from the burning tobacco. "Invading ETs are more your line than ours, so you'd better be on the lookout and get ready for anything. Full details of the sightings are being transmitted to your computers—under maximum encryption, natch—even while I'm sitting here jawin' about this. That's all for now. Let me know if we're about to be overrun by little green men. Fury out."

The screen went blank, shutting itself off as it reached the end of the communication. Cap let the ominous message sink in for a moment before speaking. He gave Iron Man a quizzical look. "I don't suppose Stark Industries is testing any experimental aircraft in this vicinity?"

"Stark Solutions," Iron Man corrected him, supplying the name of his new-and-improved corporation. He was proud of his latest enterprise. He shook his head. "I would've alerted S.H.I.E.L.D. ahead of time in any case."

"I figured as much," Cap said. "I spoke with Reed Richards earlier. The Fantastic Four don't know anything about this either."

"What about the X-Men?" Iron Man asked. Compared to the FF or the Avengers, the mutant team were renegades as far as the government was concerned. He couldn't imagine that Wolverine and company bothered to notify the authorities when they went offworld or hosted extraterrestrial visitors.

Typical, Iron Man thought, a frown marring his debonair features. He didn't buy into all the anti-mutant hysteria that sometimes got directed at the X-Men, but he had to admit that the whole bunch of them had always struck him as a pack of dangerously loose cannons, even if they had managed to cooperate (barely) with the Avengers on a couple of occasions. *Why can't they work within the system like the rest of us?*

"Apparently not," Cap answered. "I quietly dropped a line to the Beast, and he assured me that we can cross the X-Men off our list of suspects, although he couldn't vouch for all their splinter groups."

Iron Man rolled his eyes. *X-Factor. X-Force. Excalibur. Generation X . . . there's even some kid calling himself X-Man running around these days.* He couldn't blame Hank McCoy for not being able to keep track of all his fellow mutants. *I can't make sense of it myself.* He sighed wearily. *We Avengers may retool our membership periodically, but at least we always know who's who. And you can tell the good guys from the bad. . . .*

"Then it could be almost anybody behind these sightings," he objected. "The Kree, the Skrulls, the Badoon, Galactus. Even the Stone Men from Jupiter. And that's assuming that this UFO really is extraterrestrial in origin, and not just some new high-tech aircraft cooked up by Zemo or Hydra or someone."

"Fury has his own sources of information," Cap

pointed out, sitting down at the table between the Vision and Iron Man. His trusty shield rested within easy reach. "If he says that none of our local mad geniuses are responsible, I'm inclined to believe him."

That was true, Iron Man conceded. S.H.I.E.L.D wasn't known as the world's premiere intelligence operation for nothing; Fury probably knew what the Brotherhood of Evil Mutants had for breakfast. "So what do we do now?" he asked. "Take notes while we watch *The X-Files*?"

Cap raised an eyebrow under his cowl, looking a bit puzzled by the allusion. Iron Man guessed that Captain America, having grown up with old-time radio, didn't watch much TV.

"Never mind," he told Cap. "But besides notifying all our auxiliary members, I'm not sure what else Fury expects us to do."

The double doors behind him swung open and Jarvis entered the meeting room, carrying a silver tray on which Iron Man spied three china cups. "Excuse the interruption, gentlemen, but I thought you might care for a spot of refreshment." He strolled around the table, handing out the steaming cups. "A black coffee for you, sir," he said to Captain America, "and a cappuchino for you, Master Stark." The butler did not offer the third cup to the Vision, since the solar-powered synthezoid had little need of food or drink, but instead looked about the meeting room. "I say, has Mistress Wanda not yet returned? I thought sure that she would have arrived by now, perhaps while I was busying myself in the kitchen."

"I confess that I grow increasingly concerned about the Scarlet Witch's continued absence," the Vision intoned. Iron Man had heard automated answering machines that sounded warmer. "I have never known her to disregard an official summons."

He has a point, Iron Man thought. When Wanda had served as team leader for the West Coast Avengers, before that branch of the team was dissolved, she had been a stickler for punctuality, usually arriving several minutes before any planned meeting. It was always possible that her tardiness today had a perfectly innocent explanation— perhaps her I.D. card had been misplaced or malfunctioned—but Lord knows it wouldn't be the first time that an individual Avenger had been waylaid by one or more of their many foes.

"Easy enough to check out," he said, reaching for his helmet. Putting the headpiece back into place, the magnetic seals engaging automatically, he employed a cybernetic command to activate the helmet's built-in antenna array. A priority signal, keyed to Wanda's specific coded frequency, and strong enough to reach her anywhere within New York's five boroughs, issued from the powerful communications equipment embedded in Iron Man's armor.

A shame if we alarm her unnecessarily, he thought, *but better safe than sorry.*

"Iron Man to Scarlet Witch. Priority Yellow. Please reply."

To his surprise, he couldn't even get a lock on the card. Not only did Wanda not respond verbally, but there was no indication that the card was anywhere within range of the signal, which argued conclusively against it being left downstairs somewhere.

Blast it, Wanda, what the devil has happened to you?

"Iron Man to Scarlet Witch," he repeated, more urgently this time. "Let us know where you are."

Nothing.

"This isn't good," Iron Man reported to Cap and the Vision. Was that a flicker of anxiety in the synthezoid's glittering plastic eyes or merely a trick of the light? "I can't reach her at all, or even get a fix on her location." He silenced the static in his earpiece, abandoning his efforts to establish contact with the missing mutant sorceress. "I don't like this one bit. Wanda wouldn't just leave the city without telling anyone."

Not of her own free will, that is.

Chapter Five

"Let's go, people!" Cyclops shouted. "Hurry!"

A series of explosions rocked the alien space station, punctuating the X-Man's command with a string of seismic exclamation points.

I need no further urging, Storm thought, running down the quaking corridor, the diminished gravity, less than a third of Earth-normal, seeming to add wings to her feet. She was anxious to leave this cold and sterile environment behind. Transparent portholes, revealing the blackness of interstellar space, only emphasized how far this place was from the gentle winds, cool waters, and nurturing sunlight of her beloved Mother Earth. The cramped confines of the silver corridor, added to the enclosed nature of the entire station, induced an all-too-familiar sense of claustrophobia, but Storm refused to let any irrational fears, no matter how deeply ingrained, distract her from the challenge at hand.

If we can just make it to the shuttle, she thought, *before the whole station falls apart!*

They were running out of time. Already the walkway buckled beneath her feet, venting gusts of hot gas and ionized plasma which she and her two companions were forced to dodge as they ran, trusting on agility and adrenaline to avoid the hazards that sprang up in their path again and again. Ahead of her, the Beast bounded over a ruptured steam pipe, his powerful legs propelling him well above the pipe itself, so that his shaggy dark blue fur was only slightly scalded by the blistering steam spewing forth from the jagged cleft.

"Alley oop!" he called exuberantly, landing upon his massive hands, which he used to launch himself further down the corridor. "Come along, my brother- and sister-in-arms. Our heavenly chariot awaits!"

"Just have it warmed up and ready to go," Cyclops ordered him, sounding like he was only a few yards behind Storm. In contrast to the effusive Beast, his voice was brusque and humorless. "This is going to be a close one."

If we make it at all, Storm thought grimly.

The harsh clamor of metal supports crumpling and crashing upon each other came from the heart of the station, merely three levels away. Although the outer hull had not yet been breached, exposing them to the deadly vacuum outside, she knew that complete explosive decompression—and near instantaneous death—was only minutes away.

This is taking too long, she realized. *We need Rogue or Wolverine.* But the X-Men's numbers were sorely reduced today, leaving only the three of them to face this latest trial by fire.

Steaming vapor filled the corridor before her. Storm realized her own legs could hardly duplicate the Beast's spectacular leap, even allowing for the lesser gravity, so she called upon her own mutant abilities instead, taking hold of the pressurized atmosphere with her mind and shaping it to her will. Elemental energy suffused her eyes, masking the striking blue orbs behind an impenetrable white glow. A robust wind sprung to life within the ordinarily weatherless environment of the station, fluttering the wings of slick black fabric that hung beneath her arms and blowing the scalding steam away from her path. It took only seconds to disperse the hot mist, then an incandescent red beam shot past Storm to crush the exposed pipe to a flattened mass of lead, sealing the leak completely.

"Good work," said Cyclops, the source of the irresistible force beam. "Now keep moving. We haven't got much time."

I am quite aware of that, thank you, Storm thought, slightly irked by Cyclops's tone. Sometimes, Scott Summers forgot that he was no longer the sole leader of the X-Men, that indeed Storm had earned co-leader status within the group. She didn't take it personally, though, knowing that Cyclops drove everyone else almost as hard as he drove himself.

She raced over the squashed pipe, taking advantage of the sudden gale to literally take flight down the corridor, rising upon the wind currents until the vaulted ceiling hung less than an inch above her billowing crown of snow-white hair. Another flicker of claustrophobia stirred at the back of her mind, but she quashed it mercilessly. Now was no time to succumb to the terrors of the past. She looked for the Beast, but could not spot him ahead; he must have gained a considerable lead on them.

Godspeed, my friend, she urged him silently. *May we meet again soon.*

An airlock door slammed shut in front of her, the heavy bulkhead blocking her and Cyclops's escape and cutting them off from the Beast.

An automated safety measure, she guessed. *And a most inconvenient one.* Landing gracefully before the door, her feet touching down upon the shuddering walkway, she tugged at the wheel-shaped handle with both hands, but it wouldn't budge. The gray steel door remained fixed in place.

"Stand back!" Cyclops yelled, and this time she didn't object. His optic blasts were their best chance now. She flattened her back against the adjacent wall, distressed to feel the convulsive tremors vibrating through the straining steel, and watched as her fellow X-Man approached the airlock. His costume, a streamlined variation on the same blue-and-gold uniform he had worn since the bygone days of the original X-Men team, did not call attention away from the gleaming metallic visor that covered his eyes. Inside the visor, only a single ruby quartz lens, about eight inches in length, held back the awesome energies contained within Scott Summer's eyes.

The lens receded, unleashing a brilliant burst of energy that struck the sealed airlock with the force of a battering ram, knocking the airtight door off its hinges. The metal bulkhead, six inches thick, crashed onto the floor with a resounding peal that hurt Storm's ears. Nevertheless, she and Cyclops had sped past the now-open doorframe before the reverberating echoes of the crash even began to fade. The ruby lens in Cyclops's visor slid back into place, blocking his devastating eyebeams once more. A stray breeze rustled his short brown hair.

Storm galloped down the corridor as fleetly as the gazelles of the African veldt she had once called home. Her knee-high black boots pounded rapidly against the floor until, just around the next corner, she encountered a shocking sight that brought both she and Cyclops to an abrupt halt.

Bright Lady, no! she thought.

Three Brood warriors, their brown insectoid bodies hideous beyond belief, held the Beast at bay. Each hostile alien skittered across the floor on four spidery legs, hissing at the embattled blue mutant through gaping jaws filled with rows of needle-like teeth. Membranous wings vibrated furiously behind large triangular skulls. Their razor-sharp forelimbs slashed at the Beast, who hung upside-down from an exposed power conduit in the ceiling, batting away the stabbing thrusts of the Brood monsters with his disproportionally large fists.

"Paging Sigourney Weaver," he quipped in the face of danger, glimpsing his comrades' arrival out of the corner of his eye. "We appear to have an indisputable bug infestation problem on our hands."

"Do not let the mammal escape!" the central insectoid commanded its fellow Brood. A throat not meant for human speech screeched every word. Its venomous, two-pronged stinger stood poised at the far end of its tail, but, focused exclusively on the Beast, the creature had not yet spotted either Storm or Cyclops. Its demonic, serpentine eyes were fixed on the hanging mutant. "His unique genetic material will strengthen our young!"

The unforeseen appearance of the Brood caught Storm by surprise. *This is supposed to be a Shi'ar station,* she recalled. *What are the Brood doing here?*

Her astonishment slowed her only a moment, though; reflexes honed against foes even more deadly than these sent her running forward to defend her imperiled ally. As yet, the Beast seemed to have avoided serious injury, but he was clearly outnumbered, fighting a losing defensive struggle against a half-dozen segmented spears. Its wings vibrating so rapidly that they were practically invisible, the nearest Brood began to lift off from the floor, taking the battle closer to the Beast.

"Cyclops," Storm instructed hastily, "the one on the left is yours. I'll take the right."

Despite their occasional rivalry, Cyclops followed her

lead without hesitation. His forcebeam lashed out again, smiting the armored carapace of a malevolent insectoid, who let out an inhuman squawk as it tumbled backwards down the corridor. The remaining drones turned their wedge-shaped skulls toward the mutant reinforcements. Slitted red eyes, strangely reptilian in appearance, glared at Storm with unremitting virulence. Their wings buzzed as loudly as a swarm of bees. To the Brood, as she knew only too well, other species were only fit to be the involuntary hosts of their vile, invasive progeny.

They shall plant no eggs in me, she vowed, caught up in the heat of the conflict, *nor in the precious flesh of my friends.*

The starboard Brood sprang forward with alarming speed, slashing out at her exposed midriff with a barbed forelimb. "We know you, X-Men!" it squawked. "You shall not defy us again!"

Storm barely threw herself backwards in time to evade a cutting blow across her abdomen. *Gods of earth and air, defend me!* she prayed, calling upon the tempest that was her namesake.

Electrical fury coursed through her, streaming toward her fingertips, from which a sizzling bolt of lightning leapt to strike the attacking Brood upon its brow. Sparks erupted where the thunderbolt hit, followed by scintillating white-hot traceries that spread over the electrified form of the alien parasite. The noxious smell of burnt insect flesh mixed with a trace of ozone in the air. The monster's spindly legs gave out and it collapsed onto the floor, its impotent forelimbs still twitching spasmodically, its translucent wings folding in upon themselves.

Storm regarded her fallen foe with grim satisfaction. She generally strove to consider all living things sacred, but the Brood tested that resolve more than most. Not for nothing did Wolverine often refer to these beings as "sleazoids," a colorful but apt description. They were unclean creatures, existing only to propagate themselves through the pain and exploitation of others.

Would that the whole of their breed could be defeated so readily... Storm thought.

Meanwhile, the Beast, no longer compelled to battle all three Brood at once, went on the offensive against the sole Brood still intent on skewering the hirsute X-Man. Letting go of the elevated power conduit with his astonishingly dexterous feet, he flipped through the air, landing piggyback on the short, stumpy neck that connected the insectoid's flared skull to its squat torso. The Beast's added weight sank the flying creature to the floor, while squashing its buzzing wings.

"Stop! What is this?" it screeched. "Get off me, mammal! Get off, get off!"

The warrior drone shook its head violently and hopped about like a gigantic grasshopper, hoping to buck the Beast from his perch, but failed to dislodge its unwanted passenger, nor could it get at the Beast with its now useless forelimbs, which flailed angrily at the empty air. Its lethal tail twisted backwards, its lethal stingers coming dangerously close to the Beast's hairy back—until a precision blast from Cyclops's visor shattered the bony spikes, disarming the tail.

The Brood hissed in agony. "You will suffer for this, you mutated mammal!" it vowed.

"Ride 'em, cowboy," the Beast wisecracked, undaunted by the drone's threats. He straddled the creature's back, holding onto the upper portion of its skull as though it were the horn of a saddle. "I've heard of flea circuses, but this may well be the world's first insect rodeo. As-suming we were currently residing on a world, that is.''

Storm paid little attention to the Beast's typically light-hearted banter. She would never entirely understand his predilection for humorous repartee even in the midst of the most life-and-death struggle, but she had long ago grown accustomed to it. Certainly, Henry McCoy's per-petual witticisms had never interfered with his ability to hold his own in combat, at least not that she had ever been able to tell.

Perhaps he is merely blessed, she thought, *with an ex-ceptionally carefree spirit.*

Even now, as he indulged in yet more adroit japery, the Beast grabbed hold of the irate drone's upper and lower jaws, being careful to keep his oversized fingers away from the insectoid's stiletto teeth. Powerful muscles flexed beneath a thick layer of blue fuzz as he strained his simian arms to pull the ferocious jaws apart. Storm found herself reminded unexpectedly of one of the Beast's favorite old movies, *King Kong*, in particular, the scene in which the mighty ape wrestled thus with a voracious Tyrannosaurus *rex*. As in that classic film, the drone's jaws broke apart with a brutal crack, and the injured in-sectoid fell limply onto the grilled metal floor, a repugnant green ichor leaking from its mouth. Storm could not tell if the creature still lived, nor, to be honest, did she care overmuch. The floor rattled beneath the vanquished Brood, lending it a semblance of animation while remind-ing Storm of the greater danger to the station itself. The telltale clangor of imploding steel beams sounded ever closer behind them. The walls around her groaned alarm-ingly, and the smell of noxious gases permeated the en-closed atmosphere.

This delay may cost us dearly, she realized.

Was the battle concluded at last? For a second, she dared to hope so. Then, on the opposite side of the corridor, the drone sent tumbling by Cyclops re-entered the fray. Lying awkwardly upon its back, its four tiny legs kicking at the air above it, it employed its coiled tail to flip right-side up.

"Watch out!" Cyclops shouted as the Brood warrior charged at Storm, ducking around its two insensate hivemates to avoid Cyclops's line of fire before sailing through the air at the mutant weather witch. The buzzing of the monster filled her ears.

Lacking a straight shot at the insectoid, Cyclops aimed upward, ricocheting his forcebeam off the ceiling so that it slammed into the drone from above, coinciding with Storm's own defensive lightning bolt. Unable to withstand two such devastating assaults, the sleazoid's mottled brown exoskeleton exploded, spraying the walls and ceiling with pulpy goo and bits of cartilage.

"Well, that's quite revoltingly visceral," the Beast observed. He stepped away from the fractured drone beneath him, being careful to avoid stepping into a spreading puddle of viscous green fluid. Wet, scaly flakes of Brood dripped from the ceiling. "I think I prefer trashing Sentinels. At least when they come apart, all that's left are gears and computer chips."

Cyclops didn't crack a smile at the Beast's levity. He seldom did. "Time's wasting, folks," he reminded them. His trim brown hair, visible above his visor, had not a strand out of place. He nodded in the direction of their waiting shuttle. "Let's head out . . . pronto."

But, before they could even begin to leave the trio of Brood behind, the grillwork under their feet snapped like a whip, throwing them all off-balance. Storm felt the floor yanked out from beneath her, and she hastily summoned a wind to lift her off the treacherous walkway. The wrenching sound of metal sheets tearing asunder came from directly below her.

"Goddess!" she exclaimed in horror, realizing at once that they had won their fight with the Brood only to lose their race against time. Aghast, she saw the hull of the space station break apart in a dozen places.

In space, it is often said, no one can hear you scream, but within the station Storm could still hear the agonized shriek of futuristic steel alloys pushed beyond the limits of their endurance, followed by a roaring *whoosh* that sounded in her ears like the coming of a hurricane. Their air supply rushed out into the vacuum, carrying with it bits of debris and broken insect parts. Although Storm exerted all her meteorological powers to hold in the fleeing atmosphere, she could not stop the freezing emptiness outside from greedily stealing away their oxygen and their lives.

Pieces of the collapsed walkway flew past her face. Fingers aching, she clung frantically to an exposed piece of piping, watching in dismay as first Cyclops, then the Beast were sucked into the void, so that only she remained aboard the disintegrating hulk of the alien space station. The suction pulled at her remorselessly, until her fingers began to slip free from her black gloves. The silver belt around her waist succumbed to the strain, breaking apart at its weakest link and flying off into space. An icy cold enveloped her, chilling her to the bone. Her lungs gasped for air.

I can do no more, she realized with fatalistic certainty. *We have lost.*

"End simulation," she stated distinctly.

The disaster in space disappeared in a heartbeat, replaced by the familiar sights and sounds of the Danger Room. The fierce suction gave way to the ordinary pull of terrestrial gravity, and Storm found herself lying prone upon the floor. Exhausted by her ordeal, she climbed slowly to her feet, still feeling a lingering chill from the artificial environment. Shivering, her arms clutched tightly across her chest, she marveled once more at how astonishingly lifelike were the holographic simulations created by the advanced Shi'ar technology installed in the X-Men's training facility.

That was almost too *convincing,* she reflected.

Several yards away, across the empty gymnasium floor, her "deceased" teammates were recuperating as well. Judging from the deepening scowl on Cyclops's face, he was not at all pleased by their performance in this latest exercise, designed to keep their survival skills, as well as their ability to function as a team, in peak condition.

Nor should he, Storm thought, although she allowed that there were extenuating circumstances. *Where are Rogue and Wolverine?*

"Not good, people," Cyclops pronounced soberly. Storm could not see Scott's eyes through his visor, but she could imagine how frustrated and unhappy they must look. "If that had been a real space mission, we'd all be dead now." His fists remained clenched at his sides, his posture taut and unyielding. Sometimes, Storm worried about Cyclops—all the pressure he imposed on himself could not be good for his health. "I blame myself as much as anyone, of course."

"It may be that no one is to blame," Storm said

evenly. She recovered her broken belt from the floor, then walked across the chamber to join the Beast and Cyclops. After the clamorous demise of the space station, the Danger Room felt as quiet and still as a museum after hours. "As I recall, Shadowcat programmed that scenario to include Logan and Rogue, as well. With five X-Men we might well have defeated the Brood in time to reach the shuttle."

Cyclops shook his head. "That's not good enough. You know as well as I do that we can't count on having a full house the next time we come under attack." Storm noticed that some of the pouches on his yellow bandoleer and utility belt had been torn open by the holographic space station's spectacular decompression. She imagined that they all had acquired some new bruises beneath their uniforms or, in the Beast's case, below his fur.

"Take now, for instance," Cyclops continued. "Jean and the Professor and half the team are off in the Savage Land, helping out the Fall People, so they're essentially incommunicado for who knows how long. Bobby is way off in Scotland, assisting Moira's research, and none of this is very unusual. We can hardly expect our enemies to wait until everyone is home before they stage an assault on one or more of us."

"Granted," Storm said. "I was merely observing that, in this particular instance, the odds were—by design— against a successful outcome." She made no attempt to conceal a trace of irritation in her voice; although she sympathized with Cyclops's concerns, she disliked being lectured to. Storm suspected Jean's prolonged absence might also be contributing to her husband's bad mood.

Perhaps to change the subject, the Beast somersaulted through the air, landing precisely between Storm and

Cyclops. "That reminds me," he said. "Where are Rogue and Logan, anyway?"

A good question, Storm thought. "As you know, Wolverine could be almost anywhere." By temperament and inclination, Logan went his own way, and was very much in the habit of indulging his wanderlust without notice, sometimes for lengthy periods of time; this was an intrinsic aspect of his personality to which they had all become accustomed. "Rogue's absence puzzles me, however. She left this morning for a shopping expedition in the city, but I believe she had every intention of returning in time for this scheduled exercise program."

Cyclops's expression grew even more somber, if possible. "I don't like the sound of that." He adjusted his uniform as best he could, then headed for the exit. "These are dangerous times for any mutant to go AWOL. Especially an X-Man." A pair of gleaming metal doors slid apart, permitting them to leave the deceptively-empty Danger Room. "Who knows what kind of trouble she might be in this very minute?"

A healthy degree of paranoia, Storm reflected, was perhaps essential to life as an X-Man, especially for a team leader. And yet . . .

"We should not leap to the conclusion that Rogue is in danger. She may have simply lost track of time, or perhaps missed a connection at Grand Central." *Then again,* she thought, *even if the train left without her, Rogue could have always flown home under her own power.* "I share your concern, however."

"Might I suggest we resolve this conundrum by efficiently ascertaining the present location of our elusive Southern belle?" the Beast proposed. His knuckles brushed against the floor, his simian stance making him seem shorter than he actually was. Unlike the others, he wore only a pair of blue trunks, just a shade darker than his own indigo fur; with his dense, hairy pelt, he had little need for clothing, except for the minimum modesty required. A large capital "X" adorned the buckle of a bright yellow belt.

With Storm and Cyclops in tow, the Beast hopped nimbly through the lower level of the sprawling mansion that housed what was now called the Xavier Institute for Higher Learning. Safely locked away from prying eyes, this section of the mansion had the feel of a high-tech research facility. Sterile white hallways connected with well-equipped laboratories, the ground floor of the Danger Room, and an emergency medical center capable of treating everything from radiation burns to bite wounds.

"Certainly," the Beast added, "the means to do so is readily at hand."

Cyclops nodded. "Cerebro," he said tersely, leading the way to Professor X's personal laboratory.

At the center of the lab, connected to an impressive array of streamlined computer banks and monitors, was a helmet-shaped apparatus secured to the ceiling by two flexible steel cables. This was Cerebro, a cybernetic tracking system designed to locate and identify mutants throughout the world; nearly all of the X-Men had been initially recruited via Cerebro. If the device, the brainchild of Professor Charles Xavier, couldn't find a missing mutant, then that mutant had gone to enormous efforts not to be found.

Cerebro worked best, Storm knew, when used in conjunction with a powerful telepathic mind, such as Professor X's or Jean Grey's, but, in their absence, any one of those present should be able to use the device to confirm that Rogue was safely on her way home. After all, her unique mutant signature was already on file in Cerebro's capacious memory.

Bright Lady, Storm prayed, *let our fears be unfounded.*

"Would you care to do the honors, Ororo?" the Beast asked, addressing Storm by her true name. His long arms reached up and pulled the helmet down to eye-level. "I believe you may have the most affinity to our absent compatriot."

"Very well," she agreed. Although she and Rogue came from radically different backgrounds, she and the younger woman had indeed grown close over the years. Storm removed the stiff black headdress that rested upon her lustrous white hair, and placed the metallic helmet over her head. A blinking red sensor fell into place between her eyes, just above the bridge of her nose. It was a tight fit, but not uncomfortable. "You may proceed when ready."

"Just give me a second," the Beast said, the sound of his voice muffled somewhat by the helmet covering her ears, "while I call up Rogue's profile." His enormous fingers manipulated a control panel with surprising dexterity, and Storm heard Cerebro hum to life. Cyclops looked on stiffly, unable to relax until he learned the truth. "There we go. Commence scanning now."

Storm closed her eyes and visualized Rogue, looking just as she had when Storm had last seen her: casually dressed in civilian attire and enthusiastic at the prospect of a carefree day in the city. Despite the cumbersome apparatus enclosing her skull, Storm did not feel at all cramped or confined. If anything, she felt the exact opposite; she could feel her awareness radiating outward beyond the walls of the Institute, sending out finely-attuned tendrils of thought that spread out for miles and miles in every direction, with herself at the center of an unfolding psionic web. The sensation was not unlike that of calling upon the wind and the rain, except that now she was searching for a single individual spirit instead of a compliant cloud or cold front. Wherever Rogue might have strayed to, she could not remain undetected for long.

And yet, as the seconds rushed by, becoming minutes, doubts began to assail Storm. In theory, Rogue should have gone no further than Manhattan, merely a couple of hours away from the X-Men's residence in Westchester County. Why then did she continue to elude the far-reaching sensitivities of Cerebro, which had been known to chart the emergence of an unknown mutant power even half a world away? Her mind was traveling at the speed of thought, yet Rogue remained beyond her reach.

Where are you, my friend? What has become of you?

Storm opened her eyes to see her fellow X-Men watching her with growing apprehension. Even the Beast's natural ebullience appeared dampened by her continuing inability to find their missing friend.

Finally, after many long minutes that felt like hours, the Beast shook his shaggy head and deactivated the device. The blinking sensor between her eyes switched off and Storm felt the extended feelers of her artificially-amplified consciousness withdraw back into her mind, grounding her within her physical body. She slowly lifted the helmet from her head and let the steel cables retract so that the headpiece ascended toward the ceiling once more.

If only my fears could be lifted from me so readily, she thought mournfully.

"It is no use," she reported to Cyclops and the Beast, confirming what they no doubt already knew. "I could sense no trace of Rogue—anywhere upon the Earth."

Chapter Six

"So, I hear this scream and I come running, and the first thing I see is the puppets attacking the Witch—is it okay if I call her that?"

"I'm sure she wouldn't mind," Iron Man said to the nervous security guard. The Avengers interviewed the man, a retired cop named Rodriguez, in the lobby of the folk art museum. Staffers and patrons looked on excitedly, whispering among themselves, as the armored Avenger, along with Captain America and the Vision, pursued their investigation of the Scarlet Witch's apparent abduction. The Vision's knowledge of Wanda's itinerary had indeed led them to the museum—and to an increasingly bizarre mystery.

Puppets? Iron Man thought. *Wanda was ambushed by puppets?*

" 'Course I didn't know it was her at first," Rodriguez continued, gulping uneasily as he spoke to the costumed heroes, "but then she said she was an Avenger and told me to get that other girl—I mean, young woman—out of there. I didn't argue the point. I figured she knew what she was doing, especially after she started waving her hands around and all that weird stuff happened. Besides the puppets, I mean." Despite the museum's air conditioning, the guard wiped his forehead, remembering. "So, anyway, I made sure the other woman was safe, then hurried back to see if the Witch was okay. But when I got there, they were all gone. The Witch. The puppets. Everything."

"And you had never noticed anything odd about the

puppets before?'' Captain America asked. A patriotic quilt on the wall behind the guard matched Cap's uniform.

He's the only one of us who looks like he belongs here, Iron Man thought, taking in all the quaint and old-fashioned Americana on display. *The Vision and I stand out like sore thumbs.*

''No,'' Rodriguez insisted, shaking his head. ''They arrived on loan from some museum in Europe last week. I watched the curators mount them on the walls myself. There's been no problem at all, until this morning.''

When the puppets came to life, Iron Man thought. *Blast, I hope this doesn't turn out to be one of those weird sorcerous things.* A scientist by both training and inclination, he was never comfortable dealing with the supernatural. Past adventures had forced him to grudgingly concede the existence of mystical forces within the universe, like Asgardian gods or the dread Dormammu, but that didn't mean he had to like it. *Give me a horde of rampaging cyborgs and aliens any day.* Unfortunately, when it came to the Scarlet Witch, whose mutant sorcery derived from both science and the supernatural, an occult attack of some sort was a distinct possibility.

''You mentioned a security video earlier,'' he reminded the guard. ''I'd like to see that.''

''Yes,'' the Vision said emphatically. ''More data is required.'' His sepulchral voice visibly unnerved Rodriguez, who gulped and looked away to avoid meeting the synthezoid's unblinking plastic eyes. There was an intensity behind the Vision's eerie stillness, Iron Man thought, that betrayed an unmistakable concern for the safety of his former wife—at least to someone who had known the Vision for as long as Iron Man had.

The guard signaled to a young aide or intern, who hurried over to hand Rodriguez an ordinary videocassette.

"We have cameras in the ceilings," Rodriguez explained, presenting Iron Man with the tape, "to discourage vandalism, you know." He cocked his head to one side, toward a closed door beyond the front desk. "If you want, you can use the VCR in the curator's office, although it might be kind of crowded with all of you in there." Rodriguez had explained earlier that the office was not a large one, which was why they had chosen to conduct the interview in the lobby, despite the milling spectators.

"Thank you, but that won't be necessary," Iron Man replied.

Gripping the cassette gently between his armored fingers, which could have crushed it to powder had he desired, he inserted the tape into the audiovisual communications array built into the collar of his armor. Stark-designed software rapidly converted the information encoded on the tape to his private format, then routed the data to the multi-purpose beam projector embedded in his chestplate. The unbreakable polycrystal lens lit up from within and, only seconds after Iron Man received the tape, it projected a three-dimensional, holographic image onto the empty air in front of the guard and the heroes. The holograph was even colorized.

"Holy cow!" Rodriguez exclaimed, his jaw dropping open.

Iron Man peered through the eye slits in his helmet at the instant replay of Wanda's battle against, sure enough, a bunch of a very lively marionettes. He nodded in approval as the Scarlet Witch deployed her hex spheres against Baba Yaga and the other puppets, then frowned as a miniature effigy of Victor Von Doom blasted Wanda from behind with some variety of energy beam. For a second, he wondered whether the real Doom might be behind this unlikely ambush, but no, he decided, this didn't feel like Doom's style. Doom could be devious, but he had too much pride to shoot a woman in the back, especially via a puny toy version of himself.

Then who? Iron Man wondered. *The Puppet Master? Mister Doll?*

Before his eyes, the holographic Witch collapsed onto the floor and the malevolent puppets converged on her unconscious body, forming a circle around her. Iron Man held his breath, anxious to see what happened next, when the image dissolved into a blur of incoherent visual static.

"What is it?" Captain America asked, squinting at the globe of flickering electronic snow. "What's wrong?"

Iron Man called up an immediate systems report. Micro-projectors in his eyepieces aimed facts and figures directly onto his retina, causing the visual display to float before his field of vision. He scrolled quickly through the report, but the news was not encouraging. Switching off his multi-beam in disappointment, he turned toward his fellow Avengers.

"It's no good," he reported. The flexible metal of his golden faceplate mirrored his disapproving expression. "Some sort of intense electromagnetic pulse erased the tape from that point on."

"Then we have no idea where they took Wanda," Cap stated, frustration burning in his clear blue eyes, "or even how they got her out of the building."

"I'm afraid not," Iron Man confirmed. He ejected the cassette from his communications array and handed it back to Rodriguez, who still seemed amazed that such an extraordinary visual display could come from so ordinary a video cassette. "Thank you for your cooperation, sir," Iron Man said, making a mental note to have Tony Stark donate a sizable endowment to the museum. "Perhaps you can show us exactly where this occurred?"

When in doubt, inspect the scene of the crime, Iron Man thought. He was a scientist and engineer, not a detective, but maybe the marauding marionettes had left some clue to their origins or present whereabouts. Right now, that was the only chance they had to find the Scarlet Witch, hopefully in one piece.

I really, really hope we're not talking magic here, he wished. *Anything but that.*

The Vision said nothing at all.

"Oh, my stars and garters!"

Henry McCoy leaped over the camelback sofa toward the television set mounted on the wall of the X-Men's spacious rec room, the book he was reading—*Metaphor and Metaphysics: A New Interpretation of Quantum Reality*—instantly forgotten, all thought of its contents driven away by the startling pictures on the TV screen.

"Scott! Ororo! Make haste!" he called out. "The redoubtable Rogue has made the nightly news!"

His hairy blue fingers turned up the volume even as Cyclops and Storm, now garbed in everyday attire, rushed into the room. Scott Summer's eyes remained concealed behind a pair of ruby quartz glasses, but Ororo Munroe's lustrous azure orbs widened in amazement.

"Goddess!" she exclaimed.

On the screen above their heads, a familiar figure appeared to be fighting off a swarm of ... angry tee-shirts? Although the woman's features were obscured by the frenzied layers of fabric clinging to her face, it was obvious to the Beast and his teammates that the lady in question was none other than the X-Men's very own Southern rebel. The heads and shoulders of fleeing New Yorkers occasionally intruded into the frame as the jostled cameraman struggled to keep Rogue in the center of the picture. As she flailed about wildly, her super-strength tore apart what looked like some sort of flimsy showcase for anti-mutant propaganda, while the typically resonant voice of a local news anchor provided a running commentary:

"... this amateur video, taken by a quick-thinking tourist from Santa Fe, clearly shows the chaos that erupted today at a Greenwich Village street fair, turning an afternoon of outdoor entertainment into a terrifying experience for dozens of innocent fairgoers. Authorities have tentatively identified the woman in this footage as a member of the outlaw mutant organization known as the X-Men. She is believed to go by the alias of 'Rogue,' and has been linked to a number of past mutant disturbances. . . .''

An eyewitness, so named by the caption that appeared under his close-up, offered his own take on the episode. "What more proof do we need that these mutant monsters don't care who gets caught in the middle of one of their paranormal power struggles?'' Sweaty but self-satisfied, the witness eagerly launched into what sounded like a well-worn spiel. "The Friends of Humanity have documented over 875 cases of collateral damage caused by rival factions of mutant terrorists. . . .''

"These views do not necessarily represent those of this station or its management,'' the Beast interrupted, lowering the volume once more. "Or so one most fervently hopes and prays.''

Thankfully, the unsolicited editorializing quickly gave

way to further footage of the incident in the Village. Her hands and face nearly mummified by the seemingly possessed garments, Rogue lifted off from the street, the jerky eye of the camera tracking her into the sky until she flew out of the frame. This was followed by a somewhat more professional shot of a familiar stone monument that looked like it had been hit by a missile. The Washington Square Arch, the Beast recognized, although it would be better described now as the Washington Square Pillars, the arch itself having been reduced to rubble, apparently during Rogue's headlong attempt to escape the suffocating fabric.

Another landmark destroyed, the Beast thought, sighing. Through no fault of their own, the X-Men's hard-fought battles against evil mutants and other menaces often left a regrettable amount of damage and debris behind. *This is not going to help our already dubious reputation.*

Bad publicity could be dealt with another day, however; finding out what had become of Rogue was the pre-eminent matter at the moment. With Cyclops and Storm, the Beast watched the news broadcast for a few minutes more, until it became obvious that there was nothing further to be learned there. He channel-surfed rapidly, checking out the coverage on other stations, but they all seemed to be repeating the same information and footage over and over.

"So much for the mass media," he pronounced, clicking the TV off and hopping over to confer with Scott and Ororo. He perched on the back of a chair, his toes wrapped around the carved wooden ridge atop the seat. "No one seems clear on what transpired after Rogue's collision with the Arch, but this does not bode well for the ready return of our absent amigo.''

''We have to assume she's in the hands of the enemy,'' Cyclops stated. He paced behind the couch, his hands jammed into the pockets of his slacks, too engaged with the crisis to sit down. Storm, wearing a floor-length green housedress of African design, stood by the window, looking on with a deceptive aura of serenity. The Beast knew that Ororo was no doubt just as impatient to come to Rogue's aid as Cyclops.

''Ah, but which one?'' the Beast asked. ''Refresh my overtaxed memory,'' he said, balancing on one foot while he scratched his head with the other. ''Isn't there some costumed character out west—California, I believe— who's supposed to have the ability to psychically manipulate clothing and other textiles?''

''Gypsy Moth,'' Cyclops supplied, having done his homework as usual; Scott was the only person Hank knew who read super-criminal case studies in his spare time. ''But she's never had any grudge against us. More likely, we're dealing with a powerful telekinetic capable of turning inanimate objects into weapons. The Black Queen maybe, or the Shadow King.''

''It is unfortunate that Phoenix is abroad,'' Storm commented. ''In her absence, we are ill-equipped to deal with attacks of a psionic nature. Especially now that Psylocke can no longer access her telekinetic gifts.''

Betsy Braddock, the Beast recalled, had recently departed the X-Men, following her crippling psychic clash with Amahl Farouk. *A costly victory, that,* he mused, *and a reminder that we X-Men do not always emerge unscathed from our various sorties into all manner of peril.*

''We'll just have to do the best we can,'' Cyclops declared grimly. His hands gripped the back of the over-stuffed ottoman. "I'll send out a general alert, but Lord only knows when Jean and the others will wrap up that business in the Savage Land." He strode decisively for the door, turning his back on the silent television. "Into uniform, everyone. There's nothing more we can do here. I want to be in NYC by 2030 hours."

Already wearing as much of a uniform as he ever did, the Beast headed for the lab to assemble whatever equipment might be required. Somehow, he guessed that finding Rogue was going to take a lot of old-fashioned detective work, including a forensic examination of whatever evidence remained.

I mean, homicidal tee-shirts? he thought. *Well, I'll be an anthropoid's antecedent. . . .*

Yellow crime scene ribbons still cordoned off the back wing of the museum. The Vision glided right through them, leaving the banners untouched, but Iron Man and Captain America waited for the security guard to pull the tape aside before entering the site of the Scarlet Witch's abduction. Curious onlookers lingered behind the yellow banners, watching the heroes' every move through the viewfinders of clicking disposable cameras.

The walls were conspicuously bare, except for mounted plaques describing the now-missing exhibits. Spotlights shone on empty hooks where once the puppets had hung. Iron Man noted some scuff marks on the floor, possibly from the tussle earlier that day, but he imagined that the museum probably got a fair amount of foot traffic in any event.

I'm not even sure what we hope to find here, he thought. One could hardly expect puppets to leave behind fingerprints or samples of DNA. *Unless they weren't really puppets. . . .*

"The police found some torn-out hair on the floor, plus a silver earring," Rodriguez informed them, pointing to a spot on the tiles. Iron Man noticed a single speck of blood.

"Wanda has numerous earrings that fit that description," the Vision observed, his inscrutable gaze riveted to that solitary bloodstain. "My memory banks confirm that she was wearing a pair of silver earrings when she departed the Mansion this morning."

For someone with no more ties to his ex-wife, the Vision sure pays a lot of attention to her comings and goings, Iron Man noted. He also recalled that the Scarlet Witch had a fondness for bangles that reflected her gypsy roots.

"Umm, yeah," Rodriguez answered, still somewhat spooked by the Vision's icy voice. "The cops thought the earring might belong to the Witch, but you'd have to check with them about that."

"We'll be sure we do that, Mr. Rodriguez," Captain America said. "Thank you for being so helpful." As the guard departed toward the lobby, clearing away the assembled spectators, Cap searched the deserted gallery with his eyes, then turned toward Iron Man. "What do you think? Should we have those hair samples sent onto S.H.I.E.L.D. for analysis?"

"Couldn't hurt," Iron Man agreed, remembering their teleconference with Nick Fury earlier that day. *I wonder if Wanda's disappearance has anything to do with those UFOs S.H.I.E.L.D. reported?* "Fury owes us a favor or two."

Identifying Wanda as the victim wasn't the problem, though; finding out who was behind those malignant puppets was. *Puppets, dolls . . . hmm.* "Give me a second, Cap, while I check on some of the more obvious suspects."

Without budging one inch from the desolate gallery, Iron Man used the satellite link in his antenna array to go onto the Internet in search of information. A quick link to the main Avengers data base, accessible once he cybernetically keyed in the correct password, revealed that his old adversary, Mr. Doll, was still serving time for extortion and other crimes, but that Philip Masters, the so-called Puppet Master, was currently out on parole.

Interesting, Iron Man thought, although Masters was usually more a threat to the Fantastic Four than the Avengers. Justice Department records, available to all Avengers via their executive-level security clearances, further informed Iron Man of the intriguing fact that Masters' current workshop was located in SoHo, only about ten minutes away by subway. *Could be just a co-incidence,* Iron Man reminded himself. As he recalled, the Puppet Master's niece, the noted sculptor Alicia Masters, kept a studio down in SoHo, too. Sounded worth following up on, even if the Puppet Master's M.O. didn't quite fit the incident under investigation.

In the past, the Puppet Master had always used his trademark figurines to control his victims' minds, not attack them physically, but who else combined crime and puppetry? Django Maximoff, Wanda's adopted father, had once transformed both her and her brother, Quicksilver, into marionettes, and later pitted animated mannequins against the Avengers, but the old gypsy was unequivocally dead; Cap and the others had helped bury him themselves after that fracas in Transia a few years back.

That doesn't leave many other likely candidates, Iron

Man thought. Aside from assorted gods and demons, that is, whose doings and current whereabouts were not exactly the stuff of Web pages.

A copyrighted Stark search engine led him straight to the Puppet Master's personal e-mail address. An instant link to that address brought unexpectedly immediate results when Masters himself responded with a real-time transmission from his workshop.

"Iron Man?" he asked suspiciously, as an image of the Puppet Master's distinctive features, like a cross between Howdy Doody and Peter Lorre, were projected onto Iron Man's retinas. His bulging eyes protruded from beneath a shiny bald dome. "What do you Avengers want with me? I haven't done anything. Nothing at all, I tell you!" Saliva sprayed from his mouth as he sputtered vehemently, making Iron Man thankful this wasn't a genuine face-to-face encounter. "Why, I haven't left my workshop in weeks. My niece will back me on that, I assure you. Ask Alicia . . . she'll testify that I have a perfect alibi!"

"Calm down, Mr. Masters," Iron Man said, although he couldn't help thinking that the former villain was protesting a bit too much. *Maybe I should advise the Fantastic Four to keep a closer eye on him, just in case.* "No one is accusing you of anything." He briefly recounted the pertinent details of the Scarlet Witch's encounter with the rampaging puppets. "So you can see," he concluded, "why I thought to contact you. Even if you aren't guilty yourself—and no one's saying you are—maybe you can point us in the right direction."

Without mentioning it to Masters, he immediately sent an urgent e-mail to Alicia Masters, checking on her perfidious uncle's alleged alibi while keeping the line open to the Puppet Master himself. *Thank heaven for the miracles of multi-tasking,* he thought.

Looking very much like a sinister ventriloquist's dummy, Masters appeared somewhat mollified by Iron Man's attempts to keep an open mind. "Living marionettes, you say?" he said, stroking his hairless chin. "Very intriguing." Iron Man hoped Masters was not taking notes for his next criminal enterprise. "I'm afraid, though, that I can't think of any, er, former colleagues who might be responsible for the young lady's abduction. My own puppets, as you know, were constructed from radioactive clay found only on Wundagore Mountain. The clay had many unusual properties, but autonomous locomotion was not one of them." He glanced down at whatever he working on, just out of the frame of the transmission, and Iron Man would have given a month's profits at Stark Solutions to see what exactly the Puppet Master was fashioning now.

Not another of his little mind-controlling toys, he prayed, *and especially not a miniature Iron Man.*

"Now then," said Masters, "if you don't mind, I have to get back to my work."

"Fine," Iron Man said gruffly, deciding it couldn't hurt to put the fear of God into the man. He'd known a lot of criminals who had claimed to turn over a new leaf, like the Thunderbolts, and precious few who really had. "Just remember, Masters, if you're hiding anything, the Fantastic Four isn't the only super-team that's ready to throw you back behind bars if necessary. We'll be in touch—you can count on it."

"Your faith and trust touch my heart," the Puppet Master replied sarcastically, cutting off the transmission on that rather adversarial note. Iron Man wasn't too concerned about getting on the twisted toymaker's bad side; as an Avenger, he'd made too many dire enemies to worry about one more.

I can deal with Masters if I have to, he thought confidently.

Unfortunately, his exchange with the Puppet Master hadn't brought them any closer to finding Wanda.

"No luck," he reported to Cap and the Vision. "The only super-criminal puppeteers I could think of are either behind bars or appear to have alibis." He wouldn't know for sure until Alicia replied to his e-mail, but in his gut he suspected Masters was telling the truth. Why tell a lie that could be so easily checked on? Masters's niece was trustworthy, Iron Man knew, even if her uncle was not.

Cap shrugged his broad shoulders, undiscouraged by Iron Man's lack of positive results. "We'll find her, one way or another." Iron Man admired Cap's unflagging optimism and faith; the old soldier never gave up, no matter the odds against him. "Besides, the Scarlet Witch I know is perfectly capable of taking care of herself. If there's a way to get word to us, or even to escape on her own, Wanda will find it."

That's true enough, Iron Man admitted. He recalled that Cap had personally trained Wanda and her brother when they had first joined the Avengers, right after the original team—Thor, Giant-Man, the Wasp, and Iron Man—had broken up. He glanced over at the Vision, hoping that Cap's words would bring renewed hope to the synthezoid as well. The Vision floated a few feet above the floor, methodically searching the deserted gallery with his glittering plastic eyes. Iron Man found himself wishing he could offer some sort of consolation to the Witch's former husband. But how did you ease the feelings of an artificial being who rarely admitted having any?

Maybe the best thing I can do is follow Cap's example and just refuse to abandon hope.

Rapidly running out of leads and deductive leaps, Iron Man decided to fall back on the high-tech approach that usually worked for him. Activating his short-range sensors, he scanned the gallery all along the electromagnetic spectrum, searching for any anomalous readings. A beam from his chest projection unit swept the empty chamber; if there were any charged particles, unusual radiation, or unstable molecules in the vicinity, the beam would record their presence and transmit the data to the optical display in his helmet. At first, all he could detect was the solar-based bio-electricity that powered the Vision, but, after fine-tuning his instruments to compensate for the synthezoid's presence, he was surprised to register something quite unexpected.

"Well, I'll be," he murmured aloud.

"What is it?" Captain America waited expectantly, clearly confident in Iron Man's ability to provide a scientific solution to this mystery. "Have you got something?"

The Vision waited stoically behind Cap, descending to a few inches above the floor. Whatever thoughts might have been passing through his cybernetic brain remained his alone.

"It doesn't make sense," Iron Man said, checking and recalibrating his sensors just to be sure, "but I'm picking up persistent traces of radiation. Not enough to endanger anyone, but pervasive enough to have been left behind by something very recently."

His mind instantly raced through the various exhibits he had glimpsed throughout the folk art museum: hand-carved weathervanes, decorative quilts, rustic needlework and water colors. He couldn't think of a location less likely to be trafficking in radioactive materials. But there the evidence was, as clear as the illuminated read-outs before his eyes.

"What kind of radiation?" Cap asked. It occurred to Iron Man that his fellow hero had actually attended the original atomic blast at Los Alamos, another piece of history in which Captain America had personally taken part. "Anything special?"

"You bet," Iron Man answered tersely. Every sensor confirmed the same ominous truth. "It's *gamma* radiation."

The very force that created the rampaging, half-ton monster known as the incredible Hulk.

The headquarters of the 6th Precinct was a two-story building on West 10th Street, only a few city blocks away from the park where Rogue had achieved such a dubious form of TV stardom. If any vital evidence had been left behind by her struggle with the mysteriously energetic tee-shirts, it would have been taken here.

Night had descended on 10th Street, bringing with it a highly unusual visitor. Casing the police station from across the street, standing under the awning of a small antique store, the Beast shook his head and sighed philosophically.

This would be ever so much easier, he thought, *if I was still with the Avengers.* Then he could have just waltzed right in, flashed his genuine Avengers I.D. card, and received the full cooperation of the N.Y.P.D., including unrestricted access to the evidence. As an X-Man searching for another X-Man, however, he could hardly expect the same sort of VIP treatment. *Alas, our status as outlaws and renegades is the cross which all we merry mutants must bear....*

A palm-sized holographic image inducer, designed years ago by Tony Stark, allowed the otherwise eye-catching anthropoid to loiter inconspicuously upon the sidewalk; to anyone walking by, the Beast looked like merely another ordinary human—specifically, a studious-looking white male with trim brown hair, a tan trenchcoat, and slightly oversized hands. In fact, Hank McCoy had looked much the same when he was younger, before he metamorphosed into a more hirsute form of Beast. He had deliberately patterned the illusion to resemble his earlier self, for old time's sake. Just to play it safe, though, he kept a safe distance from the overhead street lamps. The antique store behind him, like most of the shops on this unprepossessing sidestreet, had been closed for hours.

A stately black limousine cruised past, steered by a serious-looking young man wearing opaque red glasses. The Beast nodded to Cyclops before the car turned onto Hudson Street, signaling to his fellow X-Men that he was ready to make his move. Buckling the belt of the rundown trenchcoat, he stepped out of the shadow of the awning and crossed the moonlit street towards the entrance to the precinct house. He had to force himself to walk normally, as any other human would, rather than bound along as he preferred.

Easy does it, he thought. *We're not invading Asteroid M here, just doing a little low-key reconnoitering.*

The sound of youthful laughter, coming from the bars and outdoor cafes on Hudson, provoked a pang of nostalgia. He and Bobby Drake, better known as Iceman, had spent many fun-filled nights in the Village during their

collegiate years, hanging out at Coffee-a-Go-Go and listening, with their girlfriends, Vera and Zelda, to the
slightly incomprehensible, Beat-styled verses of Bernard
the Poet.

Frankly, the Beast concluded, *that sounds like an em-
inently more appealing prospect than the mission on
which I am presently engaged.*

A solitary flagpole rose from the roof of the squat police station, which was flanked on both sides by much
taller brownstones. The Beast passed through a pair of
glass doors emblazoned with the badge-shaped insignia of
New York's Finest and was immediately greeted by a
large painted sign that read ALL VISITORS PROCEED TO
DESK. Rather than doing so right away, he lingered in the
entrance vestibule to inspect a directory posted on the
wall. His eyes scanned the list of departments housed
within the station house: Community Policing, Crime Prevention, Domestic Violence, Youth Officer, Auxiliary Police, Bomb Squad, Detective Squad, and something
provocatively called a Rip Unit. Nothing about Aggressive Attire or Missing Mutants, which made his task all
the more problematic.

*Let's see—if I were evidence from a paranormal epi-
sode, where would I be?*

Perhaps the Bomb Squad was the place to start; the
rambunctious Rogue had certainly left a big enough crater
in Washington Square Park. Unfortunately, by the time
Hank, Scott, and Ororo had arrived on the scene, the hole
had already been trampled on and about by too many
curious citizens, rendering whatever evidence the X-Men
might have found there hopelessly suspect. Hank could
only hope that the local constabulary had preserved their
evidence in a significantly more pristine condition.

"Can I help you?" a deep voice challenged, an intimidating tone belying the cordiality of its query.

The Beast looked up to see an imposing-looking officer watching him with a less-than-friendly expression on his face. The Beast was impressed by the officer's formidable physique . . . why, his fists looked like they were nearly half as capacious as the Beast's own gorilla-sized mitts. The undercover X-Man hoped his current disguise looked innocuous enough.

"Why, yes!" he improvised. "Is this where I go to get an exemption from jury duty? They've sent me a summons for next month, but you wouldn't believe how inexpressibly impossible that is. I'm much too busy, what with deadlines and sales conferences looming on the horizon, not to mention debugging all the software and getting ready for the end-of-the-millennium crunch. . . ."

As he rambled on, the Beast scoped out the lobby beyond, spotting a pair of stairwells located behind a metal barricade bearing a sign that read STOP. POLICE PERSONNEL ONLY.

That's surely where I want to go, he concluded. *And with all deliberate speed.*

The officer held up a hand to cut the Beast off. "You want the city courthouse, down by Wall Street. But they're closed for the weekend. You'll have to report there in person, during ordinary business hours, Monday through Friday."

"Thank you, officer," the Beast replied, even as he continued to take note of goings-on at the precinct house. "I should have known it wouldn't be that easy."

For late Saturday night, the station seemed strikingly calm and underpopulated; then again, he recalled, this had always been a relatively crime-free neighborhood, as much as any part of Manhattan was. Aside from a couple of German teenagers trying to report a stolen knapsack, all he saw were cops going in and out of the building. He glanced at an old-fashioned analog clock mounted on the wall above a convenient pay phone. It was 11:25 P.M. Almost time for the graveyard shift to come on.

Hmm. That gives me an idea.

Leaving the building, the Beast returned to the shadows across the street, then scanned one of the departing police officers with the "Record" function of the image inducer, storing the parameters of that particular officer's appearance in the device's memory. Then he sat back and waited.

Sure enough, a little after 11:30, there was suddenly a lot more activity around the entrance, with several exiting cops meeting their nocturnal replacements on the way out. The turnover between shifts was obviously well underway; the Beast realized he would never have a better opportunity to slip into the station unnoticed.

But first, he thought, *a little protective coloration.*

Changing the setting on the image inducer, the blue-furred mutant shifted in appearance to a reasonable facsimile of an officer in blue. Hank McCoy's youthful face morphed into the prerecorded visage of the officer he had just observed leaving, right down to the last mole and freckle.

You know, he reflected, considering the furry exterior hidden beneath the holographic disguise, *this brings all new meaning to the faintly archaic vernacular appellation of "fuzz."*

Striding forward with the assumed confidence of one who truly belonged there, he joined the stream of fresh officers pouring into the station house. No one challenged him as he walked past the admissions desk and beyond the metal barricade erected to discourage further passage by civilians.

Upstairs or down? he wondered, trying hard not to look at all lost. Glancing around, he saw a large bulletin board labeled Crime Prevention Center. Black-and-white crime photos shared the board with maps and charts and clipboards, only a few feet away from what, quite mysteriously, appeared to be a Canadian Mountie uniform on display. If only the elusive evidence would just call out to him . . . !

"Hey, O'Donnell," an unfamiliar voice addressed him, "I thought you left already."

It took the Beast a second or two to realize the cop was speaking to him.

"Forgot something," he muttered gruffly, hoping that his interrogator, approaching the disguised X-Man in a matching blue uniform, had not taken note of his momentary hesitation. "Cough drops," he elaborated, throwing in a raspy hack for the sake of verisimilitude.

Will my rather underdeveloped acting abilities be enough to carry the day? he fretted. *Talk about an impersonation devoutly to be wished. . . .*

"Yeah," the other cop said with a shrug. He looked like he'd been on the force for years. The nametag beneath his badge identified him as FORRESTER. "Your voice sounds a little weird. Hoarse, kind of."

The Beast issued a silent prayer of thanksgiving to Melpomene, patron muse of thespians, and started to step away. Unfortunately, the friendly officer seemed to be in no hurry to terminate the conversation. He loitered only a few steps away from the Beast; this cop and O'Donnell were obviously the best of buds.

"You know what really works for sore throats?" Forester said. "Vitamin C. You just have a coupla glasses of O.J. before you turn in tonight and you'll be amazed how much better your throat'll feel in the morning. There's gotta be some orange juice in the fridge back home, assuming Brenda's done her shopping this week."

Who in the name of domestic partnership is Brenda? the Beast wondered. *My wife? My girlfriend? My mother?* It dawned on the beleaguered X-Man that he didn't even know the first name of the man he was impersonating. He was reluctant to open his mouth for fear of blowing his cover through some innocent error. *However does Mystique manage to pull off stunts like these with such aplomb?* he thought, gaining a grudging new respect for the malevolent mutant mistress of disguise.

"Thanks for the tip," he coughed, holding his fist before his mouth. "Well, see you."

Upstairs it is, he decided, stepping decisively toward the beckoning stairwell. Anything was preferable to this torturous charade. "Hey," his newfound buddy called out, "you want a ride to the PATH train?"

Who says NY cops aren't helpful to a fault? the Beast thought, groaning inwardly. Was there no way to escape this oversolicitous officer without calling attention to himself? *For all I know, he's my partner of twenty years.*

"No thanks," he rasped. "I've got to make some calls."

"At this time of night? Like to who?" For the first time, the cop eyed him suspiciously. The Beast fingered the controls of his image inducer, just in case the jig was up and he needed to discard his disguise. What was the legal penalty for impersonating an officer anyway? "You ain't cheating on Brenda, are you?"

Heaven forbid, the Beast thought, looking past his chatty associate at the lobby beyond. The crowd of police officers was already thinning out as the transition between shifts neared completion; the longer he lingered here, the more he risked exposure.

"No way," he promised. "I just want to order some movie tickets before they're sold out."

"Oh yeah?" Forrester said, looking much more curious than the Beast would have liked. The way his luck was going, the other cop would likely turn out to be a film buff. "What flick?"

"Um, *Spider-Man: The Motion Picture,*" he improvised, vaguely remembering a "coming soon" ad he'd seen in a magazine somewhere. *Wonder if that wascally wall-crawler will see any slice of the proceeds from the box office?* Probably not; the courts had long ago ruled that costumed adventurers were public figures and thus fair game for the media. *If anyone ever films an X-Men movie, they'll no doubt pitch it as a horror flick. "Beware the bloodthirsty Beast!"*

"Oh, right," the cop agreed. "I heard that was good." The Beast expected him to launch into a lengthy discourse on the relative artistic pros and cons of the latest summer blockbusters, but, mercifully, the conversation began to show signs of winding down. The loquacious lawman peered down at his wristwatch. "Geez, look at the time. I gotta hit the road. See you tomorrow."

"Yeah, you, too," the Beast replied, breathing a sigh of relief. It looked like he was actually going to get away with this extraordinarily stressful exercise in infiltration.

Then another voice rang out across the lobby, sounding both surprised and aggrieved. "What in the world? That's me!"

The Beast looked up to see the real Officer O'Donnell staring at him, wide-eyed, from the other side of the metal barricade.

"I mean, that's *not* me!" O'Donnell amended, pointing accusingly at his doppleganger, who smiled weakly behind his false features.

Uh-oh, the Beast thought, uncharacteristically speechless.

Heads turned across the lobby as a roomful of New York cops took in the unexpected sight of twin O'Donnells. The chummy policeman with whom the Beast had been conversing for the last several minutes looked the most flabbergasted of all. His confused gaze swung back and forth between the two identical officers. He rubbed his eyes in amazement, but the paradox remained.

"Hey!" Forrester yelled. "What's going on?"

What was the real O'Donnell doing back here? The Beast was nearly as startled as the befuddled onlookers. He'd felt positive that O'Donnell had left for the night.

Probably forgot his cough drops, the Beast theorized. *How annoyingly ironic.*

Realizing that he had been scammed, Forrester lunged at the Beast, but his ordinary human reflexes could not match the X-Man's astounding agility.

"Nice talking to you," the Beast said cheerily, taking the stairs six steps at a time while simultaneously kicking out with his feet to slam a fire door shut in Forrester's face. He hopped up the steps with the utmost alacrity, realizing he had only moments before the entire precinct house would be in an uproar. Spotting a fire alarm mechanism at the top of the stairs, he briefly considered triggering the alarm to provide a much-needed diversion, but, upon rapid deliberation, decided that was simply too anti-social a ploy; what if there was an authentic four-alarm blaze going on elsewhere in the city? He'd never forgive himself if lives were lost due to a false alarm.

"Gangway! Coming through!" the Beast hollered as he careened down a corridor on the second floor, hastily scanning the labels on each door he passed. Plainclothes detectives emerged from doorways in a hurry, only to dive out of the way as the Beast bounced through the halls like an out-of-control rubber ball. One staunch officer, made of sturdier stuff than his fellows, attempted to block the disguised X-Man's path, planting himself squarely in the center of the hall, beefy arms crossed atop his chest. Without even slowing down, the Beast launched himself from the floor and somersaulted over the detective's head, landing on both feet at least a yard further down the hall.

"Alley oop!" he exclaimed.

Sorely tempted to abort his increasingly disordered and quixotic mission, the Beast nevertheless continued to peruse the label on each door that came within view. If he abandoned his quest now, he knew full well, he might also sacrifice the X-Men's only lead, however slender, toward discovering Rogue's whereabouts. He could not in good conscience allow another X-Man to suffer captivity for one instant longer than necessary, not while it remained within his power to do anything about it.

Fear not, fair damsel, he vowed extravagantly. *Help is on the way!*

Footsteps and angry voices pursued him. Doors slammed open in his wake and more officers joined the pursuit.

"Thy chase had a beast in view," he thought, quoting John Dryden, circa 1700 A.D. He was on the verge of

giving up when he spotted the stenciled lettering on a glass-and-metal door at the far end of the corridor: PROPERTY ROOM.

"Eureka!" he exclaimed, grabbing onto the doorknob and throwing it open.

A uniformed officer, seated behind a cheap and chipped wooden desk, blinked in surprise, caught off-guard by the Beast's enthusiastic entrance. "O'Donnell?"

Thank you, trusty image inducer, the Beast thought, grateful for the cop's convenient case of mistaken identity.

Before the officer could even begin to reach for his gun, the Beast seized him by the shoulders, pulled him across the desktop, sending notepads and documents flying while the startled cop yelped loudly, and threw the officer out into the hall. Then he slammed the door shut, cartwheeled over the desktop, shoved the entire piece of furniture up against the closed portal, and turned it on one side, effectively barricading the entrance.

That should buy me a second or two.

Despite his acrobatic exertions, the mutant hero wasn't even breathing hard; compared to the Danger Room, this was a leisurely stroll in the park. He quickly inspected the property room, seeing that the bulk of the physical evidence collected by the precinct's officers was locked away behind a sturdy metal cage that stretched from the floor to the ceiling. Peering through the steel bars, which were painted industrial black, he spied a stack of innocuous-seeming cotton tee-shirts resting on a shelf on the right side of the cage. Trying the door, he discovered that an old-fashioned combination lock protected the enclosure from intruders—in theory, at least.

Beyond the relocated desk, the door to the property

room rattled in its frame. Determined fists pounded against the blockade as heated voices shouted through the doorway, among them the angry tones of both Forrester and the officer the Beast had just evicted from his post. "O'Donnell—or whoever you are—open this door right now! You're not going anywhere!"

We'll cross that bridge when we come to it, the Beast thought, contemplating the cage. First, he needed to get at those shirts. Since there was clearly no time to attempt any elegant safecracking (which was more Storm's specialty, in any event), he was forced to resort to cruder methods to gain access to the cage's interior. Bracing his oversized feet against the floor, he took hold of the cage door with both hands and strained the ape-like muscles beneath his furry pelt (and holographic disguise).

While his brute physical strength wasn't nearly in the same class as, say, Colossus or Rogue, it was nothing to sneeze at, either; the Beast figured he could easily arm-wrestle Spider-Man to a draw, which should be more than enough to overcome whatever elementary metal alloy the cage was comprised of. Fortunately, the N.Y.P.D.'s budget probably didn't allow for adamantium furnishings.

The steel bars shrieked in protest as the Beast tugged on them with all his might, baring his jagged canines as he gritted his teeth. The door came free with a wrenching noise and the broken padlock crashed to the floor. Hurrying into the cage, the Beast went straight for the tee-shirts the cops must have confiscated at the scene of Rogue's apparent abduction. On closer inspection, he saw that the top shirt bore an ugly anti-mutant slogan, and that the entire stack had been stuffed into a clear plastic bag to preserve and protect the integrity of the evidence.

Excellent, he thought. *Let's hear it for professionalism in criminal investigations.*

Judging from the crashing sounds behind him, however, now was no time to conduct his own examination of the suspect shirts. That would have to wait for a more leisurely and private an occasion. He glanced back over his shoulder and saw several arms and hands pushing past the barricaded doorway, trying to get a grip on the overturned desk. The grasping arms were uncomfortably reminiscent of a George Romero zombie flick.

Time to go, the Beast concluded.

Stuffing the entire sack into the deep pocket of his trenchcoat, he glanced about for a plausible means of egress, his gaze quickly landing upon the surprising sight of an antique, standard-issue, U.S. Army bazooka, with accompanying ammunition. *I don't even want to think what criminal or street gang they took that particular piece of hardware off of.* His heart swiftly went out to Spidey, Daredevil, and the city's other urban defenders, not to mention the embattled N.Y.P.D. *Since when did everyday miscreants come complete with heavy artillery?*

Still, perhaps society's loss was his present salvation. Falling back on a bygone crash course in military ordinance conducted by none other than Captain America himself, the Beast loaded the bazooka as expeditiously as possible, then took aim at the ceiling directly overhead. A resounding explosion followed, blowing a sizable hole in the roof of the police station and raining bit-sized chunks of plaster and concrete onto the Beast's bushy head.

"Oh, dear," he murmured, wincing at the damage he had just inflicted on the building. "I'll have to persuade Warren to make a generous donation to the police department on my behalf.'' His billionaire chum could easily afford a whole new station house if necessary, let alone the cost of repairing a hole in the ceiling.

His conscience thus assuaged, the Beast returned the contraband weapon back to where it belonged, then crouched down beneath the newly-created gap, tensing the powerful muscles in his lower limbs. He sprang through the ceiling onto the roof—where he found what looked like an entire squadron of police officers waiting for him.

Well, this is certainly an unexpected and unwelcome development, he thought. *I guess I wasn't the only one who realized the only way out was up.*

''All right, stay where you are!'' a police woman ordered, taking a bead on him with her handgun. Several other officers followed her lead, the real Officer O'Donnell among them. He glowered at the camouflaged Beast with justifiable outrage in his eyes. ''Freeze!''

''I think you have me confused with my friend and associate, the illustrious Iceman,'' the Beast declared. Seeing no further point in his appropriation of O'Donnell's identity and appearance, and hoping for some slight psychological advantage, he flicked off the image inducer in his pocket, appearing before the dumbfounded law enforcement personnel in all his shaggy, simian glory. ''Behold, the bouncing, yet benevolent Beast, at your service.''

As hoped, his abrupt transformation provoked gasps and puzzled expressions. A few of the officers, including O'Donnell, stepped backward involuntarily, the muzzles of their firearms dipping toward the roof beneath their feet.

''I don't get it,'' the Beast heard O'Donnell mutter. ''I thought he was one of the good guys. . . .''

And indeed I am, he thought, although this hardly seemed the most prudent moment to explicate the matter, given that he had just been caught red-handed, as it were. *Or blue-handed, to be more precise.*

Taking advantage of his would-be detainers' momentary discomfiture, the Beast propelled himself across the open roof, his fists wrapping around the flagpole he had noticed earlier. Legs flying out parallel to the ceiling, he swung around and around the pole, his great feet knocking the guns from the hands of the nearest detectives and uniformed officers. He orbited the pole one more time, building up momentum, then let go, sending his furry form hurtling over the heads of the assembled cops and onto the eastern wall of the five-story brownstone bordering the police station. His nimble fingers and toes found purchase in the brownstone's red-brick exterior, and he swiftly began to scale the side of the building.

"Up, up, and away!" he chortled, putting as much distance as he could between himself and the police stranded on the rooftop below.

But, although taken aback by the fuzzy fugitive's spectacular gymnastics, New York's Finest quickly took action.

"Stop, or we'll shoot!" a voice (O'Donnell's?) commanded, followed by a warning shot that sent chips of stone flying off the brick facade only inches from the Beast's skull. Laser sights surrounded him with dime-sized disks of blood-red light. The smell of gunpowder reached his sensitive nostrils.

Egads! the Beast thought, gulping loudly as a second warning shot peppered him with bits of stone and mortar. *I wonder if it's too late to rejoin the Avengers?*

Suddenly, from out of a clear moonlit sky, a roll of

thunder shook the night, drowning out the echoes of the gunshots. A jagged bolt of lightning struck the punctured roof of the precinct house, scattering the throng of armed police officers threatening the Beast and leaving a charred-black scorch mark upon the cement rooftop. A rolling, pea soup fog swept over the scene, instantly reducing visibility to near zero. Immersed in the thick, gray mist, the Beast couldn't see a thing, but he heard a familiar dulcet voice calling out to him with an exotic West African accent.

"Are you ready to leave this place, my friend?" Storm asked from somewhere overhead.

"Ready and willing," he confirmed, feeling the comforting weight of the purloined evidence in his pocket. Despite a few unanticipated complications, he had gotten what he had come for. "Thanks for the airborne assist."

"Your exit could hardly have been more conspicuous," Ororo chided him. Her strong hands grabbed his wrists. With no fear of falling, trusting completely in his fellow X-Man, the Beast released his hold on the brick wall and let Storm, assisted by a powerful gust of wind, carry him aloft.

It never hurts to have a mutant weather witch on your side, he reflected. His bare feet dangled in the air, high above the rooftop below. Lost in the fog, which shortly dispersed, the 6th Precinct receded beneath him, along with several understandably thunderstruck guardians of law and order.

Somehow, the Beast thought, *I don't expect I'm getting invited to the Policeman's Ball this year....*

Later, in the luxurious back seat of Charles Xavier's customized Rolls Royce, the Beast shared the fruits of his arduous adventure with his teammates. Storm sat beside him, looking refreshed by her recent flight, while Cyclops manned the wheel, driving the limousine north and out of the city, back toward the Institute. Discarded after the Beast removed his plunder from its pockets, the wadded-up trenchcoat rested on the empty passenger seat next to Cyclops, even though the air-conditioned interior of the Rolls was significantly cooler than the night outside.

GOD MADE MAN IN HIS IMAGE, THE DEVIL MADE MU-TANTS declared the uppermost of the stolen tee-shirts. The Beast could not help scowling at the inflammatory slogan as he removed the shirt from its plastic sheath and un-folded it on the seat between Storm and himself. The tips of his fangs protruded from beneath his lower lip. It was clear from Ororo's disapproving expression that she was also disturbed by the garment's hate-filled message.

"No matter how many times I encounter such unrea-soning hostility," she commented, "it never fails to sur-prise and sadden me. You would think that such vile sentiments could not endure so long in defiance of all sense and decency."

"To quote the late, great Johann von Schiller, 'against stupidity the very gods themselves contend in vain.' " The Beast sympathized with Storm's disillusionment. Sometimes it seemed like certain regrettable tendencies were never going to change. "I fear the same may be said of prejudice and fear."

In any event, he reminded himself, there was little that could be done tonight concerning the thorny and dismay-ingly intractable problem of human/mutant relations. The most they could hope for was some clue to point the way to wherever Rogue now resided, almost certainly against her will. He declined to even consider the other, unspoken possibility: that Cerebro could not find their absent friend because she was no longer alive.

I won't believe that until I see a body, and maybe not even then. If there was one thing the Beast knew, amidst all his vast erudition, it was that X-Men were harder to kill than cockroaches.

He scanned the shirt with a handheld sensor based on advanced Shi'ar designs. The device, which he had taken care to bring along from the mansion, was several hundred times more sensitive than any equivalent Terran technology, and almost certainly many orders of magnitude more acute than any apparatus available to the N.Y.P.D. If there was anything unusual to be found, the sensor would surely alert them to its presence.

Granted, these garments were merely those left behind at the devastated fair booth, not the ones that Rogue carried away with her in her short-lived flight toward freedom. Still, these shirts presumably came from the same batch that had yielded Rogue's textile tormentors. The Beast resolved to stay wary, lest the pilfered tee-shirts suddenly turn on the limousine's passengers, but so far the cheap cotton apparel had displayed no evidence of vitality whatsoever.

Thank Providence for small favors, he thought. After successfully evading the eager clutches of the police, he had no desire to tangle with a bevy of belligerent attire.

Scanning for everything from mystical energy to signs of life, he carefully inspected the read-outs on the illuminated display panel. *I am going to feel extremely foolish,* he reflected, *if my in-depth investigation reveals nothing more ominous than a MADE IN KOREA label.*

Imagine stealing the shirts from the police for no reason at all!

But that proved not to be the case.

"Well, I'll be a primate's progenitor," he declared, staring at the results of the scan with keen scientific curiosity. His blue eyes flared with intellectual excitement. "In more ways than one."

"What is it?" Cyclops asked from the driver's seat. Eagerness and anxiety warred within his voice. "Did you find something?" Ororo listened expectantly as well.

"Indeed I have," the Beast announced, switching off the scanner and placing it gently upon the garments in question. "According to our equipment, all of these undeniably insulting items of clothing have been recently exposed to gamma radiation. Not exactly a standard feature of ordinary sweatshop output, I'm certain."

"*Gamma* radiation?" Cyclops repeated in surprise, although the Beast was pleased to see that their erstwhile leader kept his super-energized eyes on the road.

"With a capital G," he confirmed. "There's no mistaking these readings." He wondered if and when the police would have ever detected the contamination. *I didn't see any Geiger counters around the precinct house.*

"Well done, my friend," Storm said warmly. She eyed the pilfered garments with a new wariness. "But I don't understand. How can radiation bring mere clothing to life?"

"You've got me there," he admitted, considering the problem from every angle. Outside the tinted windows, the lights of the city gave way to a tree-lined highway as the car carried them toward their home in Salem Center. The Beast scratched his hairy chin. *Gamma radiation . . .*

The X-Men were often called the "Children of the Atom," based on a trendy theory relating the rapid increase in human mutations to the spread of nuclear power. There was some truth to this theory, the Beast conceded; indeed, his own parents had been employed in the fledgling atomic industry, which probably contributed to his exceptional characteristics. Subsequent work, conducted by such respected authorities as Charles Xavier and Dr. Moira MacTaggert, had also explored the potential impact of various forms of radiation on human DNA, especially during conception and fetal development. As a scientist as well as a super hero, Henry McCoy had reviewed all the pertinent literature on the subject and even written a few incisive monographs himself, probing the causes and possibilities of human mutation. Consequently, the Beast felt he knew quite a lot about the intertwined mysteries of radiation and mutation.

That being said, he also knew there was only one man on Earth who was the undisputed authority on the effects of gamma radiation in particular: Dr. Robert Bruce Banner.

The man who was also known as the unstoppable mountain of muscle that a terrified world had named . . . the Hulk.

Chapter Seven

Cruising majestically 25,000 feet above sea level, the S.H.I.E.L.D. Helicarrier was the largest moving object capable of soaring over the Earth. A huge mobile command base for the world's premiere intelligence organization, the Helicarrier looked big enough to house a couple of Boeing 747s and still have room left over for a decent-sized shopping mall. Smaller aircraft buzzed and hovered around the immense vessel like jet fighters around a Navy aircraft carrier, landing and departing constantly while the Helicarrier remained aloft twenty-four hours a day, keeping watch over the world it was built to protect. Many noted meteorologists maintained that the Helicarrier was so colossal, and its energy output so vast, that it had a direct effect on the weather conditions in whatever airspace it was currently occupying. This was probably true; certainly, it was casting a massive shadow on portions of eastern Montana at this very moment.

Aboard the Helicarrier, in the office of the Executive Director, Nicholas Fury was not having a good day.

"Blast it, Val!" he swore, pounding his fist on his desk. "How hard is it to find a UFO? It's been hours since we first tracked that thing." He gulped down a steaming cup of black coffee—his fifth that day—then took a long drag on the stump of a cigar clenched between his teeth. Technically, smoking was forbidden anywhere on the Helicarrier, but the only person who had ever had the nerve to point that out to Nick Fury quickly lived to regret it. Last anyone had heard, he was still serving extended duty in Antarctica.

LOST AND FOUND

If I can survive World War II and a coupla hundred Hydra assassins, Fury thought, as the smoke warmed his lungs, *a little caffeine and tobacco ain't about to kill me.*

"The Air Force, NASA, and our own units are searching for the mystery ship at this very moment," a tall, dark-haired woman reminded him, her voice holding a distinct European accent. Like Fury, the Countess Valentina Allegro de Fontaine wore the standard blue jumpsuit worn by any S.H.I.E.L.D. field agent, complete with shoulder holster, handgun, plasma beam projector, and other lethal accessories. Even though they were currently occupying the nerve center of the world's most formidable flying fortress, years of experience had taught both Fury and his second-in-command to be ready for anything, anytime, and anywhere. "Even the cosmonauts on Mir are keeping an eye out for this elusive UFO."

"Right!" Fury barked. The empty socket behind his trademark black eyepatch itched something terrible, like it always did when trouble was brewing, but he refused to scratch out of sheer cussedness. "Like I'd trust the Russkies to share classified intel out of the goodness of their hearts."

"The Cold War is over, Nick," Val said, sounding faintly amused by her boss's intransigent attitude. Only a white streak rising up through the lofty pile of jet-black hair above her unwrinkled brow indicated that the Countess had been in the spy game almost as long as Fury.

"Yeah, that's what they *want* us to think," Fury replied, exhaling an acrid cloud of smoke into the pressurized atmosphere of the immense airship. A half-day's growth of stubble carpeted his jaw. "You and I both know better."

Deep down, though, he knew Val had a point. This

didn't feel like a Russian operation, Red or otherwise, which was one reason he had brought Cap and the Avengers into the loop. Ordinarily, Fury preferred to handle matters of international security without relying on the Avengers, the Fantastic Four, or any other super-powered civilians, thank you very much, but if these UFO sightings were the first glimmerings of another extraterrestrial offensive, then the Avengers might be the only people equipped to handle the threat. Good as S.H.I.E.L.D.'s hardware was—the best on Earth, probably—he knew darn well that it didn't stack up against the futuristic super-science of Galactus or the Celestials.

Blasted aliens, he fumed. It's not like there weren't enough cockamamie menaces on Earth already. Faxes blanketed the top of his stainless steel desk, containing updates and status reports from field agents and regional directors all over the world, bringing him up to speed on any number of brewing situations that might soon require immediate intervention by S.H.I.E.L.D. He quickly sorted through the documents, scanning them for the pertinent details. An underground A.I.M. laboratory somewhere south of Seattle, rumored to be the site of unsanctioned time travel experiments. A reported alliance between two Hydra splinter groups, in Berlin and Stockholm, respectively. Rumors of industrial espionage at Stark-Fujikawa, including advanced computer technology diverted to the Zodiac crime cartel. Ceasefire violations along the Wakandan border. Civil unrest in Genosha. New leads pointing toward the possible hidden lairs of Baron Zemo, Modok, Viper, Fenris, the Red Skull, the Yellow Claw, and other regular fixtures on S.H.I.E.L.D.'s Ten Most Wanted List. The usual, in other words.

All in a day's work, he thought sourly.

And now, on top of everything else, an Unknown Flying Object that persisted in staying Unknown despite the best efforts of S.H.I.E.L.D.'s considerable resources, and up to who knew what. Fury ground out the remains of his stogie in the adamantium ashtray on his desk, rubbing the ashes into a scorched photo of Baron Wolfgang Von Strucker, and wished he could dispose of the nagging problem of the mystery ship as easily.

"Keep watchin' the blasted skies," he muttered under his breath. "Why can't these everlovin' ET types stick to their own backyards?"

It didn't help his mood any that the Helicarrier was carrying him farther and farther away from the vicinity of the UFO sightings. While security considerations clearly dictated that S.H.I.E.L.D.'s command center be moved away from any potentially hostile aircraft, running away always rubbed Fury the wrong way. There was a reason his office was surprisingly compact, barely large enough for a small meeting; he didn't want to get too comfortable sitting behind a desk.

If there's a nasty brawl ahead, I want to be where the action is, not sitting tight hundreds of miles away.

As if in answer to his unspoken request, a warning siren suddenly caught both Fury and the Countess by surprise.

"What the—?" he exclaimed, shooting an inquisitive glance at Val, who didn't know any more than he did. He slammed down his palm on the intercom switch on his desk, heedless of the faxes that went sliding off the edge of the desk to flutter unnoticed to the floor. "This is Fury," he snapped, spitting out the words like bullets from an automatic rifle. "What the devil is going on?"

"Intruders on Deck Four," an automated voice reported. "All security forces report to site of breach. Instituting stage-three containment procedures. . . ."

Fury was already away from his desk and out the door, with Val right on his tail, pausing only long enough to stuff a couple of particularly sensitive documents into the shredder. A Colt automatic in his hand, Fury joined a stampede of armed agents rushing to defend the Helicarrier from the still-unidentified invaders.

What's the matter with our security perimeter? he wondered. In theory, the smaller aircraft surrounding the Helicarrier should have intercepted any hostiles before they ever got close enough to board the vast airship itself. *Why wasn't there any warning?*

The shrill alarm blared in his ears. Unwilling to take a chance on the mag-rail elevators during an emergency situation, Fury shoved the Colt back into his shoulder holster and clambered hand-over-hand down a sturdy maintenance ladder, counting off the decks as he descended rapidly toward who knew what.

Deck Four, he considered as he climbed. That was mostly R&D: state-of-the-art laboratories where S.H.I.E.L.D.'s crack team of scientists and technicians developed everything from new particle-beam weapons to the latest generation of Life Model Decoys. Pretty darn convenient, Fury thought, that the invaders chose that region to stage their incursion. He'd bet his government pension, which he never expected to collect anyway, that they knew exactly what they were looking for.

Valentina's steel-toed boots rang against the metal rungs right above Fury's head. "Nick," she suggested hesitantly, "maybe you should hang back until we find out what exactly we're dealing with here." From the tone of her voice, she knew this idea wasn't going to fly with

Fury, but felt obliged to bring it up, anyway. "We can't afford to lose you."

"Not a chance," he barked gruffly. The day he had to hide behind a battalion of bodyguards, like some president or senator, was the day he'd hang up his eyepatch for good. "Nobody breaks into my HQ without an invite, not without gettin' a .45-caliber welcome from me."

As he neared his destination, Fury could hear the unmistakable sound of battle raging, like a small war had erupted on Deck Four. Gunfire crackled and voices shouted, along with a series of hisses, zaps, and buzzes of a less recognizable nature. Fury smelt both gunpowder and ozone in the air and felt the ladder tremble in his grip. A series of violent shocks shook the Helicarrier, which was swiftly losing altitude, perhaps to cope with the loss of air pressure on the research deck. Judging from the lack of explosive decompression, not to mention the fact that he could still breathe, Fury guessed that the titanic airship's automatic self-maintenance systems had already sealed whatever gap the enemy boarding party had torn in the hull. He just hoped whoever was flying the Helicarrier right now knew what they were doing. Chances were, Fury'd be too busy fighting off the bad guys to approve any flight plans for a while.

But what kind of customers was he gunning for? Who in heck had the nerve and the gall to stage a raid on S.H.I.E.L.D. HQ? Dropping from the ladder onto the quaking floor of Deck Four, Fury quickly ran through all the possibilities. Hydra? The Serpent Society? The Mutant Liberation Front? Nothing in any of his daily briefings and status reports had even hinted at an enemy operation of this magnitude.

Just that blasted UFO, he thought, all his instincts pinning the blame on the mystery ship. In his gut, he knew there had to be a connection. *Guess there's no time like the present to find out who's come knockin',* he thought, drawing his handgun. The customized blue-steel firearm fit perfectly into his hand.

"Heads up, everybody!" he hollered to Val and the other agents coming down the ladder behind him. He recognized Lee, Coning, Plummer, and Schwartz—all solid agents. They dropped onto the shaking deck without a single misstep. "Let's show these trespassers what we think of surprise visits!"

Rounding a corner into a spacious testing area, over a city block in size, he was prepared to confront anybody from foreign terrorists to alien space monsters. The last people he expected to see fighting a team of hard-pressed S.H.I.E.L.D. operatives were . . . the X-Men?

Unlike like many of his peers in the CIA and the NSA, Fury had never regarded the notorious mutant team as more dangerous to public safety than any of the other high-profile super-groups proliferating out there in this brave new world of costumed cut-ups with paranormal powers. To tell the truth, he'd always figured the X-Men served a useful strategic function in keeping tabs on the real bad apples in the mutant community, like Magneto and his fanatical Acolytes. *Let the super-weirdoes police themselves, while the rest of us take care of our own problems,* that was his philosophy, at least until one or more of the costumed clan got seriously out of line. To date, the X-Men had never risen to the top of Fury's "to-do" list. He had his hands full with *real* hard cases.

But if that was the case, then what were they doing here, wreaking havoc on the Helicarrier with their freakish talents for destruction? Before his one remaining eye, brightly-garbed figures whom Fury identified as past and present X-Men took on his own people, each in their own bizarre fashion. A jagged gap in the ceiling, nearly two yards across, testified to the mutants' initial angle of attack, but their goal appeared to be a sealed airlock at the opposite end of the staging area, which the first wave of courageous S.H.I.E.L.D operatives were doing their best to defend, despite the uncanny forces arrayed against them.

Clad in an eye-catching crimson costume, his face concealed behind a stylized mask that made him resemble some exotic Asian demon, Sunfire directed intense blasts of heat and flame at hard-pressed S.H.I.E.L.D. agents, who were forced to fall back before the thermal onslaught, despite the fire-resistant Beta Cloth (type C) in their uniforms. The Japanese mutant kept up the offensive, discharging his fusillade from both hands.

I don't get it, Fury thought. He could feel the heat from Sunfire's blasts even from a distance. *Yoshida usually sticks pretty close to his homeland. What's he doing here?*

Standing beside Sunfire, mouth wide open beneath a mop of unruly orange hair, the Irish mutant codenamed Banshee added his own powerful sonic screams to their joint assault. Although less visible than his compatriot's flashy fireworks, Banshee's wails were no less effective; stricken security officers threw their hands over their ears, letting go of their automatic rifles and high-tech ray guns even as the weapons vibrated to pieces within their grips. So tightly focused was the sonic bombardment that Fury and his reinforcements, approaching the fray at a right angle, barely heard more than a faint, high-pitched whine. Banshee's green-and-yellow costume contrasted dramatically with Sunfire's own crimson garb, making the regulation blue of the besieged S.H.I.E.L.D. agents even more uniform and interchangeable by comparison. Crinkly wrinkles around the Irishman's merry green eyes hinted at the fortyish mutant's age. Striped black-and-yellow wings hanging beneath Banshee's arms reminded Fury that, like Sunfire, the shrieking Irishman was fully capable of taking flight if necessary.

This is crazy, Fury thought, taking aim with his .45 while filling his free hand with a palm-sized fragmentation bomb from a pouch on his belt. *Sean Cassidy is an ex-Interpol agent, for pete's sakes! What the devil is he thinking?* Deciding to try the stun-bomb before resorting to deadly force, out of respect for Cassidy's roots in law enforcement, he hurled the bomb with all his strength, aiming it straight between Sunfire and Banshee. *That should knock them off their feet,* he thought, counting down to the expected detonation. "Three, two, one . . ."

A wall of solid ice formed in the grenade's path, blocking its downward arc and freezing the bomb in mid-air a heartbeat before it exploded. Fury did not have to look far to find the source of the unexpected arctic fortification—sliding forward on a swiftly-forming sheet of frictionless white ice, Iceman, his entire body seemingly sculpted from translucent blue ice, joined Banshee and Sunfire at the front line of the conflict. More ice spraying from his fingertips like water, the refrigerated X-Man defended his fellow invaders with a shield that rose in front of Sunfire and Banshee, and from behind which the other mutants continued to direct destructive volleys of sound and flame. Fury was impressed that Iceman could construct and maintain his miniature glaciers even in the presence of Sunfire's volcanic combustion.

He just keeps pouring it on, Fury noted. He could feel

the very air around him growing arid and more parched as Iceman leeched all available moisture out of the atmosphere to construct his dense, frigid barricade. Fury swallowed repeatedly to keep his throat from drying up while a trickle of blood leaked from his nostrils.

"Never did like air conditioning," he muttered to himself as he removed a thermite grenade from his belt and threw it at the wall of ice. "This ought to heat things up a bit."

Right on target, the bomb flew toward the instantly-erected snow fort—until an invisible force seized hold of the grenade and flung it back at Fury and the rest.

What the hey? Fury thought, jaw dropping in surprise only a second before battle-honed reflexes kicked in and sent him diving for safety. His palms and elbows skidded across the floor as he hit the ground.

"Incoming!" he warned Val and the other agents, squeezing his eye shut to spare it from the blinding flash he knew was coming. "Duck and cover!"

A white-hot explosion of heat and light went off less than two yards from where Fury landed, giving one side of his face a bad case of sunburn. Nick scrambled to his feet and opened his eye. His toasted profile stung like blazes.

That was a close one, he realized. The thermite charge had scorched the metal floor where Fury had stood only a moment before. *Someone is playing for keeps.*

But who? None of the X-Men he'd identified so far were reported to have that sort of telekinetic power. Peering past the three men apparently leading the assault, he spotted a striking, red-haired woman in a gleaming green-and-gold costume. A metallic gold sash clung to her hips while a generous cloud of carmine-colored curls billowed about her head, as though held aloft by the same unseen force that had snatched the firebomb in its flight. Her blue eyes glowed with psionic energy.

Figures, Fury thought, immediately I.D.ing the woman as Jean Grey, alias Marvel Girl or Phoenix or whatever she was calling herself these days. S.H.I.E.L.D. had a file on her two inches thick, including her various clones, doubles, and counterparts, even documenting one lady, also codenamed Phoenix, who was alleged to be her full-grown daughter from an alternate future!

I knew there was a reason I hated getting mixed up in this mutant stuff, Fury groused silently.

"Everyone in one piece?" he asked hastily, glancing over his shoulder to see Val and the two or three nearest agents rising to their feet. To his relief, none of them looked seriously harmed by the boomeranging grenade, although the Countess's elegant features seemed a little redder than usual and his nose detected something that smelled suspiciously like burnt hair.

"We're fine," she assured him, reasonably unruffled by their recent brush with incineration. She cradled a .30-caliber automatic machine pistol against her chest. Her keen eyes fixed on the sturdy airlock that was clearly the X-Men's objective. NO ADMITTANCE, a lighted sign above the doorway read. LEVEL 2 CLEARANCE REQUIRED. "What do you think they're after, Nick?"

"Heck if I know," Fury admitted. It was the bane of his existence that, no matter how hard he tried to stay on top of things, S.H.I.E.L.D. was simply too big and multi-purposed for any one man to keep track of, especially if he wasn't a scientist. For all he knew, any number of experiment research projects could be going on behind those polished titanium doors. Whatever it could be, it was obvious the X-Men wanted it, and Fury didn't think that a little thing like a lack of the proper security clearance was going to slow them down one bit.

That's our job, he thought, hefting his Colt.

Mindful of Banshee's acoustic powers, he took a pair of protective ear plugs from his supply belt and quickly inserted them into his auditory canals, then signaled Val and the others to do the same. The plugs couldn't protect them completely from the mutant's sonic barrage, he knew, but it might give them a moment's advantage.

Better than nothing, I guess.

The mutant boarding party made swift progress toward the laboratory entrance, Iceman's protective wall of frozen moisture advancing ahead of them while protecting them on both sides as well, forming a horseshoe of solid ice at least a foot thick at its weakest points. Sunfire kept the X-Men moving forward by melting away the ice directly in front of them even as Iceman spread more ice further ahead. By now, the first wave of defenders had been thoroughly routed, forced to abandon their positions by the relentless force of Sunfire and Banshee's dual blitzkrieg. Those agents still standing helped carry their wounded colleagues to safety as Fury fearlessly led his own team into the breach, ducking his head beneath streams of flame while firing repeated clips of ammo over the top of the icy wall.

To his chagrin, he glimpsed the bullets melting into molten lead as soon as they came within proximity of Sunfire's incandescent, super-heated aura. A hail of gunfire dissolved into a rain of liquid metal that produced rising tendrils of steam, the melted ammo tunneling through Iceman's impromptu stockade.

That's no good, Fury realized, wincing at the timbre

of Banshee's incessant wail. Even through his regulation earplugs, designed to muffle the impact of both explosions and gunfights, the eerie siren was enough to set all his nerves on edge and bring on a killer headache. Trickles of blood leaked from his ears. *Time to change tactics.*

He emptied the clip of his .45 into the oncoming ice wall, blasting gaps and fissures in the frost-covered barrier that refilled almost instantly, then he switched to the .5mm plasma projector in his side holster. The beam of ionized particles produced by the blaster proved more effective against the mutants' advance than conventional gunfire, reducing solid ice to vapor. The wall of ice receded faster than Iceman could replenish the X-Men's defenses, leaving the invaders semi-exposed.

Following his lead, Val, Lee, and the others abandoned their various firearms in favor of plasma blasters. Banshee was forced to vary the pitch and volume of his sonic output, altering the nature of the wail from a weapon to a protective force field, shielding him from the unleashed power of the energy weapons. Composed of standing sound waves, the force barrier was invisible, but Fury could see the plasma blasts swerve around it. Sunfire reeled before the surging plasma, dropping onto one knee before retreating behind Banshee and his sonic shield, joining Jean Grey who had already drawn back to put more distance between her and the plasma barrage, but not before Fury spotted the symbol spread out upon her chest: a golden silhouette of a bird in flight.

Phoenix it is, he deduced.

Streams of hot ions rippled around her, diverted by a telekinetic forcefield that he could have sworn resembled a bird. The flame-like glow in her eyes grew bright enough to hide the natural color of her pupils, giving her face an eerie appearance. Telekinetically-tossed red tresses seethed like the serpentine crown of an enraged gorgon. Only Iceman appeared to go on the offensive, showering the S.H.I.E.L.D. agents with a cannonade of icy hail even as the crystalline planes of the X-Man's frozen body began to melt away, streaming down his frame to puddle at his feet.

"Take that, you human popsicle!" Fury growled, ignoring the stinging impact of the hail against his exposed face, grateful that the 9-ply Kevlar in his uniform spared him the worst of the hailstorm. He kept squeezing the trigger of his blaster, encouraged by the beam's punitive effect. Val and other others formed a defensive phalanx around him, the agents in the back firing over the heads of Fury and the frontmost fighters.

That's the ticket, he thought. *Looks like we're starting to turn this thing around.*

Then, without warning, he felt his own gun try to tear itself free from his grip. The weapon seemed possessed of its own will, twisting and bucking with surprising strength. Nor was his the only blaster that had suddenly decided to make a break for it; out of the corner of his eye, he saw Schwartz's weapon fly from the baffled agent's hand. More blasters joined in the exodus, levitating across the open test area until they came within range of Sunfire's incendiary blasts, which reduced the runaway ray guns to molten metal in seconds, shooting them out of the air like so many flying ducks. It took all of Fury's strenuous efforts to keep his own blaster from committing mechanical suicide by joining its slagged counterparts in a lemming-like leap to destruction. The knuckles of his right hand turned white where he squeezed tightly upon the grip and trigger, while his left hand pushed down hard on the muzzle of the blaster to keep it from tilting upward against his will.

"No way, X-Gal," he grunted, recognizing Jean Grey's telekinetic prowess at work. Forget his cold, dead body—the only way anyone was prying his gun out of his hand was by vaporizing him down to the last atom.

I hope Chuck Heston appreciates this. He bet the N.R.A. had never worried about guns that tried to liberate themselves from their legal owners.

Gritting his teeth so tightly that he could have flattened a penny between his molars, while the fingers around his blaster felt like they were ready to break off, Fury kept assailing the X-Men with a cascade of hot plasma, even as doubts about the whole blasted setup began to simmer at the back of his mind.

Something's not right here, he realized, *besides the obvious.* An X-Men team consisting of Sunfire, Banshee, Iceman, and Phoenix? That didn't gibe with his most recent intel. Sure, the X-Men, like most super-squads, changed their roster more often than a major league baseball team, but this lineup sounded more fishy than most. According to reliable sources, Banshee was semi-retired these days, running some private school in Massachusetts, while Sunfire hadn't been an active member of the team for years. This was like a "Greatest Hits" version of the X-Men, put together out of personnel plucked from various eras in the team's colorful history.

A fine time to stage a class reunion, Fury thought. *If that's what this really is.*

Frankly, he was starting to have his doubts.

Any suspicions he might have been forming, however, were driven out of his head by the startling arrival of another intruder. Propelled by an impressive pair of blue metallic wings, the newcomer swooped through the gap in the ceiling and flew over the heads of his mutant cohorts to carry the fight back to Fury and his agents. The new combatant's skin and costume were as blue as his artificial wings, with only his light blonde hair providing any relief from his sleek, monochromatic appearance.

Archangel, Fury recognized at once, worried less about the winged mutant's fashion sense than the glint of the overlapping, razor-sharp blades that feathered the underside of Archangel's powerful pinions. *Wait a sec,* he objected silently. *I thought Worthington had grown a new pair of organic wings—fluffy white feathers and all . . . ?*

Belying Fury's doubts, based on meticulous and extensive intelligence on all known parahuman principals and their associates, Archangel unleashed a volley of knife-edged flechettes that shot forth from his wings to strike at the S.H.I.E.L.D. forces with merciless accuracy. To Nick's right, a flechette struck Agent Plummer in the shoulder, slicing through the reinforced Kevlar and Beta Cloth like they were tissue paper. More than simply a sharpened blade, the flechette imparted a taser-like shock to the unlucky agent's nervous system. Plummer convulsed once, his eyes rolling up until only the whites were visible, then collapsed onto the metal floor like a sack of potatoes. All around him, Fury heard agents crying out, then hitting the ground hard.

Whatever we're protecting, he thought bitterly, *I hope it's worth it.*

"Nick! Watch out!" The Countess threw herself in front of Fury, just in time to take a flechette right below her ribs. She spasmed for only a second before mercifully crumpling to the floor, landing in a heap in front of Fury's feet.

Blast it, Val, he thought, *you didn't have to do that.*

Now the last man standing, he tried to raise up his gunsight, to take out the airborne hooligan who had decked Val and the others, but his blaster still fought against his control, spurred on by the telekinetic mojo of Phoenix. He couldn't bring the weapon up fast enough to stop Archangel from releasing another salvo of flechettes, which whistled through the air toward Fury and the others.

The first blade struck him in the thigh, slashing through flesh and fabric like a scalpel, and carrying a bio-electric charge that raced through Fury's body. Every hair on his body stood on end, and he bit down on his tongue so hard he drew blood.

Metal wings again? Fury thought in the instant before losing consciousness. *Something doesn't add up. . . .*

The blaster was still clutched in his fist when his body dropped onto the floor of Deck Four.

A ⊗

Chapter Eight

"The operations went off smoothly, as you foretold."

"Of course. With my exceptional mental faculties, it was child's play to anticipate our subjects' movements and prepare appropriate receptions."

"If you say so, but do not neglect my own contributions to the success of our endeavor. The subjects could not have been so easily captured if not for the special training and talents of my lieutenants."

"Naturally. I by no means intended to discount the efforts of you and your followers. Our newly-forged alliance has already yielded positive results, in the form of our three unwilling visitors. . . ."

Logan awoke to find himself immersed in one of his least favorite memories. Or so it first seemed.

Metal restraints held him fast within what looked like the bottom half of a futuristic sarcophagus, inclined at a forty-five degree angle from the floor. Electrodes and sensors were affixed to his forehead, throat, chest, and other junctures on his body. Hypodermic needles speared his skin, threading the veins and arteries underneath. Electrical cables coiled around matching I.V. lines that snaked over the sides of the steel coffin to disappear beyond his confined field of vision. As is, the wall-sized mirror facing him showed him far more of his captive state than he would have liked: trussed up like a mummy inside the metal coffin, multicolored cables swathing him in place of dusty bandages. He had no doubt that, on the other side of the mirror, peering through a sheet of one-way glass, the unknown parties responsible for his captivity were monitoring him at this very moment.

Just like before. That lab in Canada, so many years ago. The experiments. The pain . . .

Triggered by the memories, a feral rage rose within him, threatening to swamp his hard-won rationality. A blood-red haze swam before his eyes. Jagged teeth gnashed together. Steel claws erupted from clenched fists, but clamps upon his wrists prevented him from tearing apart the apparatus that trapped him. Additional clamps held down his legs and neck.

"Gotta stay in control," he whispered to himself, holding back the bestial roar building in his throat. *Can't let the animal get loose. . . .*

It wasn't easy, though. Feverish, distorted memories of being trapped once before, of being poked and prodded like a lab animal, of being forcibly altered and made even less human than he had been before, flared within his mind, urging him to strike out blindly, unchain the raging beast at the core of his soul.

"Not again," Wolverine snarled, his eyes wild. Flecks of foam appeared at the corners of his mouth.

"Logan?"

Rogue's magnolia-tinged voice called him back to sanity. For the first time, he became aware that he was not alone in this mirrored mausoleum. *Who else got snatched?* he wondered, fearing that the rest of the X-Men had been captured as well.

Straining to lift his head despite the metal band stretched across his throat, Logan managed to crane his head enough to see two more sarcophagi reflected in the horizontal mirror, each one holding another tube-and-wire-bedecked hostage clad in matching orange plastic jumpsuits that, he assumed, looked better on Rogue and the other woman than they did on him. Rogue's elevated coffin was directly to the right of Logan, with the third prisoner farther down the row. From what he could see, she had it worse than either he or Rogue. An opaque metal visor completely covered her eyes. He guessed she couldn't see a thing, if she was even conscious at all.

Least there's only the three of us, it looks like. That's somethin', I guess.

It took him a second or two to recognize the blindfolded woman, as much by her scent as by her curly auburn hair: Wanda Maximoff, the Scarlet Witch.

Magneto's daughter, he thought uncharitably, then granted that it wasn't exactly fair to hold her old man's crimes against her. He didn't know the Witch very well, but figured she couldn't be too much like her father, otherwise a bunch of Boy Scouts like the Avengers would've never let her into their club. *Probably ought to give her the benefit of the doubt. Least for now.*

"I hear ya, Rogue," he replied. Needles in his throat made it painful to speak. He tested the bonds holding his arms and legs, with little success. *No big surprise there,* he decided; if these shiny steel manacles were strong enough to hold Rogue, there was no way he was breaking out of them anytime soon. He'd just have to wait for the right opportunity to escape. It would come; it always did. "What about you, Witchie?" he called out to their neighbor. "You with us?"

"So it appears," she answered. Her accent sounded a bit like Magneto's. Czech maybe, or Ukrainian. "And my name is Wanda."

"This here's Wolverine," Rogue volunteered, thinking perhaps that Wanda wouldn't recognize their voices.

"And ah'm Rogue. From the X-Men, you know?"

"I know who *you* are," the Witch said icily, with special emphasis on the pronoun. "Carol Danvers is a friend of mine."

Caught offguard by the rebuke, Rogue couldn't conceal her stricken expression.

Ouch, Logan thought. *That's gotta hurt.*

Rogue was carrying around a lot of guilt where Carol Danvers was concerned. Back when Carol was still calling herself Ms. Marvel, a younger Rogue, led astray by Mystique, had permanently stolen the female Avenger's strength and super-powers, along with most of Carol's memories. Carol had been a long time recovering from that devastating attack on her very identity, and, from what Logan had heard, she still suffered psychological scars from the whole crummy business.

No more so than Rogue, he knew, although he supposed he couldn't expect Carol's old Avengers buddy to understand that.

"I've known Danvers longer than either of you," Logan stated bluntly. It was true, too; he and Carol had teamed up on plenty of risky spy missions back when they were both doing the secret agent thing, way before either he or Carol got sucked into the super hero biz. "And none of that old news is goin' to do us a bit of good here. So let's put any bad blood behind us, at least 'til we bring down the house on whatever dirtbag shanghaied us."

The Scarlet Witch couldn't exactly nod her head, not with her neck pinned down, but she looked like she got the message. "Point made, X-Man," she said coolly.

Logan caught a look of relief on Rogue's face. *Remind me to teach that girl how to play poker,* he thought; sometimes her emotions were way too obvious.

"Where do you think we are?" Wanda asked.

Good question, he thought. While Rogue described their prison to the blindfolded Witch, Logan sniffed the air for clues; it smelled sterile. Antiseptic. The temperature felt like an even seventy degrees or so. His ears detected the distant thrumming of automated machinery in the walls and floors, beneath the hum of the sensors built into their high-tech coffins, but nothing that provided any hint of their present location. The only odd thing was, and he couldn't be sure of this, strapped down like he was, but his body felt *lighter* somehow. Like there was something not quite right with the gravity. Or maybe that was just a side-effect of whatever their captors used to knock him out before. He eyed the I.V. lines flowing into his arm with disgust. Who knew what kind of junk they might be feeding him?

"Hard to say where this is," he told Rogue and the Witch, making eye contact with Rogue via the mirror. "Some kind of lab, obviously."

Back in the lab again . . . Another post-traumatic flashback to his past ordeal crept up on Logan's consciousness, bringing with it an almost overwhelming fury that made it hard to concentrate on anything else. His heart pounded with remembered torment. *Tubes and needles gouging into me. Liquid metal pouring into my marrow, changing me from within. Pain and bones and spikes . . .*

Logan bit down on his lower lip—hard—to hold back an atavistic howl. He dug his fingernails into his palms, using the pain to keep himself grounded in the present, to approach their dilemma from a strictly strategic point of view.

Think like Cyke, he thought, glad that Jeannie wasn't

around to pick up that particular bit of brain activity. *Take this cool as a cucumber. All business.* He could go crazy later, when there was an enemy within slashing range. When he could slice their captors into so many bite-sized pieces of meat. *I'm looking forward to that.*

"Hey, Witch . . . er, Wanda," he said. "The way they've got us trussed up, me an' Rogue can't pull any of our usual stunts, but how 'bout you?" It dawned on him that he had only the fuzziest idea of how the Scarlet Witch's powers worked. Some kind of mutant magic or something? She'd been a regular adversary of the X-Men once, back when she was still working for her dad, but that was way before Logan hooked up with the team. "Any chance you can witch yourself loose?"

Wanda tried to shake her head, was forcibly reminded of her restraints, and abandoned the gesture. "Not really," she explained. "I use my hands to focus my powers and my eyes to pinpoint the target of my hex." Examining her more closely in the mirror, Logan noticed that, unlike he and Rogue, the Witch's hands were completely encased by solid metal hemispheres the size of boxing gloves.

Bet she can't even a wiggle a finger, he guessed.

"It's like trying to read in the dark," Wanda said, attempting to fully describe the difficulties imposed on her by her specially-designed bonds. "Or turn a page with your hands tied behind your back. Maybe in time I might be able to manage something, but it doesn't feel natural except the way that I usually project a hex sphere, if that makes any sense at all."

"I'll take your word for it," Wolverine said gruffly. Not for the first time, he was thankful his mutant senses and healing ability were simple and uncomplicated, as opposed to some sort of weird sci-fi type power. Let other mutants shoot energy beams from their bodies, read minds, or tinker with gravity.

Me, I like the basics—even if they can't do me much good under the circumstances. Too bad Witchie didn't inherit her dad's magnetic powers. Then she could dismantle this whole setup in no time at all.

Putting aside thoughts of escape, at least for the moment, Logan reviewed the unlikely chain of events that had brought him here, events that seemed crazier the more he thought about them. Shape-changing deer—what was *that* all about? The injuries inflicted by the unnatural antlers had long since healed, thanks to his mutant metabolism, but the bizarre nature of the attack lingered in his memory.

"So," he said aloud to the other prisoners, "I don't suppose you two got bushwhacked by Bambi and his folks?"

Rogue looked like she had no idea what he talking about. "What's a Disney movie got to do with all this?"

By the time they got through comparing notes, Logan felt even more in the dark than before.

"All I know," he declared, "is that a setup like this, with all this E.R. hardware and crud, wasn't built by no flamin' puppets, deer, or tee-shirts! This place stinks of the kind of preening egghead who figgers the whole blamed world would be better off under his thumb. You know the type, Rogue. We've trashed enough of them." He glanced at Wanda in the mirror, making a point to include her. "So have the Avengers, I bet."

"But *who* are they, Wolvie?" Rogue asked.

Logan had no idea. As an Avenger or an X-Man, the three of them had probably made enough enemies to fill a couple dozen penitentiaries. It was likely someone with an interest in mutants, he guessed; that was the main thing all three prisoners had in common. Besides choosing a lousy day for a little R&R, that is.

"What do you think they want with us?" Rogue wondered aloud.

"Nothing good," Logan stated with certainty. Unbidden, images from that other lab flashed through his mind, pulling back his lips until his fangs were fully bared.

Pain and bones and spikes . . .

"They are awake and aware. Are you certain your shackles can hold them?"

"Fear not, my security-conscious friend. Trust me, those adamantium restraints would hold back the Hulk . . . well, almost. Besides, even if they should escape, which is highly improbable, where could they go? Have you forgotten precisely where we are?"

"If only I could! And I still think it would have been wiser to have kept them separated. Why give them the opportunity to conspire against us?"

"The controlled interaction of their respective mutant traits is a fundamental aspect of my experiment. This arrangement simplifies procedures considerably, and it eliminates the inherent risks involved in physically transporting them from one location to another, such as from a solitary cell to a lab and back again. Indeed, statistics indicate that approximately 75.331 percent of successful escapes occur during the transportation of prisoners. You may be assured that all such logistical matters were subjected to thorough analysis and consideration during the very conception of this project."

"I am not interested in procedures, only results. How

long before you can deliver what you have promised? I have no desire to languish in this accursed place forever, not while entire worlds remain to be conquered."

"Spoken like a soldier, not a scientist. Patience. The experiment is just beginning. . . ."

The torture began without warning. Mechanical waldoes descended from the ceiling, bearing scalpels, lasers, and fiber-optic cameras at the ends of jointed metal arms.

Uh-oh. Looks like the fun's starting, Logan thought, bracing himself for what was to come.

The whirr of the servoes came ever closer. Metal rods protruded from the sarcophagus, forcing his hands open and his fingers apart. His hairy palms thus exposed, the waldoes moved in closer to commence their inhuman tasks. A remote-controlled scalpel made surgical incisions across his right palm, then retreated a few centimeters while Logan's stubborn flesh swiftly reknitted itself under the watchful eye of a miniature camera embedded in the base of the scalpel. Logan had no doubt that, besides the knife's-eye view provided by the scalpel, the various sensors affixed to his body were monitoring his heartbeat, respiration, glands, et cetera, to see how they registered during the healing process.

"Take a good look, bub," he called out to his unseen tormentor. Only the slightest trickle of blood escaped before the shallow cuts disappeared entirely. "You're the one who's goin' to need healin' after I get done with you!"

The only response to his threat came from an automated laser that directed a narrow beam of coherent light against his exposed left palm, methodically burning away the uppermost layer of skin, exposing raw, reddened tissue. Logan grimaced slightly but made no sound, even as his hyper-sensitive nostrils smelled his own vaporized flesh. He'd bite his tongue off before he'd give the sadist behind the mirror the satisfaction of hearing one peep from him. The searing heat of the laser hurt more than the scalpel, but the damage it inflicted was nothing his mutant healing factor couldn't handle.

That, he feared, was the whole point.

The scalpel sliced his right hand open again. This time, the blade struck deeper, all the way to the bone.

"A truly remarkable rate of metabolic regeneration, marked by an accelerated immune response and profuse cellular mitosis that appears to impose minimal strain on his circadian rhythms and autonomic functions. Wolverine's recuperative abilities are just as formidable as I had been led to believe; I know of only one individual whose healing powers surpass those of this specimen. I will be curious to observe how Wolverine's immune system copes with the various toxins and varieties of electromagnetic radiation I intend to subject him to. It should be a fascinating experiment."

"Fascinating to you, perhaps. Do not let your idle curiosity interfere with the timely pursuit of our objective. What about the females? When will you begin with them?"

"Time spent accumulating new scientific knowledge is never wasted. Still, if it will ease your militaristic impatience, let us proceed to the next stage of my research. Kindly observe the specimen known as Rogue."

Poor Wolvie!

Rogue could barely bring herself to watch as the robotic arms slashed and burned Logan's defenseless flesh. Sure, his special healing power would protect him from any permanent damage, but that didn't mean the busy knives and lasers didn't hurt like blazes. Her own hands, which already felt naked without their usual gloves, seemed even more exposed. She clenched her fists protectively and winced in sympathy with each new wound inflicted on Logan. What kind of no-good sidewinder could do this to another person? From what she could see in the mirror, they weren't even using any sort of anesthetic!

She was tempted to offer Wolverine whatever paltry words of comfort she could come up with, but she knew that the stoic X-Man did not want anybody's pity or sympathy, especially when a hostile party was almost certainly looking on. Her compassion might be seen as a sign of weakness or vulnerability on his part. So she kept her mouth shut, all the while wishing there was something—anything—she could do to relieve Logan's torment.

And wondering when her own turn was coming round.

"What's happening?" the Scarlet Witch asked, one coffin over. Her nose twitched beneath the metal visor. "What's that burning smell?"

Trust me, sugah, you don't want to know. Rather than keep the other woman in the dark, however, Rogue opened her mouth to respond. She hadn't forgotten the Witch's harsh remark about Carol Danvers, but no matter what the other woman thought about her, Rogue couldn't let just let Wanda suffer in sightless suspense. *'Sides, I guess she's entitled to feel the way she does, being a friend of Ms. Marvel and all.*

"They're performin' some kind of medical experiments on Wolverine," she began, wondering how much grisly detail the Scarlet Witch would want. "Ah don' know why."

Before she could explain further, the raised metal ridge running along the left side of her coffin slid downward and out of sight, at the same time that the ridge on the right side of Logan's pulled a similar disappearing act.

What now? Rogue wondered apprehensively.

A mechanical rumbling started up beneath her, like a conveyor belt coming to life, and the two metal caskets containing her and Wolverine began to slide horizontally toward each other, with not a single plate of chromed steel to separate their transfixed bodies. Rogue stared in alarm as her uncovered left hand drew steadily nearer to Logan's scarred and bleeding right palm. It wasn't the blood that frightened her, though, but the prospect of their two hands touching.

"Wait! Stop!" she cried out to whomever was operating the mechanism bringing them together. "Y'all don' know what you're doin'!"

Unfortunately, she had a sneaking suspicion that they did.

Their bare hands less than a foot apart and closing fast, Rogue's frantic eyes found Wolverine's. From the grim look on his face, it was clear he had also realized what their captors were up to.

No! she thought fervently. *I won't let it happen. I won't!* She struggled anew against the metal bonds holding her arm in place, but it was no good; not even Ms. Marvel's stolen super-strength could break the unyielding steel bands.

"Ah'm so sorry, Logan," she whispered. "Ah don' want this."

"I know that, kid," he assured her. She searched for

forgiveness in his face, finding it in his ageless black eyes. "It ain't your fault."

Somewhere to the right, now a bit further away, the Scarlet Witch demanded to know what was going on. But there was no time to explain, even if Rogue felt like sharing her profound humiliation and horror with the blindfolded Avenger, which was not exactly her first instinct.

Bad enough that I have to know what I'm going to do to Logan.

The edge of Rogue's coffin clanked against Wolverine's as the conveyances came to a halt. Her trapped hand pressed against his, flesh to flesh, and, despite herself, the young mutant gasped in anticipation. Strange new sensations, wild and unbelievably intense, flooded her mind and senses as, against her will, Logan's powers and memories flowed into her, leaving him drained and unconscious. Familiar faces and exotic places rushed the stage of her memory: Sabretooth and Mariko, the Yukon and Madripoor, Heather Hudson, Jubilee, and Krakoa. . . .

Her teeth sharpened into carnivorous fangs. Her brown hair grew stiffer and more fur-like in a matter of instants. Her eyes blazed with predatory fury as her senses came alive, smell and touch and hearing suddenly magnified a hundredfold. The whole world became brighter and richer and more vivid. Feral passions surged inside her, even as Wolverine slumped within his coffin, his drooping lips finally releasing the anguished moan that neither slicing blades nor scorching laser fire had succeeded in extracting before.

This is glorious, Rogue thought, torn between shame and exultation.

The damage done, hidden gears engaged and the two caskets began to withdraw to their original positions. Next to Rogue, the left-hand wall of her coffin slid upward, back into place, cutting her off from the man whose vitality and unique attributes she had just leeched. It didn't matter, though. Only a moment's touch had been enough to effect the transference.

The shocking clarity and impact of her newly-heightened senses stunned Rogue. The light seemed brighter, throwing her surroundings into extreme focus, so that every edge and surface stood out with a distinctness that went beyond three-dimensional. She could practically feel textures with her eyes alone: the cool smoothness of the mirror, the leathery feel of Logan's weathered face, the stickiness of his drying blood. Her ears brought her sounds that now seemed unnaturally amplified; her own heartbeat pounded like a kettle drum, nearly drowning out the sibilant hiss of electrons coursing through myriad electrical cables, while Wolverine's pulse faded to a slow, dim rumble. Her nose twitched, alerted to both Logan's musky odor and the faint scent of fear rising off the blinded witch. Her fists flexed against the sides of the coffin, instinctively trying to extend claws that weren't really there.

She had only seconds, though, to take in Wolverine's perceptions of the present, before his borrowed memories thrust her into a past that was not her own.

All at once, she was in another lab, floating in a tank of liquid nutrients while bubbles rose through the murky red fluid, obscuring her view of the facility beyond the transparent walls of the tank. Some sort of breathing apparatus covered her mouth, tasting coppery upon her tongue and forcing a plastic tube partway down her windpipe. More tubes dug into veins and arteries all over her body; she couldn't move without getting tangled in a web of cables and thin capillary tubing. Metal spikes, attached to flexible steel cables, dug deeply into her bones, producing agonizing pain as her body tried to reject the foreign matter. The spikes, though, were embedded too firmly to be dislodged. Her eyes tearing up from the agony, she peered through the rising bubbles at the dimly-glimpsed silhouettes of nameless figures looking on, charting her ordeal on clipboards and computers. The lukewarm fluid raised goosebumps up and down her arms and legs. Her feet floated freely, unable to touch the floor of the tank.

This never happened, Rogue tried to remember. *Not to me. Not now.*

But Wolverine's memories, dragged to the surface by more recent tortures, were too vivid to ignore, no matter how hard Rogue fought to regain control of her mind. She could not escape the crimson tank, could not distance herself from the spikes and tubes even as they began pouring something alien into her body, her bones. The forced infusion was cold and hot at the same time and made her flesh crawl; she could feel it spreading over her skeleton, bonding to the calcified hardness supporting her flesh and blood.

The adamantium! she realized in a precious moment of lucidity. *This must be when they put the metal in Wolvie's bones.*

Sharp, throbbing pains stabbed at her hands and she brought them up before her eyes, dragging I.V. lines and cables from her elbows and wrists. Her bottom knuckles swelled and ached, pulsating in synch, like there was something beneath her skin trying to get out. And there was: blood spurted from the backs of her hands as six sharp metal claws, three on each hand, tore their way through the fragile epidermis that stretched across her knuckles. The curved silver daggers sliced through the thick red liquid, further churning the bubbling solution surrounding Rogue. Her spilled blood joined the tepid fluid surrounding her.

No, she thought emphatically, still locked in the unfolding nightmare. *Not me. Wolverine.*

Looking through Logan's eyes, she glared past the gleaming claws at the shadowy figures lurking outside the tank, staring dispassionately at her grueling transformation. It was all their doing, she knew; they were the ones who had done this to him/her/whatever. An anger of frightening intensity seethed inside her. Beyond the pain, the violation, the icy dread at what she had become, her fury raged, savage and uncontrollable, like no anger she had ever experienced before. It didn't even feel human, this rabid, instinctual frenzy. Her heart pounded ferociously in her chest. Her phantom claws ached for action. She craved her enemies' blood, hungered for their deaths. Only the metal mouthpiece between her jaws kept her from gnashing her teeth in a bestial rage. All she could think of was tearing her foes apart with her hands and teeth and claws.

Good Lord, she thought, with the tiny spark of sanity remaining to her. *Is this what Wolvie feels like when he loses his temper? How in the world does he ever keep this . . . madness . . . under control?*

Then, from beyond yesterday, something sharp cut into her hand, yanking her back into the present at the same time that she suddenly felt a laser beam burning through her skin. . . .

• • •

"Observe carefully. Note the subtle feral rearrangement of her features, the predatory glint in her eyes which mimics that displayed earlier by her primitive confederate. Her heartbeat, adrenaline output, and metabolism have increased by a factor of ten, while, according to my instrumentation, the transfer itself required less than one-point-eight-seven seconds to take effect, with a corresponding diminution in the life energies of Wolverine.

"Also, as you can see for yourself, her newfound ability to heal herself at an accelerated rate appears indistinguishable from Wolverine's, even to the exact amount of time required to repair identical third-degree burns. As nearly as I can tell, there is no statistical difference between the attributes originally manifested by the first subject and those duplicated by the second. I wonder how prolonged the physical contact must be to ensure that the transference is permanent? Perhaps I will conduct that test—when our work is complete, of course."

"You can do as you like once we achieve the object of our ambitions. I will have more important matters to concern me than the fate of three human lab animals."

"Do not underestimate all we might learn from such unique specimens. Take our final specimen, for instance—the one who calls herself the Scarlet Witch. Who knows what the full potential of her unlikely abilities might be, once harnessed effectively? Behold."

Alone in the darkness, her torn ear still throbbing where the Peter puppet had yanked her earring free, Wanda heard an animal growling far too close for comfort. Or was it an animal? She couldn't be sure, but she thought the bone-chilling snarl sounded like it might be coming from . . . Rogue?

LOST AND FOUND

I knew she was a vampire at heart, Wanda thought, *but I didn't expect her to actually growl like a wolf!*

"Rogue? Wolverine?" For about the two hundredth time, she wished that she was sharing a cell with a couple of her fellow Avengers instead. She had a long history with the X-Men, none of it very good, even if the two teams had managed to successfully join forces now and again, if only during the most dire of emergencies. And of all the X-Men to be trapped with . . . ! A homicidal maniac with a bad attitude and the drawling little succubus who literally stole poor Carol's soul. It was all Rogue's fault that the former Ms. Marvel had been driven to alcoholism and disgrace, of that Wanda was utterly convinced. With cellmates like these, who needed enemies?

At least they'd had the decency to describe their mutual prison to her, even though both X-Men seemed to have fallen silent for the time being. Had something happened to them? Rogue had mentioned medical experiments, before her ominous words gave way to incoherent growls. Not exactly the most comforting note on which to leave things. What *kind* of medical experiments?

If only she could see what was going on! The blindfold over her eyes added to her understandable anxiety at being captured so easily. So far she didn't even know *who* had abducted them, let alone how and why. With nothing else to gaze upon, the leering faces of past enemies passed before Wanda's mind's eye as she tried to guess the villain responsible for her captivity. The Grim Reaper? Ultron? Kang the Conqueror? It could be any of them, or even a new alliance between previously independent menaces. She racked her brain in search of a foe she shared in common with Wolverine and Rogue, but the only one that came to mind was Magneto and this didn't feel like her father's work.

Magneto could never be so anonymous, she decided, knowing the tyrannical mutant mastermind's ways too well. *He would have to gloat out loud, justifying his crimes by invoking the sacred destiny of* homo superior.

Besides, if her natural father was involved, where was her brother? Surely Magneto would have rounded up Pietro as well, and maybe even little Luna, her brother's infant daughter. With Wolverine and Rogue sharing her prison instead, she felt sure this was no family affair. But then what was it?

This is getting me nowhere, she thought, squirming impatiently within the confines of her cold, metallic sarcophagus. Lack of motion had caused both her legs to fall asleep and she struggled to rouse them despite the bonds hindering her. Wanda had no doubt that Captain America and the other Avengers were already searching for her, but she didn't intend to simply hang around waiting to be rescued. Yet how could she escape on her own? Her fingers, eager to perform the gestures that summoned her magic, felt like they were immersed in solid cement. *I suppose I could try just projecting a hex at random, but there'd be no way to predict the results. I could end up making things worse, maybe by triggering a short-circuit or electrical fire that kills all three of us.*

"Hello?" she tried again. Like it or not, her best chance to escape might be to work together with her fellow captives. "X-Men?" She knew they were still nearby; she could hear their ragged, unsteady breathing. Why wouldn't they answer her? Unseen machines whirred and hummed in the background, along with the sizzle of something burning. "Wolverine? Rogue?"

An agonized gasp was the only response.

That was definitely Rogue, Wanda thought, which did not bode well for her next-door neighbor. Despite the younger woman's unquestionably guilty past, Wanda could not help feeling a pang of sympathy for a person who was obviously in pain. No one deserved to be tortured, not even Carol Danver's heartless victimizer.

"What is it, Rogue?" she asked, more gently than before. "Are you all right?"

An unexpected light appeared before her eyes. She blinked in surprise as a glowing disk, about a foot in diameter, materialized only a few inches away from her face—even though her blindfold remained securely in place.

An illusion, Wanda realized instantly. Probably some sort of virtual reality projection. Iron Man, she knew, had a similar gadget inside his helmet to provide him with visual displays and data that only he could see; Tony would surely be able to explain exactly how this disk was projected. For herself, she didn't much care about the mechanics involved, as long as it meant that something was happening at last. After lying here in the dark for who knew how long, blind and paralyzed, she felt genuinely relieved that her nameless captor was finally making his or her next move, even if Rogue's pain-wracked moans hardly led one to hope for easy treatment at the hands of their foe.

Let's get this over with, she resolved, bracing herself for whatever the enemy had in store. *Chances are, it's nothing I haven't endured before.*

"Greetings, Ms. Maximoff." The voice, electronically distorted, was unfamiliar to her. It sounded like it was coming from miniature speakers implanted in her visor, which implied that the speaker was not actually near enough to hex.

Too bad, she thought, as the voice continued to whisper into her ears.

"My apologies for keeping you waiting, but I have a number of experiments to conduct on you and my other test subjects, so I am afraid you simply had to wait your turn."

"Who are you?" Wanda demanded, refusing to be patronized by the anonymous voice. "Don't hide behind a microphone. Show your face."

"My identity, and that of my partner in this endeavor, is irrelevant, at least as far as you are concerned."

Yes, definitely not Magneto, Wanda concluded from the speaker's reticence and relative lack of egomania. *Probably not Kang or Graviton, either.*

"All that matters," the disembodied voice continued, "is that you pay close attention to what I am about to explain to you. The rules of the game, as it were."

Before Wanda's eyes, the virtual disk began to spin counter-clockwise. Luminescent lines, radiating from the center of the disk like the spokes of a wheel, divided the disk into wedge-shaped slices that alternated in color from red to black to red and so on.

Like a roulette wheel, she noted, a comparison that grew even more apt as a white virtual sphere, about the size of a Ping-Pong ball, was ejected from the center of the wheel, whose centrifugal force drew the sphere to the outer rim of the wheel. It bounced from wedge to wedge exactly like a ball upon a real, non-virtual roulette wheel. A clicking noise accompanied each bounce, presumably to enhance the illusion.

"Your genetic gift, as I understand it, involves the manipulation of probability upon on the physical plane. Taking a leaf from the professional gambling industry, I have prepared a simple game with which to test your celebrated abilities.''

That's it? They snatch me in broad daylight, lay me out like a mummy in a tomb, just to make me play some glorified video game? Wanda was unimpressed.

''Why should I play along?'' she asked. ''Frankly, I prefer games of skill, like chess or tennis. If I wanted to cheat at gambling, I could have made a fortune in Monte Carlo years ago.''

The faceless voice assumed a note of impatience. ''Spare me your tiresome displays of defiance. You *will* take part in the experiment because the stakes are such that you have no choice. Let me demonstrate.''

The spinning wheel slowed to a stop and the bouncing sphere came to rest at the wide end of a glowing red wedge. Wanda held her breath, expecting the worst, but nothing happened, leaving her relieved but somewhat puzzled. Then the wheel began spinning again, gaining speed so that the ball skipped along the circumference of the wheel, bounding clockwise from wedge to wedge so quickly that Wanda could barely keep track of it until the wheel decelerated again. This time the computer-generated sphere landed squarely within a black wedge.

Excruciating pain, sharper than the most unbearable toothache, convulsed her body, causing her to writhe within her constraints. The pain passed in an instant, leaving Wanda pale-faced and shaking.

Where did that come from? she thought, shocked by the depth of the agony she had experienced. *I've been blasted by Kree death-rays that didn't hurt that much!*

''Perhaps I should have mentioned earlier,'' the voice

said, affecting a thoroughly unconvincing simulation of remorse, "that electrodes affixed to your skull provide me with direct access to your brain's pain centers. I do not intend to employ this option arbitrarily, however. The parameters are simple: when the sphere stops in red, you will be spared, but when the sphere stops in black, you will receive another jolt of the same magnitude. Ordinarily, the program will yield 50/50 odds, so that the sphere will be deposited within a black region roughly half the time—unless you bring your distinctive talents to bear."

On that note, the wheel started revolving once more. The bouncing ball clicked in her ears.

"Wait!" Wanda called out. "Why are you doing this? What do you hope to gain?"

The mysterious architect of this sadistic exercise said nothing more; apparently, he had told her all that he felt she needed to know. Wanda watched intently as the bouncing ball followed its preordained path, then flinched involuntarily as the wheel's dizzying speed began to slacken.

Not the black, she silently commanded the ball. *Not the black.*

Her ensnared fingers ached to point at the virtual roulette game, even though she knew it wasn't really there. Could her hexes even affect a computer-generated simulation? Despite years of training and adventures in the field, the precise limits of her powers remained slippery and elusive, sometimes changing without notice. Half scientific, half sorcerous, her hex spheres stemmed from a unique confluence of mutant DNA and ancient mystical energies present at her birth, making them almost as mutable as the weather and just as hard to predict. Recently, there had been an attempt to explain her abilities in terms of "chaos theory," but Wanda remained skeptical that anyone, her unknown jailer included, would ever fully account for the peculiar and mercurial gift that was her birthright.

Just so long as it's there when I need it . . . like right about now!

Her gaze fixed upon the ball as it hopped, now with maddening slowness, around the edge of the wheel, her heart missing a beat everytime the sphere touched down within an ebony wedge. She focused all her concentration, all her willpower, upon the glowing ball—and was heartened to feel a familiar buzz at the back of her brain, like a circuit had suddenly switched on.

"Not the black," she whispered vehemently, her lips echoing the constant refrain of her thoughts. "Not the black."

The wheel froze in place and the sphere tottered on the brink between adjacent red and black wedges. Crossing her fingers figuratively, if not in reality, Wanda waited anxiously, already stiffening in expectation of another fierce burst of pain. Which would it be, suffering or salvation? Red or black?

Red.

She exhaled slowly, grateful for her deliverance. Granted, the odds had been only one out of two, but she felt certain that her powers had tipped the scales in her favor. Before she could savor her temporary triumph, the wheel resumed its relentless spinning. The game commenced again, and she grimly set about repeating her success of moments before, for the second in who knew how many trials.

Here we go again, she thought, as she petitioned the

laws of chance as only she could. *Not the black, not the black, not the black.* . . .

Red. Red. Red. Red.

So far, so good, but the strain was telling on her. The unseen experimenter allowed her no respite, starting each new round fast on the heels of the previous victory. Her head began to pound, mildly at first, but growing more painful and distracting by the minute. The queasy throbbing threatened to supplant the reassuring tingle that heralded the exercise of her power. The constant clicking nibbled away at her nerves, like a leaky faucet that, left untended, could drown all her hopes. The virtual roulette wheel swam before her eyes, and she had to blink repeatedly to keep the game in focus. Beads of perspiration ran down her forehead, dripping from her nose. She could taste the salt upon her lips, feel the fatigue creeping up on her. Beating the odds time after time was hard work, and still the ball kept rolling.

Red. Red. Red. Red. Red.

I can't keep this up much longer, she thought, wondering if the faceless instigator of the game was pleased or disappointed by her consistent string of victories. What were the odds of coming up red a dozen times in a row? The Vision could tell her if he was here; his computerized mind was good at that sort of thing, even if he couldn't figure out how to save their marriage. *Is he worried at all about what's happened to me? Can his memory banks call up some vestige of the love we once shared?*

Red. Red. Red.

Black.

Her concentration slipped for a moment, and she was rewarded with a brutal shock that seemed to set her entire nervous system on fire. The searing jolt came from nowhere and everywhere at the same time, sparing no part of her convulsing body. The pain faded quickly, but the ceaseless game gave her no time to recover. Shaking off the lingering after-effects of the jolt, she collected her faculties and focused on the virtual game with renewed determination yet depleted strength. A blinding migraine pulsed without mercy within her skull, squeezing her aching head like one of Moon Dragon's vicious telepathic attacks. Her breathing grew ragged. Sleep beckoned, and she had to struggle to keep her eyes open.

"Not the black," she whispered over and over like a mantra. She heard another desperate moan, but couldn't tell if it was coming from Rogue, Wolverine, or herself.

Red. Red. Red.

Empathy warred with exhaustion, and she found herself wondering what sort of ordeals the two unlucky X-Men had been forced to endure.

If they were anything like this, she thought sadly, *then heaven help both of them.*

Red. Red. Red. Red. Red. Red . . .

"Excellent. I could not have asked for better results, from any of our subjects. I look forward to the next round of tests, which should bring us even closer to the culmination of our plans—and the destruction of all who oppose us."

Chapter Nine

A gloomy hush hung over the Avengers' elegantly appointed reception room as Captain America stared at the ornately framed portrait mounted over the marble fireplace. The color photo captured all the founding members of the Avengers, only days after the team's historic inception—there was Iron Man, in his original golden armor, along with the mighty Thor, Ant-Man, the Wasp . . . and the Hulk.

The green-skinned, gamma-spawned behemoth glowered from the portrait, a surly expression on his Neanderthal-like features, angry emerald eyes glaring out from under heavy brows that always reminded Cap of Boris Karloff in the movie *Frankenstein*. His brawny arms were crossed defiantly atop his massive chest. Even in those halcyon days following the Avengers' debut, the Hulk looked uncomfortable and irritated to be part of the team.

Too bad, Cap reflected. They could use the Hulk right now, or at least his human alter ego, Dr. Robert Bruce Banner.

"Shame the Hulk never worked out as an Avenger," Iron Man said, echoing Cap's own sentiments. His gleaming faceplate was elevated, exposing Tony Stark's dashing features. His pale blue eyes followed Cap's gaze to the portrait above the mantle. "I remember the day we took that photo. The Hulk was in such a bad temper that Jarvis could barely look at him without trembling, let alone hold the camera steady." He raised a crystal champagne glass filled with sparkling ginger ale to his lips. "It wasn't long after that he teamed up with the Sub-Mariner to try to destroy us, and things went downhill from there.''

True enough, Captain America thought. Over the years, the Hulk had fought against the Avengers more often than he had fought beside them. It was more than a little tragic, he mused; all that awesome strength, not to mention Bruce Banner's unquestioned genius, wasted on a pointless, never-ending war with the rest of the world. Just think of all the good the Hulk could have done if only he had been capable of obeying his duty and conscience instead of his unquenchable rage.

''You don't think he has anything to do with Wanda's disappearance?'' he asked.

Iron Man shook his head. He paced away from the fireplace, his heavy boots leaving deep impressions in the Persian carpet. As if to compensate, the Vision hovered weightlessly not far away, the soles of his feet barely grazing the floor.

''I doubt it,'' Iron Man said. ''There wasn't enough damage at the museum. I mean, animated puppets? That's hardly the Hulk's M.O.'' His futuristic armor looked out of place among the antique furnishings, and Cap noticed that the armored warrior took care not to brush against the Ming Dynasty vase resting atop the small lacquered end table beside him. ''For another thing, he's never had any particular grudge against Wanda. He'd quit the team long before she and her brother joined the Avengers, and before that she'd mostly fought the X-Men.''

''I can confirm,'' the Vision stated, ''that Wanda bore the Hulk no special animosity.'' His immaterial body passed through a polished mahogany coffee table on his way to join Cap and Iron Man; the Vision was one person who never had to worry about breaking anything. ''I cannot recall that we ever had a significant discussion on the subject of the Hulk during the years of our marriage.''

He says that so coldly, Cap thought, struck by the synthezoid's unemotional demeanor, so unlike the android Human Torch whom Cap had battled beside during World War II; that artificial man, constructed decades earlier, had possessed the same feelings as any other man or woman. By contrast, the Vision's implacable calm hardly struck Cap as progress. *Poor Wanda,* he thought.

As team leader, Cap couldn't be unaware of all the pain that the Scarlet Witch had endured during the dissolution of her marriage. Sometimes he wondered about the wisdom of keeping the estranged couple on the same team, although, to their credit, neither Wanda nor the Vision had ever let their personal difficulties interfere with the performance of their duties. All the more reason, he resolved, to use every resource at their disposal to recover Wanda safely; it was the least they could do for a valiant teammate who had always been willing to put her life on the line for the sake of the Avengers, America, and the world.

''We can rule out the Puppet Master, too,'' Iron Man reported. ''I got an e-mail from his niece a few minutes ago, confirming her uncle's alibi. Seems she was with him this morning, around the same time Wanda was apparently abducted.''

Left unspoken was the grim possibility that the Scarlet Witch was no longer alive, but Cap refused to accept that she might have already paid the last full measure of devotion. *As long as there's hope,* he vowed, *the Avengers will never abandon one of their own.*

''Even if the Hulk *is* innocent,'' Iron Man added, ''I wouldn't mind a chance to ask Banner some pertinent questions about those traces of gamma radiation at the museum. I like to think that I'm a pretty savvy engineer, but I'm not ashamed to say that I'm stumped when it comes to figuring out how in the world you could use gamma rays to bring a bunch of puppets to life.''

''All available databases report that the Hulk's whereabouts are presently unknown,'' the Vision reminded them. Cap knew that the Vision remained in contact with the mansion's ultra-sophisticated computer systems via a direct cybernetic link. ''Every search engine is now engaged in searching for clues that might lead us to the Hulk, as are as many of our auxiliary members as I have been able to contact.''

That's good to know, Cap thought, but was it enough? As Iron Man had so astutely pointed out, the Hulk's connection to Wanda's abduction was an extremely tenuous one, even if it was the only lead they had. Their lack of progress frustrated him. They also serve who only stand and wait, he knew, but it was hard to just cool their heels in the opulent comfort of Avengers Mansion when another team member was in jeopardy.

His resolute gaze drifted to another portrait, occupying a place of honor on the west wall of the reception room. The framed photograph depicted the second wave of Avengers, consisting of himself, Hawkeye the Archer, Quicksilver, and the Scarlet Witch.

Those were the days, Cap thought. It had been his privilege to sponsor and train both Wanda and her brother when they first resolved to turn their backs on their criminal pasts, and he had never had cause to regret his decision to give the homeless young mutants a second chance. *That reminds me. I should probably try contacting Pietro again.* Previous attempts to notify Quicksilver of his sister's disappearance had proven useless; neither the Inhumans nor the Knights of Wundagore knew where Pietro could be found. Given the speed at which the super-fast mutant traveled, he could be anywhere in the world at any given moment, making him a hard man to catch up with.

An electronic beep distracted Cap from his somber ruminations. He extracted his Avengers I.D. card from the flared cuff of his right glove. An emergency signal flashed upon the laminated card.

"It's S.H.I.E.L.D.," he announced to the other heroes. "A priority transmission."

He aimed the card at the framed photo above the fireplace and clicked twice on the touch-sensitive card. The portrait slid to one side, gilded frame and all, revealing a largish monitor not unlike the one in their communications center upstairs; thanks to Tony Stark's renovations, the venerable mansion was full of such hidden technological surprises. With another click, he transferred the incoming message to the screen above the mantle. For the second time that day, the Star-Spangled Avenger contemplated an over-sized close-up of Nick Fury's grizzled features.

"Captain America here," he addressed the screen. "What's up, Nick? More about that UFO you mentioned before?" He would have preferred news of Wanda, but duty called.

Fury chomped down mercilessly upon a cigar. "Yeah, you might say we had a bit of a close encounter ourselves." He had obviously seen recent action; a dark purple bruise discolored his unshaven chin while a fresh bandage was wrapped around his shoulder. "At approximately 2100 hours, Eastern Standard Time, the Helicarrier was attacked and boarded by the X-Men.''

The X-Men? Cap couldn't believe his ears. Their unsavory reputation notwithstanding, he knew that the mutant heroes generally fought on the side of the angels. ''Are you sure, Nick? I know the tabloids make them out to be the biggest threat this side of the Masters of Evil, but I've stood by them in the line of fire and I can tell you that their hearts are in the right place. The Beast even served as an Avenger once.''

''I know where you're coming from, Cap,'' Fury admitted, ''but take a gander at some of this combat footage, captured by our own security cameras.''

Fury's scowling visage surrendered the screen to chaotic images of desperate S.H.I.E.L.D. agents fighting back against brightly-costumed invaders wielding fire, ice, flying blades, and what looked like telekinesis. The pictures were several orders of magnitude clearer and more vivid than the security videotape Cap had watched earlier that day; obviously, S.H.I.E.L.D. could afford better equipment than the American Museum of Folk Art. Despite frequent gusts of flame and steam, Cap easily recognized the faces and distinctive uniforms of the intruders: Sunfire, Banshee, Archangel, Phoenix, and Iceman. All mutants, right enough, and all linked to the X-Men. Watching the footage, he could tell that the apparent X-Men were clearly on the offensive; he winced in sympathy as one of Archangel's barbed feathers struck the Countess Valentina, rendering her unconscious. Moments later, Fury himself succumbed to the mutants' onslaught; S.H.I.E.L.D.'s irascible director dropped face-first onto the floor of the Helicarrier, multiple flechettes jutting from his punctured body.

He went down fighting, Cap noted, impressed by any strike force that could overcome Fury and his people on their own turf. He watched with growing concern as Banshee's supersonic scream, which registered upon the videotape as an ear-piercing squeal, knocked a massive steel airlock off its hinges. The X-Men stormed over the fallen bodies of Fury and his people to enter what was clearly labeled as a top-security laboratory. *What are they after?* Cap wondered.

The security footage blanked out, replaced by a very unhappy Nick Fury. "It's just as bad as it looks, maybe worse." Having shared some of the darkest hours of World War II with Fury, Cap knew that the old warhorse wasn't prone to exaggeration. "Not only did we get our butts kicked, but your mutant buddies also absconded with some choice classified hardware, zipping away in their flying saucer before we knew what hit us. We figure it's got some sort of stealth capacity, that's how it got in past our defenses."

"What kind of classified hardware got stolen?" Iron Man asked urgently, his metallic faceplate back in place. Cap recalled that Tony Stark had provided S.H.I.E.L.D. with much of its state-of-the-art technology. The thought of his own discoveries falling into the wrong hands surely preyed on the armored Avenger's mind.

An uncomfortable look came over Fury's face, like he didn't much like the taste of the words in his mouth. "Well, that's kind of a problem, actually. I can tell you already that you're not going to like what I have to say."

"What is it, Nick?" Cap asked, puzzled by Fury's visible reluctance to spit out the truth. He didn't always approve of S.H.I.E.L.D.'s more clandestine operations, but he knew that Fury was a man of integrity, stuck in a dirtier job than Cap would have ever chosen for himself. *I always want to give America's officially-sanctioned defenders the benefit of the doubt, even though I'm sometimes disappointed by what our own leaders can stoop to.*

Fury could not conceal his distaste for what he said next. "Turns out a handful of our resident science whiz-kids had just finishing assembling the prototypes for a new generation of Sentinels."

The black sedan rolled through Westchester County, down tree-lined avenues that led toward the quiet suburban community of Salem Center, New York. Behind the wheel, Scott Summers resisted the temptation to put on the gas now that they were almost home. After the Beast's narrow escape from the police, the last thing they needed was to be pulled over for speeding.

Impatience gnawed at him, however. For all they knew, Rogue could be in desperate straits at this very minute. He was anxious to get back to the Institute and continue the search for her. With any luck, Wolverine would have returned from his solitary roaming in time to help with the hunt; they might have need of his tracking skills.

I just hope Logan's not slumming in Madripoor again, Cyclops thought. *We might not see him for weeks.*

If it was anybody else, Cyclops would never tolerate an X-Man going AWOL as often as Wolverine did, but he had learned from hard experience that there was little hope of getting Wolverine to change his ways, and the diminutive Canadian was too valuable an asset to the team to do without. Over the years, he had grudgingly come to accept Logan's singular idiosyncrasies, just as the habitual loner had adjusted to being part of a team . . . sort of.

If necessary, we'll have to make do without him, Cyclops decided. With or without Wolverine, there was no time to spare.

Keeping his foot firmly on the gas pedal and his eyes on the lonely road ahead, he called back to his companions. "Any luck?"

"Not yet, I'm afraid," the Beast replied from the back seat. Scott heard Hank tapping away at the customized keyboard of his portable computer, handcrafted to accommodate the Beast's gorilla-sized digits. "I'm searching the Internet for any new developments concerning Rogue, gamma radiation, or even the Hulk, but so far there's been nothing worth noting, although I did stumble onto a couple of intriguing new scientific treatises that I've bookmarked for later study. Purely of academic interest, alas; nothing that points the way to our comrade's safe recovery."

"Didn't I read something recently about the Hulk's wife dying?" Cyclops asked. As team leader—well, co-leader—he tried to stay abreast of current events in the superhuman community. You never knew when some obscure old villain might suddenly stage a comeback in your own backyard.

"Yes," Hank said, his tone somewhat heavier than usual, "from an overdose of gamma radiation. There was considerable controversy over whether she could have been irradiated simply through prolonged contact with the Hulk."

"How tragic and unfortunate," Ororo sympathized. The X-Men, too, had known their share of sorrow, and controversy as well. If anything, the Hulk got even worse press than they did.

"All the more reason to try to contact Banner,"

Cyclops declared. "If anybody can explain what the radiation on those shirts means, it's him." He steered onto a back road leading toward the Institute; no need to attract attention by driving through the town proper during the wee hours of the night. "I just hope he's in a, well, approachable state if and when we find him. I don't relish another run-in with the Hulk."

Might be just as well that Logan's trekked out for parts unknown, he reflected. Wolverine and the Hulk had an adversarial relationship that dated back years, to way before Logan even joined the X-Men. Cyclops scowled at the thought; he didn't want their search for Rogue to get derailed by yet another grudge match between the volatile Canadian and Banner's monstrous alter ego.

"I know what you mean," Hank agreed. Strong as he was, the Beast was nowhere near the Hulk's weight class. "Here's hoping that Dr. Banner is not looking notably chartreuse when we come calling."

First we need to find him, Cyclops remembered. With luck, that wouldn't take long; there weren't many places where a thousand-pound green monstrosity could avoid attracting attention. Unlike Scott Summers, Banner could not conceal his curse behind a simple pair of quartz glasses.

Besides being merely elegant in appearance, the luxurious limousine came equipped with all the latest features, including sophisticated night vision technology. An infrared heat sensor mounted in the front grill scanned the darkened road ahead for over five hundred yards, five times farther than the sedan's headlights could reach, and projected a long-distance image onto a ten-inch screen above the steering wheel and just below the top of the dashboard. Consequently, he spotted the barricade well before it came within ordinary sight; on the photonegative screen, the blockage on the road registered as a long white cylinder, glowing warmly against a dark background.

A fallen tree, Cyclops wondered, *or something more sinister?*

"Eyes up, folks," he urged his passengers as the limo slowed to a stop along the side of the road. It was probably nothing, Scott realized, but X-Men couldn't afford to take chances. Too many of their enemies knew their home address, even if the world at large did not; an ambush was always a possibility.

He relaxed only slightly when the car's high beams bounced off the gnarled trunk of an elderly maple tree. Judging from the fresh dirt coating the ruin's exposed roots, the tree had crashed onto the road within the last few hours.

Just what we didn't *need,* Cyclops thought impatiently. They had lost too much time driving back from the city already.

"Better step out while I handle this," he advised the others; even if there was nothing amiss, he saw no reason why Hank and Ororo should remain sitting ducks within the car. He stepped from the car and walked along the side of the road until he was only a few feet away from the imposing wooden barricade. Gravel crunched beneath his feet and he heard both rear doors of the limo open and shut. A pondful of frogs croaked somewhere behind the remaining trees.

"Do you require assistance, Scott?" Ororo volunteered. A few well-placed lightning bolts, he knew, would clear the road quite effectively.

"No thanks," he replied. Storm had already done her share back at the police station, airlifting the Beast away from those trigger-happy boys in blue. Time for him to pull his own weight on this expedition.

He glanced around to make sure no one was watching, but the silent woods appeared deserted nor were there any approaching headlights in either direction.

Perfect, he thought. Taking hold of his glasses with one hand, he carefully lifted the red-tinted shades off his nose.

It was like removing a dam from the mouth of a rushing river. Unchecked by the ruby quartz lenses, crimson energy poured out of his eyes, merging to form a single incandescent beam that raced toward the toppled maple at the speed of light. Raw power, beyond Cyclops's conscious control, slammed into the tree trunk, reducing it to splinters. A violent crash violated the quiet serenity of the countryside, momentarily silencing the steady murmur of the frogs. Only fragments of the shattered obstacle remained upon the pavement.

"That should do it," Scott said, lowering the glasses back onto his nose. He took a deep breath; although his mutant eyes tapped into a seemingly inexhaustible reservoir of extradimensional energy, he always felt slightly depleted after channeling that much power through his mortal flesh. He blinked rapidly behind the protective lenses; his eyes burned a bit, but it was nothing he hadn't experienced hundred of times before. *I wonder what's harder on my system, providing a conduit for all that energy—or holding it back the rest of the time?*

Thankfully, his eyes could be used for more conventional purposes as well. Cyclops scanned the empty stretch of road, half expecting Juggernaut or the Blob to come barreling out of the woods at any moment, but only the rustle of wind through the trees hinted at life behind the still nocturnal tableau. Apparently, the fallen tree had been just that, not the opening move in another unprovoked assault on the X-Men. Scott shrugged his shoulders.

Better safe than sorry, he thought.

"Okay, everyone, back into the car." He bent over to pick up one of the larger pieces of the broken wood off the pavement, then flung it into the shadows. Slipping back into the driver's seat, he was gratified to see that the Beast was already back at work on his laptop. At least somebody was getting work done while Scott played chauffeur. The limo pulled back onto the road and Scott mentally counted the miles remaining back to the Xavier Institute for Higher Learning.

"Voila!" the Beast exuberantly declared, only minutes after their trip resumed. "My humble hacking has borne fruit at last. CNN.com reports that an individual believed to be Dr. Robert Bruce Banner has been spotted at Niagara Falls, not far from the Canadian border."

"Good work," Cyclops said. Hank's breakthrough was not enough, however, to remove the worried expression from his face; they were still a long way from locating their missing teammate. "Anything about Rogue?"

The Beast shook his bushy head. "Not a word." His gaze bounced between Storm and Cyclops. "What now, o' glorious co-leaders?"

Cyclops glanced at the dashboard clock. It was close to two in the morning. Niagara Falls was several hours away by car, but if they used the aircraft hangared beneath the Institute, they could be there before sunrise.

"What do you think?" he asked Storm, peeking at her pensive features in the rearview mirror. "The Blackbird?"

"My thoughts exactly," she said.

• • •

Sentinels! Cap's jaw dropped in dismay, much as he imagined Tony's mouth must have fallen open beneath his gilded mask. *I don't believe it.*

Sentinels, in whatever form, had to count as one of the U.S. government's most shameful ideas: a species of powerful and implacable robot policemen specifically designed to track down and apprehend mutants. Mechanized discrimination . . . he could scarcely imagine a more blatant violation of the Constitution and the Declaration of Independence. He had hoped that, after the last Sentinel-inspired orgy of strife and destruction, the whole pernicious notion had retired permanently.

But apparently not.

"Don't give me that look," Fury grumbled, spitting out his stogie in disgust. He stared down at the Avengers from the color monitor. "I don't like this any better than you do. Mama Fury didn't raise no bigots."

"Then how did S.H.I.E.L.D. end up in the business of manufacturing Sentinels?" Iron Man asked indignantly. No doubt he was wondering whether any classified Stark technology had gone into the construction of the new robots.

"I'd like to hear the answer to that myself," Cap said. The government's occasional efforts to pander to all the anti-mutant hysteria out there invariably reminded him of the relocation camps that Japanese-American citizens were herded into during the last big war. He had personally toured several of those camps, and it remained a lasting source of regret to him that he had never been able to persuade President Roosevelt and his advisors to reject that ignoble enterprise.

And now here we are, he thought, *fifty years later and*

heading down that same sad road. As far as he was concerned, building Sentinels to round up mutants was no different from imprisoning innocent men, women, and children simply because of their ancestry.

"Blame bureaucracy in action," Fury snorted. "After Senator Kelly shut down Bastion's little witchhunt, the Sentinel development program was folded into S.H.I.E.L.D.'s larger robotics R&D department. I never cottoned onto what those busy little techies were up to because the whole project showed up on the budget as just specialized Life Model Decoys."

Cap nodded, comprehending. S.H.I.E.L.D. frequently used artificial LMDs to impersonate both agents and adversaries, not to mention the occasional targets of assassination plots. There was a world of difference between LMDs and Sentinels, especially where their objectives were concerned, but he could see where the basic robotics technology would tend to overlap.

One man's defense is another man's weapon of destruction, he reflected. Even his own shield could be used for offensive purposes.

"I hate to point this out," Iron Man commented, "but the existence of these new Sentinels gives the X-Men a plausible motive for attacking the Helicarrier. They could have seen it as a preemptive strike against a new anti-mutant crusade."

Or maybe that's what someone wants *us to think,* Cap considered. It certainly wouldn't be the first time villains impersonated heroes to destroy the reputations of their enemies; less than a year ago, an alien Skrull had briefly taken Cap's own place as part of a plot to deceive the American public. *To my mind, the X-Men are innocent until proven guilty—just like any other citizens.*

The Vision spoke up, his sepulchral voice practically lowering the temperature in the room. "Given that the express purpose of Sentinels is to apprehend mutants, perhaps there is some connection here to the unexplained disappearance of the Scarlet Witch."

"Good point," Captain America said. He tersely informed Fury of the circumstances surrounding Wanda's abduction. "The only problem is that she was attacked by the puppets several hours before the prototype Sentinels were snatched from S.H.I.E.L.D. Still, I can't help feeling in my gut that there's a link between these two incidents. A missing mutant. Stolen Sentinels. It's just too much of a coincidence."

Iron Man raised another question. "You said these were a new type of Sentinels. What exactly was so special about them?"

Fury shrugged. He was a soldier, not a science whiz. "You'd have to ask the eggheads for the real nitty-gritty, but what they told me is that these tin woodsmen have gamma reactors for hearts. Supposed to make them a whole lot stronger than the last batch."

"*Gamma* reactors?" Cap asked, incredulous. He exchanged meaningful glances with Iron Man and the Vision.

"You bet," Fury confirmed. "More government restructuring—seems covert research into gamma weaponry got lumped in with this new Sentinels initiative as part of a campaign to simplify government spending. Blame Al Gore." He glanced down at notes or reports below the view of the screen. He paused for emphasis and Cap leaned forward, wanting to know all he could about what the Avengers might be running up against.

"That's even what they called these blasted things," Fury said ominously. "The Gamma Sentinels."

Chapter Ten

A few hours before:

Close to a hundred thousand gallons a minute poured over the two great Falls at Niagara. Multicolored lights, projected from both the American and Canadian sides of the Falls, cast a brilliant radiance over the vast cascades of roaring water as they tumbled more than a hundred feet to the breakers below. Defying gravity, a constant spray of polychromatic mist rose from the rocky base of the American Falls, reaching all the way up to where awestruck spectators stood on the shore, looking out over the brink of the precipice, watching the Niagara river plunge furiously over the crests of the Falls with irresistible force.

Bruce Banner knew all about irresistible forces, having shared his life with one for over a decade now. The damp mist cooling his bearded face, he paused upon the lighted walkway running along the southern shore of the river and leaned against the guardrail. Preoccupied with other matters, Banner nonetheless spared a moment or two to take advantage of the spectacular view. Closest to him, the American Falls stretched over eight hundred feet across, while farther away, on the other side of Goat Island, the Canadian Horseshoe Falls, so named because of their distinctive shape, could be seen streaming down into a deep, mist-shrouded pool. The muted roar of the Falls filled his ears. People came from all over the world to witness the Falls, he reasoned, so he might as well take in the show while he could. And, to be perfectly honest with himself, he didn't mind stalling a bit before facing the ordeal ahead.

I wonder if this is really such a good idea? he thought.

Newlyweds and other tourists strolled leisurely along the path, their hushed *ooh*s and *ah*s barely audible over the crashing water. None of them took any heed of the solitary individual, clad in a navy blue windbreaker and faded purple jeans, leaning upon the rail. Unlike his alternate persona, Banner was of average build and unexceptional appearance. A cheap box of hair coloring, purchased only hours before at a local drug store and applied at a convenient public restroom, had lightened his customarily brown hair to bleached blond. Only the haunted look of his eyes, and the weary shadows beneath them, distinguished him from the gaily-chattering vacationers also visiting the Falls tonight. That and the fact that he was conspicuously alone.

Taking one last look at the breathtaking magnificence of the American Falls, Banner sighed and pushed away from the rail. *Time to get it over with,* he decided as he continued on toward the Rainbow Bridge farther on down the river, past the Falls. Getting past Customs was going to be tricky, but, all his doubts notwithstanding, he didn't have any better options. With General Ross and his Hulkbusters back on the warpath, now struck him as an ideal time to get out of the country for a while; God willing, Ross's battalions wouldn't be so gung-ho as to pursue him beyond the Canadian border, which might at least buy him a little time to figure out what to do next.

The longer they leave me alone, he mused, *the longer I may be able to keep the Hulk under control.*

Sometimes that was the most he could hope for.

The American customs station was far from impressive, being basically a one-story aluminum shack flanked by a wire fence to keep people from skipping around it on their way to the bridge; it looked like a temporary shelter intended to make do until the *real* station was built, but Banner remembered it looking much the same the last time he passed through. Not exactly a triumph of public architecture; he'd seen DMVs with more grandeur and gravitas. Impressing visiting Canadians, it seemed, was low on the federal government's list of priorities.

He trudged up the wooden steps to the front door, doing his best to affect a jaunty, carefree attitude. *Just another tourist out for an evening excursion,* he thought. *Nothing suspicious here, nope, not at all.* He wished he was really as confident as he hoped he looked, and that his heart wasn't racing so fast. Maybe he should have bought some false glasses as well, to go along with the dyed hair. His baggy purple jeans, held up by a cheap leather belt, were several sizes too big, just in case.

A bored-looking customs official, seated behind a desk to Banner's right, waved him on. Apparently, you didn't get the third-degree until you tried to get *into* the country. Breathing a sigh of relief, he exited the shack at the rear and stepped onto the pedestrian walkway on the Rainbow Bridge. Traffic across the bridge was light; only a few stray vehicles drove past him. A hundred-some feet below, the coursing river continued on its way to the Whirlpool further north. Banner would have been more impressed had he not once beheld another Rainbow Bridge, the one that stretched across the heavens to fabled Asgard, home of the mighty Norse Gods.

Now that *was a bridge,* Banner thought. If nothing else, his tumultuous career as the Hulk's saner half had taken him to some interesting places. Meager consolation, perhaps, for a life spent on the run.

It was perhaps a reflection of some deep-rooted national inferiority complex that the Canadian customs station, at the opposite end of the bridge, was as opulent and imposing as the American station was minimalist. Surrounded by impeccably landscaped gardens, the white marble facade looked like it should house the sacred remains of some historic figure instead of what was basically an ornate tollbooth; it was like going from a low-rent mobile home to the palace at Versailles. Taking a deep breath to steady his nerves, Banner opened the door to let a party of Norwegian tourists through, then stepped inside.

Easy does it, he cautioned himself. *Just another tourist, remember?*

The Canadian border guard, a big man with a stern expression, looked Banner over more thoroughly than his Yankee counterpart. "Purpose of visit?"

"Checking out the sights," Banner said casually. He considered shrugging, but decided that might be pushing it. "I hear there's a pretty good view from this side."

"Uh-huh," the Mountie grunted. The name on his badge read CRAIGIE; Banner assumed that was his surname. The guard glanced at the clock over the door. "Kind of late," he commented.

Banner's mouth went dry and he fought an urge to gulp. "Don't tell me the Falls close at midnight," he said with a smile, trying to make it sound like a joke. He jammed both hands into the pockets of his windbreaker to keep them from fidgeting nervously.

Let it go, he silently begged the Mountie. *Don't make me get too upset—or I might not be responsible for what happens.*

"Just saying it's late," Officer Craigie said, not cracking a smile. He eyed Banner suspiciously, his gaze intermittently dropping down to inspect something below the edge of the counter. A wanted poster, Banner fretted, or some sort of alert? Beneath his jacket and calm exterior, sweat began to soak through his cotton shirt, gluing the fabric to his back. "May I see your passport, sir?"

Something's wrong. Banner was convinced of it. He glanced back over his shoulder, hoping to see more travelers approaching. Maybe a line of impatient tourists would speed the process up, but, no, he was on his own. The Mountie held out his hand, waiting for the passport while Banner fumbled around in his pockets. *I should have waited until morning,* the fugitive scientist castigated himself, *when there was more of a crowd.*

It was too late to back out now, though, not with this overeager Mountie already watching him like he was the second coming of Al Capone.

"Here they are, officer," Banner said, handing Craigie the phony papers he had bought in Times Square with nearly the last of his hard cash. They had looked convincing to him, but what did he know? *I'm a nuclear physicist, blast it, not an international smuggler.*

The border guard inspected the fake passport longer than Banner liked. Long, sweaty seconds ticked by.

"Is there something the matter, officer?" he asked. He probably should have kept quiet, he realized, but maintaining the semblance of calm was rapidly turning into a losing battle. His heart pounded in his chest, raising the terrifying prospect of an unplanned and very unwanted transformation.

No, not now, Banner prayed, even as a dozen familiar sensations alerted him to the change commencing within his body. His skin felt raw and exposed, stretched tightly over rebellious, rippling muscles, and burning as if being roasted from within by a tremendous inner heat. His teeth and gums tingled while an angry pulse started throbbing behind his eyes. His breathing grew shallow at the same time that his lungs expanded against his ribcage. The collar of his shirt felt tight around his neck, choking him. His belt dug into his waist and too-small shoes squeezed his feet. *Not now,* he wished fervently. *Anything but this.* He stared at his hands in alarm. Was he only imagining it, or was his skin already starting to take on a greenish tint?

Maybe it wasn't too late to halt the metamorphosis! He tried counting backwards from one hundred, in hopes of calming his agitated nervous, but it was growing harder and harder to think clearly. Counting back, he never got further than ninety before losing count and having to start over again. The very nature of his thoughts seemed to be changing, growing thicker and harsher and more elemental. How dare this puny human soldier interfere with him anyway? And why did he want to stop the change? Banner had obviously failed. He had been too weak again, as usual. Banner was always too weak.

"Sorry, sir," the Mountie said, still squinting at the forged passport, "but I'm afraid you're going to have to come with—"

Officer Craigie's stern declaration fell silent as he looked up from the papers in his hand to the man he meant to detain. His jaw fell open in astonishment, nothing he might or might not have read about the stranger preparing him for the shocking and grotesque sight before him.

Less than a foot away, Banner was changing into . . . something else. His light brown beard shrunk into his face as his head expanded outward, the features of his face melting and reforming into a visage far more brutish and inhuman, the nose a flattened snout above a mouthful of large, jutting teeth. Pale pink skin darkened to an unnatural shade of yellowish green. Dark pea-green hair spread like fresh grass through the *faux* blond hair until only a shaggy, emerald mop remained atop an immense, box-like skull. Banner's eyes receded beneath heavy, hanging brows so that only a pair of glinting emerald marbles could be seen where his haunted brown eyes had been.

"Ohmigod," Craigie exclaimed, his eyes wide. He backed away from the counter, his ruddy face going pale. "It really is you. It's actually happening!"

Agonized grunts and gasps escaped from Banner as his entire body rebuilt itself with frightening speed. Mundane clothing came apart at the seams, exposing bulging green flesh that ripped through fragile garments that were suddenly many sizes too small. The blue windbreaker was torn into shreds, along with the plain white shirt underneath; both hung in ribbons from impossibly broad shoulders. Immense green feet pushed their way free from the sneakers that tried unsuccessfully to confine them, leaving scraps of rubber soles and broken shoelaces upon the floor. Only the worn violet trousers, deliberately purchased to accommodate Banner's increasing dimensions, hung together, even though the cheap belt snapped like a rubber band stretched too far.

Hunched over in pain, clutching his head in his hands, Banner's posture partially concealed the full extent of his transformation.

Stop it! he thought desperately, already forgetting why as another personality subsumed his own, forcing its way into his thoughts like a rampaging invader from the darkest depths of his unconscious mind and shoving his own hopes and fears into some desolate psychological limbo. Anxiety gave way to defiance—and a seething sense of anger at the entire world.

Stop it? Stop who? Nobody stops the Hulk!

With a deep, full-throated roar, a colossal green ogre, nearly three meters tall, raised his monstrous head high and shook fists the size of anvils. The last tatters of his shirt and jacket fell off his massive frame, to be trampled beneath Sasquatch-sized feet. His hairless chartreuse chest was at least a meter across and looked constructed of solid muscle. Disordered, emerald hair scraped the ceiling as the Hulk rose to his full height, towering over the flabbergasted border guard, who stammered incoherently and reached for his revolver. Banner's ersatz passport slipped from the Mountie's fingers, fluttering unnoticed to the floor.

Sergeant Cameron Craigie considered himself a large man and a tough customer, fully capable of handling himself in a tight spot, but the genuinely incredible Hulk would have dwarfed even the most steroid-enhanced bodybuilder. His looming shadow eclipsed the guard. Photos and film clips of the legendary monster, which Craigie had occasionally seen on the news, had failed to fully convey just how intimidating the Hulk was in the flesh.

I don't believe it, Craigie thought, part of him sincerely wishing that he had never recognized Dr. Banner from the fax pinned behind the counter. *Just look at him. Even his muscles have muscles!*

The Hulk's head swung slowly atop a neck that looked as squat and wide as a fireplug. Beady green eyes swept the customs station, as if he were newly orienting himself to his surroundings. A thuggish sneer suggested he didn't like what he saw, not that he looked terribly worried about anything.

"Hmmph!" he grunted. Without giving Craigie a second glance, he took one enormous step toward the exit, leaving the remains of his wrecked garments and footwear behind him. His heavy tread shook the floor.

"H-hold it," Craigie ordered, an atypical quaver in his command. He barely recognized his own voice. *Just my luck somebody spotted him in town earlier,* he thought. Nervously, he raised his gun and aimed it right at the back of the Hulk's head. "Stop or I'll shoot."

With ominous indifference, the Hulk turned his head and eyed the Mountie balefully. Bushy green eyebrows met above his nose. Hostile green eyes narrowed ominously. "Go ahead," he rumbled in a deep baritone that made James Earl Jones sound like a castrato. "Try it."

"Just stay where you are," Craigie insisted, backing farther away from the gargantuan monstrosity. His gaze darted quickly to the phone on the desk behind the counter. If he could just call for help, maybe someone could send an army or two to deal with the Hulk.

Yeah, he thought, *let the Yanks handle it. They're the ones who wanted him caught.* He inched closer to the phone, keeping the Hulk safely between his sights. Just because the bloody brute was as big as house didn't mean that he was bulletproof, right? Heck, at close range, he was practically impossible to miss!

"Don't go anywhere," he warned, his voice sounding a trifle more confident this time. "I'll fire if I have to."

"So what?" the Hulk grunted, a smirk upon his prehistoric features. Without warning, he spun around and brought down a heavy fist to crash against the counter. The blow shattered both the counter and the desk as well, leaving nothing but a pile of splintered debris between Craigie and the Hulk. Echoes of the deafening impact hung in the air, and the Mountie almost forgot to breathe. He staggered backwards, barely managing to hang onto his revolver. Suddenly, he wished devoutly that he had never heard of Bruce Banner.

The Hulk snarled, baring enormous incisors, and Craigie feared for his life. The Hulk's thunderous footsteps rattled the floor as he stepped toward the Mountie. Craigie squeezed the trigger and fired three times, only to watch in dismay as the bullets bounced harmlessly off the Hulk's bare chest, ricocheting around the room. Panicked, Craigie ducked his head, hearing glass and plaster explode as the deflected bullets wreaked havoc on the walls and furnishings. A framed photo of the Prime Minister crashed to the floor, symbolically assassinated by a stray shot.

Please, Craigie prayed, *let me get out of this alive and I'll never hassle another tourist again!*

"Give me that!" the Hulk bellowed. He snatched the smoking gun from the guard's quaking hand and fumbled with it awkwardly. The blue steel service revolver looked like a toy in the Hulk's massive grip. For a second, Craigie thought that the Hulk was going to shoot him with his own gun, then the looming green-skinned titan raised the gun over his left shoulder, pointing the muzzle between his own oar-sized shoulderblades. Unable to stick a meaty finger past the trigger guard, the Hulk simply squeezed the entire grip so hard that it collapsed into a flattened wad of metal at the same moment that gunpowder ignited, blasting live ammo at the Hulk's spine.

"Ah," he rasped in satisfaction, acrid wisps of smoke rising from his clenched fist. "The only way to scratch those hard-to-reach spots. Thanks a heap," he said disdainfully, tossing the crumpled revolver at Craigie's feet.

"You're welcome," the border guard whimpered weakly, but the Hulk wasn't listening. Turning his back on Craigie, and ignoring the clearly-posted EXIT sign, the Hulk walked straight through the solid stone wall across from the smashed counter, leaving a three-meter tall, one-meter wide hole that opened onto the previously tranquil garden outside. Fallen chunks of marble and concrete were crushed to powder beneath the Hulk's bare feet as he casually brushed a layer of dust and plaster from his shoulders. Screams of panic erupted outside as dozens of startled tourists witnessed the Hulk's first steps onto Canadian soil.

Nerves frayed almost to the breaking point, every muscle quivering, Sergeant Craigie got down on his hands and started rooting around in the ruins of his office. Through the newly-created door in front of him, he heard the Hulk stomp through the landscaped garden, to the accompaniment of frightened shouting.

Help, he thought numbly. *We need help. Lots of help.*

He knew there had to be a phone buried somewhere in the rubble.

By the time the X-Men arrived on the scene, the Hulk's arrival at Niagara had become a full-fledged media event. Competing news helicopters circled overhead, jockeying for the best perspectives on the telegenic crisis. Both the American and Canadian armies lined their respective shores, holding back crowds of excited onlookers and scoop-hungry reporters. The nightly light show had been replaced by glaring spotlights, all focused on the wooded island between the Falls, where the rampaging Hulk roared his defiance.

"Leave me alone!" he shouted, his huge feet planted on the northern tip of the island, facing the Falls. He pounded his fists against his chest. "Get outta my sight or you'll be looking at one less national landmark!"

Viewing the chaos from a video monitor in the cockpit of the Blackbird, Storm felt her spirits sag. "It is far more . . . public . . . than I would have preferred," she commented.

The Blackbird, a sleek black aircraft equipped with the finest in stealth technology, closed on Niagara. Cyclops manned the helm, no doubt watching carefully for the copters occupying the airspace ahead. To the east, Storm glimpsed the first rosy hints of dawn and held back a yawn. By car or by plane, they had been traveling all night in their thus-far fruitless search for Rogue. She rubbed her tired eyes. Lack of sleep did nothing to ease her anxiety. *How can we possibly confer with Banner under such volatile circumstances?*

"That's why we wear masks," Cyclops stated. He took another look at Storm and the Beast. Like Cyclops, they had shed their civilian garb for their X-Men uniforms, but only Scott's face was covered by his costume; specifically, by his polished gold visor. The Beast, in fact, was wearing nothing more than a pair of black shorts and his own furry pelt. "Well, some of us do. In any case, we might not get a better chance. If the military actually manage to apprehend the Hulk, there's no way they're letting us anywhere near him."

"Perhaps," the Beast suggested, peering over Storm's shoulder at the television footage, "our favorite gamma-spawned gargantua might appreciate a timely lift at this particular juncture?"

"Perhaps," Storm agreed. Aiding and abetting the

Hulk in an escape from the authorities would hardly help the X-Men's embattled reputation, but, realistically, they had very little to lose in that regard. And it might make the Hulk more inclined to assist them in their quest. "What do you think, Scott?"

Cyclops kept his golden visor fixed on the Blackbird's instrumentation. "Let's go for it—if we can get the Hulk to cooperate."

That, Storm knew, was a very big if. Compared to the Hulk, Wolverine was a gentle pacifist. She leaned back into the passenger seat and closed her eyes, the better to concentrate her powers. "I believe a degree of cloud cover may help ensure a measure of privacy."

At her command, a heavy fog abruptly rose from the river below, blanketing the small island entirely and shielding the Hulk from curious eyes. Forced to retreat by the instant lack of visibility, the news copters turned their floodlights on the roiling mist, but their beams failed to penetrate the dense gray fog, as did the powerful searchlights upon the shore. The mist crouched atop the island like a living entity.

Shrouded by the mist, the Blackbird touched down on Goat Island, executing a pinpoint VTOL descent onto a wide stretch of paved roadway near the center of the island.

"Hurry," Storm urged her teammates as they vacated the plane. "The conditions here are conducive to fog, but I cannot sustain such an opaque atmosphere indefinitely." Even now she could feel the early morning breeze attempting to dissipate her fog; it required conscious effort on her part to redirect the winds around the island.

They rushed through the forest, Cyclops in the lead, clearing a path through the brush with his eyebeams, whose incandescent glow also provided a beacon to follow through the clammy mist and shadows that made the woods a murky tangle of flailing branches and clotted undergrowth. Storm almost tripped more than once, her heels sinking into the mossy loam, but managed to maintain a steady pace that still fell far short of the Beast's rapid progress through the branches overhead. He swung nimbly from trees, as much in his element now as Storm would have been soaring above the clouds.

To each his own, she thought.

Her rough trek neared its end as she saw the densely planted trees begin to thin out ahead. Beyond the obedient fog, she sensed the newborn sun rising above the horizon, casting its warmth upon the early morning hours. Cyclops shut off his beam, their way now clear, only to drop speedily to the forest floor, surprising Storm.

"Watch out!" he warned her, flattening himself against the damp, dewy earth.

Storm glimpsed a full-sized tree swinging toward her like a club and took to the air. A hasty gust of wind carried her aloft, safely above the uprooted spruce tree that swung in a wide arc through the very space that she and Cyclops had occupied only a moment before. The branch-strewn log whooshed beneath her and over Cyclops's prostrate form.

"Holy moley!" the Beast exclaimed from his vantage point in a nearby bough. "Where in the name of Paul Bunyan did that come from?"

The answer emerged from the fog, still clutching the base of the spruce in one capacious fist.

"Thought you could sneak up on me, didya?" the Hulk thundered savagely. Green eyes squinted through the haze, fixing on Storm and the others. "Well, well. If it isn't the world's most famous mutant misfits.'' He tapped his leafy cudgel upon the ground threateningly, not far from where Cyclops cautiously rose to his feet, his visor at the ready. ''Where's that sawed-off Canuck, Wolverine?'' The Hulk sneered at Cyclops, seemingly unafraid of the X-Man's potent eyebeams. ''He's the only one in your bunch worth brawlin' with.''

''Believe it or not, Hulk,'' Storm declared, ''we are here to help you.'' A tamed breeze swelled the cloth wings beneath her arms as she gracefully descended to earth. *I had forgotten quite how large he is,* she thought, contemplating the Hulk's tremendous physique. Not even the Juggernaut was as imposing in his proportions, nor as grotesque in countenance.

''Who asked you?'' the Hulk growled. His manners were comparable to Cain Marko's as well, it seemed. He peered about him suspiciously, an idea forming within his misshapen skull. ''You responsible for this pea soup muck, weather girl?'' he asked her, sweeping his free hand through the fog.

Although still worshipped as a goddess in parts of Africa, Ororo chose to ignore the Hulk's disrespect. The savage creature could not help his lack of common courtesy, or so she decided to assume. ''I had thought that you might appreciate the seclusion,'' she explained. ''Free from prying eyes.''

He threw the uprooted tree to the ground with surprising force, startling Storm with his sudden fury.

''You thought I needed to hide? From a coupla wimpy armies?'' Indignation distorted his already primeval features. Titanic muscles flexed along prodigious arms, the veins standing out like heavy cables. ''Listen to me,

X-Lady, and listen good. The Hulk don't hide from no-body!"

Two gigantic hands slammed together, producing a shock wave that tore apart her carefully constructed fog bank like a child's birthday candle blown out in a single huff. The congealed mist blew off the island, propelled by a hurricane-strength force that also sent Storm and Cyclops tumbling backward, somersaulting out of control through the brush while the Beast hung onto to a sheltering tree trunk with both hands, flapping like a furry blue flag above the forest floor. Branches and brambles whipped past Storm, but more than the physical impact buffeted her; a portion of her consciousness had been intertwined with the foggy atmosphere she had fostered, and the violent disruption of her creation sent a psychic shock through her mind that left her dazed and speechless.

Goddess! she thought, ending up sprawled upon the ground, dozens of tiny scratches and scrapes stinging her skin, her brain aching from the neurological trauma. Cyclops groaned nearby, but she lacked the strength to lift her head right at this moment. *He's like a force of nature all his own.*

"That's more like it," the Hulk grunted, placing his hands upon his hips. His cataclysmic clap had cleared all the foliage from a spit of land at the northern tip of the land, exposing him further to the armed forces mustered on both sides of the Falls, as well as to the hovering news copters. The Hulk clearly couldn't care less; beneath the bright morning sun, surrounded by a stretch of blasted earth, he roared a challenge to all within earshot.

And then the Avengers arrived.

· · ·

"The Hulk—and the X-Men? This can't be a coincidence," Iron Man blurted through his metal mask. "Gamma rays. Gamma Sentinels. And now this." His automatic vocalizer amplified his voice, making him easily audible over the roar of both the Hulk and the Falls. The motile metal of his gilded faceplate allowed a semblance of his grim expression to come through the mask. "I don't know about you, Cap, but from where I'm standing two plus two sure doesn't equal an innocent misunderstanding."

"I concur," the Vision intoned. "According to my computations, there is a 98.76 percent probability that this incident is related to Wanda's disappearance."

The trio of Avengers had taken a position upon the Robert Moss Parkway, overlooking the American Falls. Their Avengers Quinjet, designed by Tony Stark, was parked at Niagara Falls airport, a few miles away. A brigade of U.S. soldiers, led by their commanding officer, Colonel Arturo Lopez, shared the parkway with the newly-arrived heroes. The colonel himself looked more than a little relieved that Captain America had shown up to take charge of the crisis.

"Confound it," he shouted into a handheld walkie-talkie, close enough for Cap and the other Avengers to hear. "Somebody get those news choppers out of there. Threaten to revoke their FCC licenses if you have to, but clear that airspace!"

Shaking his head angrily, he handed Cap a pair of field binoculars that Cap used to scope out the situation. The Hulk's bestial visage came sharply into focus, looking more savage than ever. At least two of the X-Men were down on the ground, looking like they'd experienced the Hulk's infamously bad temper firsthand. Cyclops recovered first, and hurried to check on Storm, who appeared somewhat worse off, perhaps in a state of shock. He was quickly joined by the Beast, who dropped from the tree-tops onto the rocky soil. Cap wished he could hear whatever the Hulk and the X-Men might be saying to each other. That way he might feel a little less in the dark.

"I don't know," he said cautiously, lowering the binoculars. His unbreakable shield was strapped to his back, just as ready as Iron Man and the Vision, who stood nearby, awaiting his instructions. As immobile as a statue, the synthezoid kept his unblinking eyes fixed on the Hulk while Iron Man listened to Cap confer with the colonel. "Let's not rush into anything before we get our facts straight." It was practically a tradition for costumed heroes to bump heads whenever their paths crossed, with the X-Men and the Avengers being no exception, but Cap saw no reason to let this stand-off devolve into an out-and-out free-for-all if there was any way to prevent it. He handed the binoculars back to Lopez. "Tell your soldiers not to fire except in self-defense."

"I understand," the colonel said. His lean, prematurely furrowed face was grave. "I have my orders, though. Not only has General Ross ordered me by telephone to engage the Hulk, but the X-Men are also wanted for an attack upon a high-security government installation. I cannot allow them to escape without making some effort to take them into custody."

"Perhaps I can persuade them to turn themselves in for questioning," Cap suggested. Despite the Sentinel connection, and the X-Men's surprising appearance alongside the Hulk, he was not convinced of the mutants' guilt where the assault on S.H.I.E.L.D. was concerned. There was something fishy about everything that had happened since the Scarlet Witch was abducted from the museum.

Maybe if we all work together, he thought, *we can get to the bottom of this.* If nothing else, he knew he could count on the Beast to cooperate—if that really was Hank McCoy on the island.

"I can hold off for a while longer," Lopez admitted. He peered through his binoculars at the drama unfolding at the once-wooded tip of the isle, where the Hulk still faced off against Cyclops and his team. "I'm in no hurry to throw my troops up against those freaks and their powers." He shook his head, scowling. "Give me a good natural disaster or bomb scare any day."

"Thank you, Colonel," Cap said sincerely. With luck, the Canadian troops across the river would show the same restraint. He turned to Iron Man and saw his own face reflected in the sheen of the golden Avenger's helmet. "Iron Man, can you amplify my voice so that the Hulk can hear me over there? I want to try to reason with him."

"Are we thinking of the same Hulk?" Iron Man said dubiously. Cap knew what he meant; the Hulk was hardly the most reasonable of individuals.

"Worth a try," Captain America said. Before resorting to force, he always made sure that all peaceful avenues had been explored; that was the American way.

"We are losing valuable time," the Vision announced brusquely. The soles of his canary-yellow boots began to lift off the pavement as he made his artificial body lighter than air and assumed a more aerodynamic posture, arms stretched out in front of him as though he was merely diving upward into the sky. His cape rustled softly in the wind as he wafted away from the parkway, toward the Falls. "I will confront the Hulk," he stated.

"Stand down, Vision," Cap ordered firmly before the

synthezoid could put too much distance between them. The Vision's impatience and impulsiveness surprised Cap; it wasn't like him to jump the gun like this. *Maybe he's more worried about Wanda than he lets on,* he surmised. The Vision paused in midair, his saffron cloak billowing around him, then reluctantly returned to the side of his fellow Avengers, but not without a lingering glance over his shoulder at the Hulk's island refuge. His waxen expression never changed.

"Here, Cap." Iron Man removed a capsule-shaped component from the neckpiece of his armor. His voice suddenly acquired a more human, less amplified tone. "Just speak into this."

The miniature mike fit easily into Cap's palm. Raising the mechanism to his lips, he addressed the distant green giant. "Hulk, this is Captain America. I know we've had our differences in the past, but there's no need to make things any worse. From one Avenger to another, I promise you that we just want to talk to you and the X-Men. Give me a chance to straighten things out."

Hoping for the best, he lowered the mike and waited expectantly. "You really think you can get through to him?" Iron Man asked skeptically. "I doubt that old Avengers ties carry much weight where the Hulk is concerned."

Confirming Iron Man's worst expectations, the Hulk responded by digging his hands into the soil of Goat Island and tearing out a large, gray boulder the size of a washing machine. Raising the colossal rock above his head, he hurled the boulder at the shore, sending it soaring over the entire width of the American Falls, nearly clipping the propellers of one of the buzzing TV choppers.

"Watch out!" Captain America warned Lopez and his soldiers. "Incoming!"

The rock came whistling at them, descending in an arc from the sky above. Snatching his shield off his back, Cap raised it above him and braced himself for the impact. Iron Man had another idea. Bright orange repulsor beams issued from his metal gauntlets, twin streams of accelerated neutrons pulverizing the boulder only instants before it crashed down upon Cap and the others. Bits of stony debris rained down on Cap instead, deflected by his upraised shield.

So much for peaceful negotiations, Iron Man thought. The Hulk was clearly in no mood to talk.

The unprovoked attack was the spark that set off a wildfire of retaliation, and drove the intrusive helicopters away from the Falls. Artillery fired on both sides of the river, all targeted at the berserk, green-skinned monster on the island. The unleashed firepower was deafening; romantic Niagara, the honeymoon capital of the U.S.A., suddenly sounded like Omaha Beach on D-Day. The smell of gunpowder filled the air, along with the *rat-ta-tat-tat* of machine guns. Neither the Canadian nor the Americans, it was obvious, intended to give the Hulk a chance to launch another projectile assault. Cap couldn't much blame them.

Unfortunately, their efforts generated more sound and fury than results. Missiles and automatic weapons fire exploded all around the Hulk, raising clouds of dust and smoke, but leaving him entirely unscathed. Rockets detonated against his chest, and the indestructible behemoth merely bared his teeth and shook his fists at the armed forces doing their best to destroy him. He broke off another chunk of island and catapulted it into the air, this time at the Canadian forces assembled on the other side of the Horseshoe Falls. With no Iron Man to defend them, the flying boulder smashed into the armored chassis of a tank, smashing the gun turret to a pulp while nearby soldiers ran for cover.

Hopefully, nobody in the tank got hurt, Cap thought. But it was only a matter of time before someone was seriously injured or worse.

The X-Men were also under siege from both armies. Cyclops's ocular energy beams swept in a wide swath, shielding his comrades from the deadly fusillade while the Beast helped the stricken Storm limp toward the partial safety of the beckoning woods. Was he trying to defend the Hulk as well? Captain America couldn't tell. The crimson beams, similar in effect to Iron Man's repulsor rays, blocked whatever firepower came their way.

Almost. As the Beast pulled away from his visored leader, one hairy blue arm supporting Storm, an errant shell detonated less than a yard away from him. The Beast took the brunt of the blast, sparing Storm, but the shock wave slammed the one-time Avenger into the base of an old maple so hard that the tree crashed down on top of him, pinning the agile mutant to the ground.

Watching from the shore, Cap was distressed to see the Beast lying immobile beneath the downed tree. *Was he just unconscious or . . . ?*

"Blast it!" Captain America exclaimed, his words lost in the din of the battle. "This is just what I *didn't* want!"

The Vision gave Captain America a questioning look. The Captain nodded solemnly, and, without a word, the Vision launched silently off the parkway once more, leaving Captain America and Iron Man to defend the American troops as best they could. The artificial Avenger flew over the Falls, rockets and live ammunition passing harmlessly through his intangible body.

A curious urgency compelled him. The prospect of engaging the Hulk in combat seemed vastly preferable to continued inaction, especially while the Scarlet Witch remained unaccounted for. It was only logical, of course, to desire the safe return of a valued team member, but was that the only source of such uncharacteristic haste? A rigorous self-diagnostic could not ignore the potentially significant factor that the Avenger at risk in this instance was, as a matter of biographical record, his former wife.

Wanda. His emotional responses were not what they once were, having suffered significant degradation over the course of various episodes of major repair and reconstruction, but he could not rule out the possibility that some residual subroutines, left over from an earlier generation of himself, might still linger in his software, lending additional impetus to his current priorities. *Wanda is in danger. Wanda.*

An intriguing hypothesis, but now was the not the time for further introspection. The Hulk loomed before him, glaring at the Vision's spectral form with unconcealed antagonism as the synthezoid descended from the sky by minutely increasing his mass. The Vision's plastic face was as impassive in appearance as the Hulk's was fierce.

"Do not attempt to resist, Hulk," he warned. "Willingly or not, you will answer our questions."

"Questions?" the Hulk echoed. For a moment, he looked more puzzled than aggrieved, as though unable to imagine what manner of questions the Avenger might have for him, then his customary belligerence returned. A contemptuous sneer further marred the aesthetic of his primordial features. "What do I look like, an information booth?"

It was difficult to comprehend the Hulk's words over the cacophonous tumult of the military armaments deployed against him, so the Vision adjusted the sensitivity of his auditory receptors, filtering out a statistically significant portion of the explosive background noise. His boots touched down lightly upon the soil of Goat Island, directly in front of the Hulk. The green-skinned goliath towered over the slender synthezoid by more than a head, but the Vision was undaunted; as long as he remained intangible, the Hulk's physical strength, however formidable, could not touch him.

The Vision glanced quickly to the left, ascertaining the current status of the X-Men. Captain America would want to interrogate the mutant adventurers as well, he knew, but they did not appear to be in danger of escaping in the immediate future; Cyclops remained fully occupied by the task of fending off the barrage from the two armies while the Beast and Storm had not yet recovered from previous injuries. *I will deal with them shortly,* he resolved, giving the Hulk his full attention.

"I require data, Hulk, which either you or Dr. Banner may be able to provide. What do you know of the Gamma Sentinels and/or the abduction of Wanda Maximoff, also known as the Scarlet Witch?"

"Don't talk to me about Banner!" the Hulk snarled, saliva spraying from his prognathous jaws. He tried to bat the Vision away with the back of his hand, but the slap passed through the synthezoid as if he wasn't there. The Hulk glared at his own splayed fingers with open annoyance.

"I am waiting for your answers," the Vision said with

implacable calm. His arms were crossed below the yellow diamond symbol on his chest. His boots left no impression in the ground below. "Will you surrender them voluntarily, or will I be forced to resort to physical coercion?" The amber gem embedded in his crimson forehead started to glow forbiddingly.

"Don't pull your spooky act on me, robot!" the Hulk growled. He walked straight through the Vision, effectively leaving them back-to-back instead of face-to-face. "Get real enough to fight, or leave me alone." He strode arrogantly across the tiny spit of land, not giving the Vision so much as a single backwards glance.

But the artificial Avenger declined to be dismissed. Turning his head, he tapped into the solar energy absorbed by the amber jewel and redirected it out through the projective lenses in his eyes. Red-hot thermoscopic beams streaked toward the Hulk, intersecting at the base of his neck. For a nanosecond, the chartreuse flesh turned red and raw, before the Hulk's legendary invulnerability asserted itself, restoring the damaged skin to a healthy green hue. With the sun now shining brightly overhead, however, the Vision kept up the bombardment of concentrated photons, his gaze literally burning into the back of the Hulk's neck.

It was enough to make the Hulk slap a Brobdingnagian paw over the afflicted area.

"What the—!" he exclaimed, than yanked his huge mitt away in a hurry as the Vision's thermoscopic vision seared the back of his hand, which healed almost instantly. "Cute," he said sourly, giving the Vision a dirty look, "but you're goin' to have to do better than that."

Before the Vision could reply, a new voice called out, significantly complicating the situation.

"Hulk!" Cyclops shouted. He rose from the Beast's side, where he had knelt only seconds before.

From Cyclops's behavior, the Vision deduced that the X-Men's leader had not discovered the Beast's injuries to be life-threatening. *This is well,* he concluded. *The Beast has been a valued comrade in the past, albeit with an unnecessarily active sense of humor.* The Vision further noted that a shaky Storm stood once more upon her own feet, although with obvious effort.

"It's not too late to make a clean getaway," Cyclops urged, daring the fusillade to approach the Hulk at a run. "Our aircraft is nearby. Come with me. Now."

Fascinating, the Vision observed, extinguishing his heat beams. His initial analysis of the situation had suggested that the Hulk and the X-Men were pitted against each other as adversaries, but perhaps that assessment needed to be revised. Cyclops now appeared to be siding with the Hulk, despite their earlier confrontation. Regardless, the Vision decided, he could not permit either party to depart before their role in Wanda's abduction could be determined.

Wanda.

Without warning or conscious volition, a picture-perfect recollection of his wedding to Wanda, conducted years ago in the garden of a Vietnamese temple by none other than Immortus, the enigmatic Master of Time, surfaced in his mind, momentarily disorienting him with its vivid clarity and unexpected emotional resonance. For approximately .791 seconds, he could almost smell the overpowering fragrance of the tropical blossoms, sense once more the joyful camaraderie of their assembled friends and allies.

Happy, he recalled with a twinge of regret, the bittersweet jolt of remembered emotion threatening to disrupt the ordered procession of his computations. *We had both been so happy. . . .*

Cyclops's forcebeam swept harmlessly through the Vision, leaving the synthezoid untouched but successfully deflecting another hail of bullets and missiles. Ricocheting rockets detonated at a safe distance from the determined X-Man, who tugged on the Hulk's mighty bicep. "Hurry," he exhorted the immovable green goliath. "Let us help you get away from this chaos."

The Hulk was no more interested in Cyclops's assistance than he was in the Vision's questions. "Bah!" he grunted loudly. "This island is getting too crowded."

Shrugging off Cyclops's grip as easily as he might a flea, the Hulk squatted upon bended legs, then leapt into the air, his tremendous strength propelling him over thirty feet above the Vision and Cyclops, who had to tilt back their respective heads to follow his ascent as he rose like a rocket into the clouds. His departure left gallon-sized footprints in the ravaged soil.

"Wait!" Cyclops yelled after him. His blazing eyebeams chased the Hulk, who quickly outdistanced them. "I need to talk to you!"

No less than I, the Vision thought, resolving that the Hulk would not elude him so easily. It seemed he could still smell the flowers in the garden of a temple many thousands of miles, and a lifetime, away. . . .

From the shore, Captain America took in every detail of the Vision's confrontation with both the Hulk and Cyclops. If nothing else, the Vision had distracted the Hulk from his attacks on the various military personnel, freeing him and Iron Man from the challenge of defending Colonel Lopez's troops from soaring boulders and the like. He tapped on Iron Man's crimson shoulderplate, attracting the armored Avenger's attention. Holding the miniature microphone before his lips, to ensure that Tony could hear him over all the racket produced by the artillery and the Falls, Cap pointed toward the tiny island where the Vision had established a beachhead of sorts.

"Get me over there," he requested, before handing the mike back to Iron Man, who replaced it in his neck assembly while Cap strapped his shield back onto his back.

The golden Avenger nodded. "You want a ride, you got it," he said, his voice mechanically amplified once more. He clamped his iron gauntlets around Cap's wrists and ignited his boot jets.

Cap felt the wind rushing against his face as Iron Man carried him into the air with impressive speed and much more volume than the Vision had produced in his takeoff; it was like hitching a ride on a man-sized 747. Cap's own red boots dangled above the rushing Niagara River for only a second or two, then he spotted dry land beneath him. Working together like a piece of flawless Stark technology, Iron Man released his grip on Captain America, who somersaulted through the air, landing on his feet just in time to see the Hulk hurling back to Earth, with the Vision flying away in hot pursuit of Bruce Banner's green-skinned alter ego. Iron Man circled overhead, keeping a careful watch over both his teammates, ready to intervene wherever he was most needed.

Cap looked around him, appalled at the devastation. The northern tip of the island looked like No Man's Land, with flattened trees and gaping craters, the latter where the Hulk had yanked his boulders from the ground. Shield in hand to defend himself from the whizzing rockets and gunfire, Cap raced across the battlefield, nimbly evading every pitfall, until he came to face-to-face with the X-Men's youthful leader.

"All right, son," he informed Cyclops sternly, raising his voice over the hubbub, "I'm giving you a chance to explain what this is all about."

The scarlet glow behind the X-Man's visor made it impossible to read the younger man's eyes. Cap waited tensely for Cyclops's reply, ready to raise his shield at the first sign of hostile action on the X-Man's part, but hoping sincerely that further violence could be avoided. Bombs exploded in the background, as, beneath his shining visor, Cyclops's lips moved urgently.

Cap couldn't make out a word he said.

The Hulk had become nothing more than a faint green speck in the sky before gravity finally caught up with him. As the Vision tracked his quarry's progress via artificial eyes, the Hulk accelerated downward almost as steeply as he had climbed, landing feetfirst midway across the crestline of the Horseshoe Falls. The splash created by his semi-seismic return drenched onlookers all along the Canadian border and soaked the super-powered occupants of the island as well, all except for the Vision who let the inundating spray of droplets pass through his immaterial form.

I cannot allow obsolete and outdated memory files to distract me from my task, he affirmed, letting the unsolicited recollections of his wedding slip back into his memory banks. Instead he carefully considered the Hulk's latest tactic.

The raging current rushing over the Falls would be more than enough to push anyone else over the brink, but not the Hulk. He stood hip-deep in the cascading foam, adamantly immobile despite the countless gallons of water surging past him.

"You clowns want me?" he hollered at the Vision and the X-Men, as fixed in his footing as the ancient cliff itself. Surging white water was forced to flow around the pillars of his legs. "Come and get me!"

Cyclops's mouth gaped open, only half of his startled expression concealed by his gleaming metal visor. Wet brown hair lay plastered atop his skull and water dripped from his soaked blue uniform. Obviously, there was no way the X-Man could follow the Hulk out into the river; the torrential current would wash him over the Falls almost instantly, eyebeams or no eyebeams.

The Vision was not so readily thwarted. Leaving the X-Man behind, he reduced his weight as well as his density and floated off the ground and out over that fork of the river which flowed between Goat Island and Ontario. "Stay where you are, Hulk," he commanded coldly, the wind blowing *through* his face. "I do not fear to join you upon the very precipice you have chosen."

As easily as he could make himself lightweight, he could also increase his density until he became as hard as diamond and as heavy as solid neutronium. Sinking into the frothing white water only a few feet away from the Hulk, he let his swiftly-accumulating mass anchor him to the rocky riverbed no less steadfastly than his emerald opponent, until his boots were deeply embedded in the silt and stone below the rushing current. Epidermal sensors in his legs registered the lower temperature of the icy water as opposed to the open air, but he experienced little discomfort; the solar energy that powered him also helped his more heat-sensitive components resist the sudden chill.

His lengthy yellow cloak, composed of unstable molecules, remained selectively intangible, the better to avoid becoming tangled in the rapids.

"So, just can't take a hint, huh?" the Hulk rumbled, his words almost lost beneath the clamor of the Falls at their feet. He leered barbarically, savoring the prospect of physical violence. "Okay, let's do this the hard way . . . just the way I like it."

He reached out for the Vision, presumably with the intent of breaking the synthezoid in two, but the Vision grabbed onto the Hulk's wrists, holding him back for a few moments. His gloved fingers failed to reach all the way around the Hulk's thick wrists, making it difficult to keep his grip as the Hulk leaned forward, pushing against the Vision's defense with all the force of oncoming bullet train. The Vision had to increase his corporeal density to its utmost limit, his feet sinking deep into solid rock, just to keep the Hulk out of arm's reach.

"You're tough, robot," the Hulk grudgingly admitted, "but not tough enough. Get ready for a really big fall."

They grappled like mythic champions above the awesome spectacle of the Falls, the dark green of the Vision's skintight costume contrasting against the chartreuse hue of the Hulk's coarse hide, the synthezoid's spectral cape spreading out from his shoulders like a streaming yellow banner. Despite his considerable mass, the Vision felt his heels sliding backward, digging parallel trenches into the stony riverbed. He fought to regain his footing, only to realize that he could not long resist the unremitting pressure of the Hulk's advance. But perhaps his opponent's overpowering momentum could be turned against him?

With an instant's thought, the Vision shed his dense solidity, becoming vaporous once more. The sudden evaporation of all resistance caused the Hulk to topple forward, falling face-first into the foaming water, which rolled him inexorably toward the crest of the awesome cataract—and a staggeringly rough descent.

Weightless and watchful, The Vision levitated in the air a few feet past the brink, not to mention over one hundred and fifty feet above the misty pool below. He had no fear that an unwanted trip over the Horseshoe Falls would kill or even seriously injure the Hulk, but perhaps the rocky plunge would knock some of the combative spirit out of the ferocious malefactor, making him more amenable to the Vision's planned interrogation. There was even some slight possibility, which the synthezoid estimated at approximately 15.64%, that the arduous plunge would be sufficient to trigger the Hulk's metamorphosis back into Bruce Banner, who was, in fact, the very individual the Avengers most desired to question.

I can only hope for such a fortuitous development, the Vision thought, looking on dispassionately as the Hulk clung desperately to the crest of the cataract, struggling to keep from washing over the edge. The Vision began to descend slowly toward the pool, readying himself to fish either Banner or the Hulk from the churning water at the foot of the Falls.

But, to the Vision's surprise, the Hulk did not plunge as promptly as the android Avenger expected. Instead, the Hulk fought back against the relentless current, rising slowly to his hands and knees amidst the savage torrent, throwing back his head to gasp for air above the waves crashing against his head and shoulders. He sputtered, coughing out great mouthfuls of water that ran down his chin and back into the river. Even the Vision's imperturbable plastic face displayed a degree of astonishment and open wonder as, defying all probability and reasonable expectation, the obstinate green titan rose again to his feet.

"Gutless coward!" he accused the hovering Vision. Water streamed from his matted emerald hair, irrigating the crevices between his bulging muscles. "A cheap trick like that can't stop the Hulk! Come back and fight me like a man, you chicken-hearted mannequin!"

The Vision felt no need to defend his man-made masculinity, but acknowledged that his ploy had failed to overcome the Hulk's truly remarkable perseverance and stamina.

Very well, he cogitated. *I have other strategies to employ.*

Reversing his gradual descent, the Vision floated back to the crestline. "This conflict is unnecessary," he reminded the Hulk, regaining sufficient mass to immerse his legs in the current a second time. He waded across the rapids, waist-deep in the spewing water, until he came close enough to thrust an intangible arm deep into the Hulk's inhumanly broad chest. His right forearm disappeared entirely within the Hulk. The tips of his ethereal fingers emerged from the monster's back. "All we desire is information, followed by your peaceful departure from this venue. Spare yourself further discomfort."

"Spare this!" the Hulk bellowed, throwing a gigantic fist at the Vision's face.

Simultaneously, the Avenger resorted to his most aggressive, and consistently effective, offensive tactic, partially materializing his arm within the very substance of the Hulk's body. As two solid objects could not occupy the same space at the same time, the subject of such an invasion invariably suffered intense and incapacitating pain. It was a delicate procedure, requiring acute concentration; if he allowed his arm to become too fully solid, he could easily kill even so indestructible entity as the Hulk.

Said concentration was not made any easier by the physical shock of the Hulk's fist smashing into the Vision's face. Knuckles like concrete slammed into a diamond-hard mask, although some portion of the force of the blow was sapped at the last minute by the convulsive agony that spread from the Hulk's chest to the rest of his Herculean body. Even still, the punch rattled the Vision's cybernetic synapses and knocked his entire super-hard body back a few inches, dangerously dislodging his precarious footing upon the watery ledge. On the other side of the Hulk's thick torso, the Vision's extended fingers sank back into the chartreuse flesh as it were a pool of quicksand. ·

"Arrgh!" the Hulk howled, throwing back his head in agony, his emerald eyes bulging from their sockets. He clutched at the phantom arm invading his flesh, but his beefy fingers passed through it fruitlessly. "What are you doin' to me?"

"Surrender," the Vision said concisely, declining to explain the precise nature of his attack. Still reeling from the Hulk's single blow, he considered rendering his entire body as insubstantial as his arm, but feared that he would not being able to hold his position without the excess mass weighing him to the rocky floor below. No matter what other blows he might endure, he could not allow the Hulk the slightest chance of dislodging the synthezoid's invasive arm before it had completed its task of subduing the bellicose colossus.

Already the Hulk had resisted his transcorporeal assault

longer than the average organic being. Most foes succumbed almost immediately, the acute systemic shock reducing even the most intransigent of adversaries to unconsciousness within a matter of seconds. As with the Hulk's triumph over the current only moments ago, however, the verdant giant's astonishing recuperative powers again undid the Vision's carefully reasoned calculations. To his confoundment, the very substance of the Hulk's being seemed to resist the synthezoid's intrusion on a cellular, even a molecular, level. The Vision grimaced in unaccustomed discomfort as the Hulk's atomic structure refused to give way to his own synthetic flesh and bone, squeezing his semi-solid atoms all the way down to their collapsing nuclei. A surprisingly human gasp escaped the Vision's sculpted lips.

"Hah! Didn't expect that, did you?" the Hulk gloated. His enormous body quivered in pain, but the Hulk somehow managed a malignant sneer, as if daring the synthezoid to push the fight further. The surface of his skin seethed and bubbled where it intersected with the Vision's ethereal limb, a visible symptom of his flesh's tireless struggle to expel the foreign material. Irrationally, or perhaps not, the Vision imagined that he was trying to subdue an unusually malignant, humanoid form of cancer. "Give me your best shot!" the living green cancer dared him.

Wanda is in danger, the Vision recalled. *I cannot fail.* The Hulk's gamma-charged body had become a battleground upon which the Vision knew he dared not lose. The Hulk defied logic, overthrew all standards of rationality; if unreliable emotional responses could provide him with whatever extra capacity he required to vanquish this indefatigable beast, then for once the Vision welcomed them. He thrust his arm so deep into the Hulk's breast that his gloved yellow hand penetrated straight through the monstrosity's spine and came out the other side. *Wanda, my wife . . .*

"You don't get it, do you?" the Hulk mocked him. Spidery tracings of green streaked the Hulk's bloodshot eyes. "You can't beat me. You can just make me mad." The Hulk glared at him with gleeful malice, a rictus-like sneer distorting his bestial countenance. His hot, foul breath offended the Vision's olfactory sensors. Stubborn green flesh writhed at the point of contact between the Vision's untouchable limb and the Hulk's palpitating muscles. "And you know what? The madder I get, the stronger I get . . . !"

That is scientifically improbable, the Vision thought, with something resembling desperation. Nonetheless, the Hulk's endurance indeed appeared to be increasing at a geometric rate; new muscles, unseen in any anatomy text, formed atop preexisting layers of sinew. The Vision willed his arm to near full substantiality, exceeding every humane safety limit he had ever maintained, yet the Hulk remained standing. Beads of greenish sweat broke out on his sloping brow, and his rippling thews pulsated convulsively, but he stayed fixed in place like some solid green outcropping of the cliff beneath him.

The Vision looked no less unbending, his arm thrust out in front of him, buried up to his elbow in the Hulk's breastbone, a yellow hand protruding between the monster's shoulderblades. Spasms of pseudo-pain ran up the Vision's arm, triggering his innate programming for self-preservation, but he did not withdraw his arm or abandon his attack—until the Hulk, grinding his teeth together loud enough to be heard over both the Falls and the artillery, grabbed onto the not quite solidified arm at the shoulder, right where it connected with the rest of the Vision's ultra-dense body, and ripped the entire limb from its socket.

Sparks flared from the ruptured torso. Oily lubricants and hydraulic fluid sprayed from severed tubing, disappearing rapidly into the constant flow of the river. The Vision's head jerked spastically, his overloaded circuits struggling to process the full effect of his arm's brutal amputation.

"W-w-warning," he stuttered, like a malfunctioning tape recording. The jewel in his brow flashed on and off. "M-m-major damage to structural integrity. Im-imediate repair is nec-necessary—"

The severed arm, semi-liquid in appearance, dangled like a tendril of green and yellow jelly from the Hulk's chest. He raised a dark green eyebrow and, with a surly wince, plucked the invading arm out of his body, producing a slight sucking sound that the Vision was in no position to hear. He carelessly tossed the gelid limb over the Falls, then shoved the tottering, sparking synthezoid with the flat of his hand.

"W-w-warning," the Vision repeated automatically. He was dimly aware of gravity seizing him as he toppled over the brink of the Horseshoe. "W-w-w-warning—"

The Hulk vanished from his field of vision, supplanted by a kaleidoscope of rotating images that spun in front of him as he accelerated downward through empty space, unable to stabilize his internal systems fast enough to discard the weight that was pulling him toward a rough landing in turbulent waters. His yellow cloak wrapped around him like a cocoon.

My apologies, Wanda, the Vision thought, as he hurtled toward the churning surface of the pool. *This mechanism has failed you again. . . .*

LOST AND FOUND

• • •

"I'm not sure this is such a good idea," the cameraman said as he climbed aboard the boat, stepping awkwardly off the gangplank onto the riveted steel deck. He stared nervously at the looming Falls, towering above them at the far end of the pool. His blue rain slicker was already damp from the spray.

"Don't be ridiculous," the anchorman replied, a note of impatience marring his mellifluous baritone. He paced impatiently toward the prow, leading the way. "This is the biggest story to hit Niagara since Marilyn filmed that movie here in 1952."

Not to mention my ticket to the big time, Cliff Barron thought; he'd spent enough time paying his dues at that dinky local station in Buffalo. This was his chance to impress the bigwigs at the networks, maybe even land a spot on the evening news. "This story belongs to me, and I want to be live on the scene, right at ground zero!"

"Yeah, sure," the cameraman said unenthusiastically. His name was Muckerheide, but everyone called him Muck. His portable camera sat poised upon his shoulder. "But what about the cannons and stuff?" Even as he spoke, shells exploded at the top of the Horseshoe Falls, adding to the chaos in the distance.

The flunky's foot-dragging just annoyed Barron, who was anxious to be underway. *What if the Hulk surrenders before we get there?* "They're firing at the Hulk, not us," he insisted. "Besides, they wouldn't dare put us in danger. We're the press. We have a First Amendment right to be here." He paused and looked to the west, toward scenic Ontario. "Um, they *do* have a First Amendment in Canada, right?"

Muck shrugged, apparently resigned to his fate. He

dabbed at the lens of his camera with a dry cloth while Barron nodded at the ship's captain to set sail. The grizzled boatman muttered under his breath, like he was already regretting his decision to ferry the avid newsmen in exchange for a generous bribe, but took his place at the helm, a deck above his two passengers. A few minutes later, the all-steel, double-deck tour ship chugged away from the dock, with Barron and his one-man film crew standing at the prow. A matched set of American and Canadian flags waved from the back of the small craft.

The *Maid of the Mist* was the latest in a string of vessels, all bearing the same name, that had taken sightseers for a close-up look at the Falls since the middle of the nineteenth century. Under ordinary circumstances, the ship could carry up to six hundred passengers, but Barron and Muck had the boat to themselves, given that the Hulk crisis had pretty much curtailed tourism as usual.

Nothing like a berserk monster and frightening mutant terrorists to put a damper on a vacation, Barron thought. As the *Maid* sailed upstream toward the Horseshoe Falls, carefully skirting the rocks below the American Falls, the ambitious reporter experienced a troubling moment of anxiety when he recalled that he had forgotten to get a receipt for his expense account. *Maybe I can get the boat guy to write something up later,* he speculated.

The crescent-shaped curtain of water that was the Canadian Falls grew larger and more impressive as the *Maid* came within a few hundred yards of the wide, cascading spume. Staring upward through the thickening mist, Barron could barely see the superhuman figures of the Vision and the Hulk fighting it out at the brink of the Falls, close to two hundred feet above him. From where he now stood, upon the increasingly slippery deck of the prow, they looked like a pair of dueling green action figures. Barron assumed that Muck's telephoto lens was getting a better view of the action; after all, that's what the fainthearted cameraman got paid for.

It took a few minutes for Barron to decide on the ideal spot for his soon-to-be-historic broadcast, with just enough mist and spray to look dangerous and authentic, but not enough to mess up his hair or make-up. The Falls providing a magnificent backdrop behind him, he carefully adjusted his own blue slicker, now bcdcwcd with condensation, while he waited for his cue, smugly noting the absence of any other boats on the river. He had this scoop locked up tight.

Eat your heart out, Dan Rather, he gloated.

Muck signaled him they were about to go live, counting down on his fingers, so Barron cleared his throat, slicked back his dyed chestnut hair, held onto his microphone, and launched into his spiel:

"This is Cliff Barron of WDRP, on the scene beneath Niagara Falls, where an apocalyptic confrontation with the incredible Hulk and the infamous X-Men has escalated into open warfare, transforming this otherwise peaceful and romantic vacation spot into a veritable battleground, and pitting an unholy alliance of mutants and monster against the armed forces of two nations, as well as the Avengers themselves."

Not a bad intro, he congratulated himself, although describing the Hulk as "incredible" was a bit of a cliché. *I probably should have used another adjective.* The crashing water and ear-splitting explosions were making quite a racket, he fretted; hopefully, the sound guys back at the studio could filter out most of the background noise. *If not,* he vowed, *heads will roll.*

"As this exclusive live footage shows, Earth's Mightiest Heroes are leading the fight against the . . . dreaded . . . Hulk and his mutant confederates, but whether their unquestioned courage and power can prevail remains to be seen. Even now, the . . . stupendous . . . Hulk is locked in mortal combat with the android Avenger known only as the Vision."

He winced inwardly at his own words. Mortal combat? That sounded too much like a video game. Probably a licensed trademark, too. *Just what I need,* he groused. *Another whiny memo from Legal.*

Muck took advantage of his pause to tilt his camera back up toward the top of the Falls, where the fighting was. "Make sure you're getting all this," Barron whispered to him urgently, placing his hand over his mike. *Should've had two cameramen,* he realized. One for the action footage and one for his close-ups. But what could you expect from a mom-and-pop operation like WDRP? *I won't have to put up with shortcuts like this after I make my move to the networks. Then it'll be first-class production values all the way. Maybe a couple of Emmys, too.*

The cool, misty air was refreshing and invigorating; Barron recalled that the Falls supposedly produced "negative ions" that were highly conducive to romance, part of the region's claim to fame as the honeymoon capital of the U.S.A. *Maybe I should bring the wife up here for a weekend,* he thought idly, while Muck kept his telephoto lens focused on the ratings-grabbing spectacle above. *Better yet, maybe I should bring Tiffany. Why waste all those ions on the spouse?*

Squinting through the viewfinder, Muck kept his camera rolling—until his jaw dropped unexpectedly and he scurried backward upon the deck, almost losing his balance atop the slippery metal. Lowering his camera, he started shouting at the captain in the wheelhouse.

"Back up! Back up!" he shrieked in panic, waving his free arm wildly in a desperate attempt to attract the boatman's attention. "We have to get out of here!"

Barron was shocked by the cameraman's unprofessional behavior, and right in the middle of Barron's big break. What did this clown think he was doing? Who the heck did he think he was to decide when the broadcast was over? Barron saw his future Emmys going down the drain and wanted to shoot Muck. He was spoiling everything!

The *Maid* sluggishly began to turn around, but not quickly enough for the hysterical photog. Clutching the camera under one arm, Muck pointed frantically at the Falls and yelled at the indignant anchorman, practically jumping up and down in his anxiety.

"Look out!" he cried.

A sliver of urgency penetrated Barron's frustrated ambitions and preoccupations. Still fuming indignantly, he turned around and looked up, his telegenic blue eyes widening at the sight of a green-and-yellow figure plummeting toward them.

"Ohmigod," he whispered, unintentionally sharing his surprise with countless TV viewers. "We're all going to die!"

Instantly abandoning any semblance of journalistic dignity, Barron darted madly away from the prow, colliding with Muck in his frenzied stampede to safety. They tottered upon the deck, grabbing onto each for balance while the expensive camera crashed upon the wet steel flooring, accompanied by the ominous sound of something crucial breaking inside the apparatus.

A moment later, the ultra-dense form of the Vision smashed through the deck, leaving a gaping hole in the prow. He tore through the bottom of the hull as well, as evidenced by the huge gush of water that came spewing up from below deck. The river poured through the Vision-sized rupture, swamping the deck, which tilted beneath Barron's feet as the *Maid of the Mist* rapidly reenacted the last moments of the *Titanic*.

"Abandon ship!" the captain cried, giving Barron a murderous stare before leaping from the forecastle to the relative safety of the river. Muck merely shrugged once more, too much in a hurry to even say "I told you so" as he climbed over the rail, dutifully reclaiming the dropped camera before he splashed into the water, leaving the distraught anchor man alone aboard the sinking tour ship.

Afraid that it would make him look fat, Barron had declined to wear a life jacket under his plastic wrap. Now he groped desperately for a donut-shaped life preserver, his dreams of network glory supplanted by eyewitness imaginings of drowning beneath the waves.

So help me, he thought, scrambling off the stern just before it slid beneath surface of the river, the freezing water swallowing him up to his head and shoulders, *I knew I should've taken that sportscaster job in Pough-keepsie....*

"Good Lord," Iron Man exclaimed, shocked at what he beheld through the rectangular eyeslits in his faceplate. The Hulk had ripped the Vision's arm off! Or ripped the Vision off his arm, which amounted to the same thing.

Iron Man watched in horror as first the severed mechanical arm, then the rest of the heroic synthezoid, went plummeting over the Falls without so much as a barrel to protect him. Thank goodness, he thought, that the Vision wasn't remotely human; there was always a chance that he could be salvaged and repaired, unlike a flesh-and-blood human being suffering the same fate. *I've helped rebuild the Vision before,* he remembered. *I can do it again.*

But first he had to stop the Hulk from hurting anyone else. Already the Hulk's titanic temper tantrum had yielded collateral damage in the form of what looked like a small tour boat, now foundering below the Falls.

"That does it," he decided, diving to the rescue, his arms rigidly held out above his head to maximize his aerodynamic potential. "No more Mr. Nice Guy." As far as he was concerned, the Hulk had used up whatever sympathy or special consideration he might be entitled to from his days as an Avenger; that karmic investment had been spent. The mutated missing link was a menace, pure and simple, and Iron Man wasn't afraid to take him on.

To his relief, the torpedoed ship had apparently carried only three passengers, all of whom were now floating down the river toward the Whirlpool waiting beyond the Rainbow Bridge. Wondering briefly who in their right minds would pilot a boat *toward* the Hulk, he plucked all three survivors from the current, grabbing a soggy refugee by the collar with each hand while lifting the third victim, who held onto a circular life preserver for dear life, by means of a tractor beam issuing from the projection unit in his chest. The glowing purple ray held the pale, dripping castaway suspended in the air while Iron Man flew toward the nearest shore. Was that make-up, the Avenger wondered, running down the unlucky man's face?

It took Iron Man only minutes to deposit his three hitchhikers safely on the Canadian shore, where cooperative soldiers quickly took custody of them. Iron Man's boots barely touched the ground before, his mission of mercy completed, he doubled back into the sky above the Hulk. Going into a power dive, he jetted toward the Falls headfirst, the palms of his gauntlets held out in front of him. Display panels before his eyes charted his acceleration and energy output, the latter spiking dramatically as he unleashed his repulsors from both metal gloves.

"Okay, Hulk," he murmured to himself. Laser targeting systems drew a bead on his gargantuan target. "Here's what you get for mutilating an Avenger, even an artificial one."

Orange beams of force struck the Hulk head-on, staggering him. Iron Man upped the intensity, diverting power from secondary systems into the neutron projectors in his gauntlets, each one costing close to two million dollars.

"Let's see how *you* like a trip over the Falls, *sans* barrel," he said, wishing now that he had joined the fight against the Hulk immediately, rather than conducting an aerial reconnaissance first. If he had gone on the offensive earlier, maybe the Vision would still be intact. But how could he have known at once who required the most immediate assistance, Cap, the Vision, or even the Beast? He had also wanted to scan the vicinity for the rest of the X-Men, particularly Banshee, Iceman, and the other mutants known to have invaded the S.H.I.E.L.D. Helicarrier. Even now, he kept expecting more of Xavier's renegades to appear on the scene. *If Wolverine shows up, a major brawl is almost guaranteed.*

More provoked than punished by Iron Man's repulsors,

the implacable Hulk struck back, leaping at the golden Avenger as if fired by a cannon, his open hands reaching out for his foe. But Iron Man's forward proximity sensors detected the oncoming threat even before it registered on Tony Stark's human brain, and the computerized armor automatically took evasive action. Retro rockets surged in his starboard boot, causing him to execute a sharp left turn at the last minute. Prodigious as the Hulk's leaping abilities were, he could not change course in midair, so the enraged brute zoomed past Iron Man, missing his intended target by several feet.

That was a close one, Iron Man thought. If he had been only a few seconds slower, the Hulk would have grabbed him for sure. *Have to keep out of his hands or I'll end up like the Vision.* The latest generation of his armor was pretty darn indestructible, but he knew better than to underestimate the Hulk's phenomenal strength. After all, not even the mighty Thor had ever managed to surpass the Hulk where raw physical power was concerned—and Thor was a bona fide god! Iron Man's armored exoskeleton amplified his strength a hundredfold, but that wasn't enough to put him in the same class as the Hulk, so the Avenger intended to take full advantage of his aerial abilities and long-distance weaponry in this particular contest of arms. *Against the Hulk, I'll take every edge I can get.*

Howling in frustration, the thwarted Hulk landed right back where he'd started, at the very crest of the Canadian Falls. His face contorted with savage fury, he glared at Iron Man with crazed green eyes; even though he knew better, Iron Man found it hard to accept that a brilliant physicist was locked away somewhere inside the bestial creature he saw below him. The Hulk looked more like a sub-human evolutionary throwback than a mutated scientific genius.

Iron Man decided to keep the Hulk off-balance by varying his attack. Giving his gauntlets a chance to cool off, he activated the vari-beam projector at the center of his chestplate. Incandescent blue pulse bolts fired at the Hulk, gaining in power as they accelerated through the open space between Iron Man and his foe. One after another, the plasma bolts hit the Hulk, releasing all their accumulated energy on impact with his head and shoulders. Bright cerulean flashes briefly obscured the Hulk's face, only to fade within heartbeats, leaving the man-monster looking even more frenzied than before. Bristling green eyebrows, seared away by the hot plasma, grew back instantly while the Hulk rubbed watery eyes with his huge fists. The bolts had hurt him, obviously, but had not succeeded in budging him an inch closer to the steep, watery drop-off behind him.

"Good God," Iron Man whispered within his helmet, impressed despite too many past encounters with the Hulk. "What's it going to take to faze him? A couple of low-grade nukes?"

The pulse bolts were too energy-expensive to employ for a prolonged period of time, so he switched back to his repulsors, swooping in closer to the Hulk in hopes of increasing their impact. He wasn't thrilled about getting any nearer to the Hulk's destructive wrath, but it was a calculated risk; hopefully, his superior maneuverability would still keep him out of range of those piledriver fists.

"This would be a lot easier if you'd just change back to Banner," Iron Man muttered with more than a trace of irritation in his voice. Repulsor rays battered futilely against the Hulk's impervious hide.

Right now, Tony Stark wished Bruce had never passed high school physics, let alone heard of gamma rays.

The flattened forest swam before Storm's eyes. The pounding of explosives, coupled with the continual tumult of the nearby Falls, matched the throbbing in her head. Blood trickled from numerous small cuts and scratches on her head, arms and legs, stinging every inch of exposed skin.

What is happening? she wondered, teetering upon rubbery legs as she tried to orient herself. *Who is firing upon us, and why?* The last thing she remembered was summoning a fog to hide the Hulk from his tormentors. *That's right,* she recalled, the painful memory gradually resurfacing through the haze within her mind. *The Hulk . . . he hurt my fog, hurt me. . . .*

"Ororo," a plaintive voice cried out weakly. Struggling to clear her head, she glanced around her and was distressed to see the Beast, laying on his back beneath an overturned tree trunk several yards away. His eyelids flickered as if he was barely conscious. "I fear I am in unqualified need of a certain degree of succor," he confessed during a momentary lull in the thundering report of the guns, "as well as extrication from my present circumstances." His inimitable vocabulary deteriorated as his alertness ebbed. "Help me, Ororo. Help. . . ."

"I am coming, my friend," she called out to him. Her own pains temporarily forgotten, she rushed to his aid, dropping down on her knees beside him. Scattered leaves and broken branches littered the ground. The matted twigs and pine needles stung the scrapes on her knees as she promptly took stock of the Beast's predicament. *Bright Lady,* she prayed, *let his injuries be minor.*

The fundamentals of first aid came back to her quickly, so she hesitated to move him too quickly. Climbing over the heavy log that weighed upon the Beast, she prodded the calloused soles of his hairy feet with a gentle finger.

"Can you feel this?" she asked, having to repeat her query twice before the dazed Beast responded with a nod. *The Goddess be praised,* she thought in relief, but carefully checked each limb before returning to the other side of the log and cradling the Beast's shaggy head in her lap. His bristling blue hair scratched against her already abraded legs, but she made no complaint, instead laying a hand against his neck to check his pulse, which proved to be reassuringly steady. Although she held no medical degree, it seemed likely that Henry McCoy had merely been trapped and knocked unconscious by the falling maple. Grateful, she suspected that he would soon recover, although she might need Cyclops's assistance to free their comrade from the sturdy wooden encumbrance that pinned him to the forest floor.

"Hold on, my friend," she counseled the Beast, raising her head to search for their absent teammate.

A gush of icy water struck her in the face, soaking her to the skin and chilling her to the bone. Her snowy tresses hung limply over her shoulders as she sputtered and coughed, clearing her lungs of the liquid she had inadvertently inhaled. Water streamed down her body, pooling around her legs.

"Who dares?" she demanded indignantly; shock, fatigue, and lack of sleep doing nothing to improve her temper. She looked up, surprised to see a gleaming metal figure cruising through the sky above her.

A Sentinel? she thought at first, blinking against the

glare of the sunlight reflected off his shining armor before recognizing the robotic figure as Iron Man. *The Avenger here?* she wondered. *Is he responsible for this affront?*

The deluge had turned the forest floor to mud. Twigs, leaves, and needles floated atop filmy puddles all around Storm. Lying in the ooze beneath her, the Beast coughed up a mouthful of cold water. His furry pelt was drenched, making him look thoroughly miserable if slightly more alert. The smell of wet fur filled the air.

Nothing like a bucket of water in the face to restore one's clarity, she reflected ruefully. He mumbled what Storm assumed was an amusing witticism, even if she could not hear it over the renewed fury of the guns. Removing her headdress, she used the stiff crown to cushion the Beast's head, and lift it above the mire, before she rose to survey her surroundings.

Iron Man was not alone, she observed. Many yards away, at the very tip of the island, Captain America faced off opposite Cyclops, the two men circling each other warily. Iron Man dived toward the Hulk, who had apparently been driven out into the seething torrent of the river by his antagonists. Storm looked about for the other Avengers, perhaps the Scarlet Witch or Thor, but saw only the costumed crusaders she had already spotted: Iron Man and Captain America.

It matters not, Ororo decided, ready to defend her allies against any number of new assailants. She knew not why the pair of Avengers had laid siege to the embattled Hulk, and to the X-Men as well, but she determined that they would not strike another blow without suffering the consequences. Rogue, she recalled, had begun her short-lived career as an Evil Mutant by striking out at Captain America, Iron Man, and the other Avengers, permanently crippling Ms. Marvel. Could it be that Rogue's disappearance, and the Avengers' unexpected arrival here, were all part of some long-delayed act of retaliation? Stranger things had happened in this uncertain life they led. In any event, she had no intention of remaining soggily upon the sidelines, not while the elements remained hers to command. *It is just as well,* she mused, *that the Thunder God has not accompanied his allies. No Asgardian deity shall dispute my dominion over the skies.*

"Be well, my friend," she whispered to the Beast. She shook her flowing white mane, throwing off a spray of tiny droplets. Mud caked her long legs from the knees down, but she paid it no heed, throwing out her arms to capture a sudden breeze beneath her wings. Her ascendant will, and eternal empathy with the elements, fed the breeze, lending it strength. "I will return shortly."

Disregarding the throbbing of her head, Storm rose upon the wind to a vertiginous height above the Horseshoe Falls. There she saw Iron Man blasting the Hulk with his celebrated repulsor rays, apparently intent on pushing the persecuted brute over the crest of the Falls. Unnatural orange beams, unlike anything in nature, emanated from the Avenger's metal gauntlets.

Sentinels wield weapons such as those, Storm thought, finding the armored warrior's resemblance to those hated mechanical storm troopers quite unsettling. *But the heavens harbor weapons of their own, purer and cleaner than those spawned by science.*

She summoned her own power to her, the idea occurring to her that this coming battle might well be what the Fates had intended all along. Perhaps only by defending the Hulk against a common foe could they persuade the surly and suspicious monster that their interests were his own.

Genuine thunder, like the crashing of gigantic atmospheric cymbals, joined the pandemonium of noises clanging discordantly about and above Niagara. All of Storm's frustration and discomfort, which had been building ever since her "demise" in the Danger Room, merged with the tempest building around her, flowing out from her fingertips in the form of a crackling lightning bolt that lit up the sky between her and Iron Man. Raw electrical fire converged on the metallic Avenger as if he were a living lightning rod.

"Leave the Hulk alone!" she commanded Iron Man from on high. "Pit your vaunted technology against the untamed power of Nature herself!"

No sooner had Iron Man's repulsors started pushing once more against the Hulk's immovable bulk, the accelerated neutrons colliding with the densely-packed atoms making up the Hulk's lime-green epidermis, when the Avenger was struck from behind by a powerful electrical charge strong enough to overload the EMF force-field that was his armor's first line of defense. Tony felt the shock all the way through multiple layers of tessellated metal tiles.

"What the devil was that?" he exclaimed as soon as the muscles in his face stopped twitching. Emergency displays reported that his armor had been subjected to over 350 gigawatts of electrical force. Since when did the Hulk fight back with energy powers?

Breaking off his assault on the Hulk, he performed a flawless barrel roll that left him facing upward at the sky. Sunlight in his eyes kept him from seeing anything at first, until his polarized lenses kicked in, and he spied Storm aloft above him, angry thunderclouds roiling behind her outstretched arms. The whole sky turned overcast quickly, nearly turning day to night as the sun disappeared behind gray and tempestuous clouds. Thunder rolled across the heavens. Violent winds whipped the clouds into a threatening display of nimbostratus fury.

Guess there's no doubt now whose side the X-Men are on, he thought resentfully.

The cloud cover above the female X-Man grew darker and more turbulent with each passing moment. The polarized lenses lightened automatically in response to the changing light. Sensors in his armor reported an unnaturally rapid increase in the barometric pressure and humidity. Storm's doing, no doubt; Iron Man wondered if the mounting intensity of the atmospheric disturbances were any measure of the woman's mood.

If so, he decided, *I'm in serious trouble.*

A gale force wind blew him farther away from his green-skinned quarry, out over the American Falls on the other side of the island.

Talk about getting the brush-off, Iron Man thought wryly, using his boot jets to halt his involuntary retreat. Gouts of orange flame spewed from the soles of his boots as he fought back against the zealous zephyr, slowing advancing into the wind toward its imperious mistress.

"Sorry, Miss," he informed her, even though the deafening clamor made any real attempt at verbal communication a lost cause, "but you can't blow Avengers away like old leaves."

A lifelong ladies' man, Tony could not help noticing the female X-Man's exotic allure. The combination of stark white hair, dark skin, and captivating blue eyes produced a singular beauty that Iron Man didn't need any high-tech sensors to appreciate. It seemed a shame to lash out at such a strikingly attractive woman, but years of contention against the likes of Madame Masque and the Viper had seriously eroded whatever chauvinism and/or chivalry might once have restrained him.

She started this, he remembered, so he wasn't about to play sitting duck. *Maybe she can explain what this is all about later—after I shut down this meteorological menace of hers.*

He fired his repulsors at her, ready to catch Storm before she fell unconscious into the river. "Careful," he reminded himself; the X-Man was nowhere near as indestructible as the Hulk. He wanted her contained, not a casualty.

He shouldn't have worried. The orange repulsor rays fell far short of their target, dissipating completely several yards before they came within striking range of Storm.

Of course! he realized, mentally (but not physically) slapping his forehead. The accelerated neutrons that gave his repulsors their punch traveled along a shaft of ionized air projected from his gauntlets; obviously, that conductive shaft had been unable to make headway against the tremendous atmospheric forces controlled by the mutant heroine.

Her own thunderbolts, needless to say, encountered no such resistance. Even as Iron Man watched his repulsor rays fade away, Storm let loose with another concentrated blast of lightning. He tried to evade the bolt, but the jagged electrical spear followed him wherever he flew, drawn by the crystallized iron in his armored suit.

Zap! Sparks flew as lightning struck his helmet, sizzling in his ears. The refractory coating over the outer layer of high temperature enamel shielded his flesh and blood from much of the lightning bolt's charge. The armor's internal displays, though, flickered alarmingly, before coming back on-line. Diagnostic routines reported minor malfunctions throughout the sophisticated circuitry of the suit, including damage to the secondary neural net processor, the ventral foot altitude sensor, and even, ironically, the LIDAR weather scan sensor port.

Ouch, he thought.

Storm had drawn both first and second blood. Iron Man realized he had to strike back, ideally with a weapon that didn't depend on the atmosphere as a conductive medium. His plasma bolts were not an option; they were too powerful to use against an opponent who was neither armored nor invulnerable.

Never mind whose side she's on, I don't want to blow her to atoms. Tight-beam sonics were less lethal, but Storm might be able to deflect the sound waves by manipulating the very air through which they traveled.

Magnetism, on the other hand, functioned just as well in a vacuum as it did in a gaseous environment. Maybe that was the ticket. Iron Man arced above Storm, swooping around to catch her from behind. The projector in his chestplate flared brightly as he attempted to snare Storm with his tractor beam, the same beam he had used to pluck that unfortunate shipwreck victim from the river. In theory, the magnetic beam would seize hold of the iron in Storm's blood, holding her fast within the beam while he towed her back to the authorities.

A little trick I learned, Iron Man recalled, *from the X-Men's old nemesis, Magneto.*

The irony was not lost on him.

Catching Storm with the beam proved easier said than done, though. At the last minute, the flying mutant banked to the left, escaping the beam, then performed a graceful loop-the-loop that left Iron Man sweeping an empty swath of sky with the tractor beam while Storm climbed toward the clouds above him. Iron Man hastily adjusted his own trajectory to try to bring her back in line with the brilliant purple ray emanating from his chest. The chase turned into an intricate aerial ballet that tested the limits of Iron Man's maneuverability. He had always thought that his sleek metal armor was the last word in aerodynamic design, but Storm not only glided effortlessly upon the prevailing winds, the very currents of the air seemed to go out of their way to accommodate her every swoop and spiral. No matter which way she turned, she always had a strong tailwind at her back, whereas he was constantly buffeted by an opposing squall. Iron Man started to feel like he was competing in a game that had been stacked against him from the start. How did you win an air battle when the air itself was fighting for the other side?

All he needs to do is strike me with that ray once, Storm thought, redoubling her efforts to stay one cloud ahead of her mechanized adversary.

She had no idea what sort of energies were at work within that radiant purple beam, but thought it best to stay well clear of its path. Too much was at stake to risk being immobilized once more; her head still ached from the psychic and physical toll of the Hulk's shock wave while the Beast remained out of commission, so that only she and Cyclops remained to stand against the Avengers, the authorities, and, quite possibly, the Hulk. One mistake, she knew, and she would feel the unguessable effect of Iron Man's weapon upon her own form and flight. Such a defeat would leave Cyclops alone and outnumbered.

Never! she vowed. Despite the occasional tensions between them, Cyclops was a dear friend whom she was not about to surrender to the uncertain mercies of their present adversaries.

And then there was Rogue, who might be at greater risk than them all. . . .

For all that was at stake, the skyborne pursuit was exhilarating in its way. Mighty winds blew her through the firmament, drying her hair, skin, and garments as she soared up and down and back and forth, changing direction constantly so as to confound her armored opponent. Bursts of cleansing rain washed the island's mud from her limbs. Only soaring thus through the open sky did she ever feel truly free, unhemmed by walls or ceilings, and at one with the elements. Thunder pounded in perfect synch with her heartbeat while lightning gathered behind her eyes and within her fingertips. She pitied Iron Man; trapped as he was in his cold metal shell, how could he possibly savor the miracle of flight as she did? He was cut off from nature, not to mention his fellow man.

I could not endure that, Storm knew. The very thought of trapping her body and soul inside a cramped, lifeless machine made her shudder.

A luciferous streak of light fell across her path, and she barely dived beneath its ominous glow in time. Glancing to left, she caught a glimpse of Iron Man zooming toward her on an intercept course, steel-clad fists tearing through the gossamer fabric of her clouds. His gilded mask was surprisingly expressive, the angled slits of his mouth and eyes conveying grim determination. Parallel rows of signal lights ran along the top of his helmet, blinking in sequence according to some unknown computer program.

Computers. Storm had no doubt that computers controlled many of the functions in Iron Man's armor, just as they did in most technology these days. Despite her reverence for the natural world and its ancient ways, she was not uninformed about modern computers—and their weaknesses. An electromagnetic pulse of the right magnitude, she recalled, could seriously disrupt a computer and its operations. Shadowcat, the X-Men's resident computer genius, had explained this to Storm rather vigorously after a couple of unfortunate accidents involving Ororo's powers and the Xavier Institute's computers. She and Kitty Pryde had even managed to duplicate the phenomenon in the Danger Room.

Let us see, she resolved, *if Iron Man's formidable technology can be as temperamental and touchy as Kitty's precious programs.*

A luminescent white glow filled her eyes, masking her vibrant blue irises and dark pupils. Calling upon memories honed through constant repetition, she released the pent-up electrical energy in her fingertips in a single high-intensity pulse that flared so briefly that it had vanished completely from sight before its effect was felt. . . .

"What the heck?" Colonel Lopez exclaimed as a harsh burst of static assailed his ear.

He yanked his walkie-talkie, which he had been using to converse with the commander of the Canadian forces across the river, away from his head and glared at the malfunctioning device. "Hello?" he asked, cautiously raising the walkie-talkie back toward his ear, but the line was as dead as his chance at a promotion after this fiasco. He shot a blistering glance at his second-in-command, who looked just as befuddled as the rest of his troops.

Judging from the confused and/or irritated faces he saw along the front lines, his walkie-talkie wasn't all that had screwed up. Suddenly, in a single instant, all their expensive electronic hardware had just gone completely FUBAR: Fouled Up Beyond All Recognition.

Playing a hunch, he checked his pocket compass just in time to see the needle swing toward Goat Island, southwest from where he was standing, then back again toward magnetic north.

''Typical,'' Lopez muttered. The supertypes' freakish powers were even messing with his compass. Not to mention the drastic changes in the weather. He felt another layer of stomach lining burn away and searched his pockets for a Tums. Blast it, he thought, why couldn't all these heroes and mutants and monsters stay in the Big Apple where they belonged?

First, his computer crashed. Then Iron Man did.

The luminescent displays before his eyes blinked out of existence. His glowing chest unit went dark. The limbs of his armor locked into place, the servos that amplified the motion of his muscles grinding to a halt. And, perhaps most significantly, given his current altitude and position, all six micro-turbines in his boots shut down at once, turning the world's most sophisticated man-shaped flying machine into several hundred pounds of dead weight.

''Whaaaaaaaaaaaaa—!'' Iron Man exclaimed, the single syllable stretched across a vertical drop of over a thousand feet.

He hit the river with an enormous splash. Ordinarily, a Plexiglas layer would automatically drop into place to prevent water from entering through the mouth slit in his helmet. But with the armor frozen until the computer rebooted, Tony found himself coughing and sputtering in a desperate attempt to keep from drowning in the icy water. The wild rapids tossed him about like a piece of drift-wood. Rocks clanged against his helmet he took a bumpy ride down the river. Fragmented glimpses of sky and spray spun before his eyes when his head wasn't dunked beneath the waves altogether. Blurry smears of water speckled his protective lenses.

Have to hang on, he thought fiercely, guessing at once what had happened. He knew too well what the right kind of EMP could do to his armor, and how long he needed to recover. Thanks to constant improvements in the software, it took precisely 2.34 minutes for his armor to re-boot, a significant gain on earlier systems which had needed a full three minutes to come back to life. All he needed was a couple of minutes and he'd be raring to go again.

Unfortunately, he went over the Falls in seconds.

Using the Internet, Iron Man had scanned the history of Niagara during the flight from Manhattan. Over the years, he had learned, at least fifteen people had deliber-ately gone over the Falls in barrels and other "protective" devices, five of whom had met horrible deaths. Now, against his will, Iron Man's armor had become merely the latest high-tech barrel.

Beneath multiple layers of diamond dust, enamel, iron, and micro-circuitry, a comfort layer of firm rubber pad-ding cushioned Tony Stark's vulnerable human flesh. Tony had never been more thankful for that padding than now, when he abruptly found himself bouncing roughly over the rapids at the crest of the Falls, then smashing repeatedly against the side of a cliff as he plummeted downward, spinning helplessly out of control. A hundred bumps and jolts jarred his bones while the omnipresent pealing of millions of gallons of cascading water drowned out the rest of the world. Frothing chaos was all he could see, rotating wildly before his eyes. Inside the armor, Tony held his breath as he braced himself for the worst, i.e. hitting the bottom.

But which Falls had he gone over? The Horseshoe Falls, which emptied into the fabled Maid of the Mist pool, or the American Falls, which fell directly onto a deadly pile of rocks at the base of the cataract? Not even the most reckless daredevils of yore had ever risked a trip over the American Falls; the unlucky souls who accidentally took that fatal plunge *never* survived. To his horror, Iron Man realized he had no idea over which Falls he had been flying when the EMP knocked his armor for a loop; his extended dogfight with Storm could have taken him over either drop. Could even his armor, its protective force field off-line, protect him from a crash landing upon those deadly rocks? He had to admit he wasn't sure.

Thanks to Storm, I've gone from super hero to crash test dummy in one fell swoop . . . !

An anxious moment of uncertainty stretched on for what felt like forever until he slammed into something hard—and kept on sinking. After falling a hundred-plus feet, the surface of the pool felt like cement, but it was still only water. He'd gone over the Horseshoe Falls after all! His entire body felt like one big bruise, and he was dizzier than the Human Top, but he was still in one piece.

Let's hear it for Stark Solutions quality control! he thought jubilantly. Niagara could enter an eleventh documented survivor into their record books, provided he didn't drown in the next few minutes.

His heavy armor weighed him down like an anchor as

he sunk to the bottom of the pool, landing with a dull thud upon the silty floor. Holding onto his breath for as long as he could, Tony waited desperately for his armor to reactivate. His lungs ached for fresh air, his cheeks bulged with carbon dioxide. It took all his will and self-control to keep his jaws tightly clenched together, holding onto the stale air pouring out of his lungs. Tiny bubbles escaped through the cracks between his teeth, rising toward the surface, leaving him behind. With his lights and sensors dead, he could see nothing through the murky liquid, not even a glint of daylight. He started feeling light-headed, a sure sign of oxygen deprivation; unlike the infamous Sub-Mariner, Tony Stark couldn't breathe underwater.

Just when he felt like he was going to have to try, gills or no gills, his armor came humming back to life all around him. The start-up sequence initiated on schedule, redundant circuits and auxiliary systems coping with whatever components had been burnt out by the EMP. The plexiglass mouth shield slid smoothly into place, and none too soon. Automated breathing tanks, utilizing cutting-edge rebreather technology, pumped a precisely calibrated mixture of oxygen and nitrogen into his helmet, which he inhaled as eagerly as if it were the world's most intoxicating perfume.

When I build a barrel, I build it right, Tony Stark thought proudly. Systems reports scrolled before his eyes and he scanned them feverishly, scoping out the extent of the damage that the armor had incurred during its jarring trip over the violent cataract.

The bad news: the chest projector was thoroughly trashed, the primary lens cracked into three pieces, which meant no tractor beam until he had a chance to make some needed repairs, nor even a spotlight to shine through the murk at the bottom of the pool. A slurry of silt and water, left behind when the mouthpiece sealed itself off from its aqueous surroundings, trickled down through the neck assembly, raising goosebumps on his skin.

He figured he'd probably picked up a few dents as well.

The good news: the jet turbines in his boots had survived intact, meaning he had the means to escape this watery launching pad.

About time, Iron Man thought; he would have to do something about speeding up the whole rebooting procedure. Maybe there was a way to get it down to a minute or less, possibly by streamlining the primary initialization codes. . . .

Part of his mind already grappling with the technical problems involved, he took a few more deep breaths to clear his head, then used a cybernetic command to activate his boot jets. A half-dozen micro-turbines ignited at once, generating over two thousands pounds of thrust, enough to send him rocketing up through the gloom to the churning surface of the pool. Radio signals from orbiting satellites told him where he was and which direction to fly, so that he took the straightest route possible to the open air, emerging dramatically from the Maid of the Mist pool like Excalibur thrust upward by the Lady of the Lake. Cool-air venting, ringing the soles of the boots, mixed chilled air with the jet exhaust, so as to avoid cooking every fish in the pool.

"All right," the golden Avenger said, searching the sky. Nano-wipes cleared the silt and water specks from his optical lenses. "Where's that tricky weather witch?"

Storm had not flown far since dropping Iron Man from

the heights. Perhaps she had lingered overhead to ascertain whether Iron Man had indeed survived his plunge, maybe even contemplating a rescue attempt. Whatever her intentions, her influence over the environment remained readily apparent; looming gray thunderheads, swollen with unspilled rain, blotted out the sun, throwing a gloomy shadow over the world-famous scenery. External sensors in Iron Man's armor registered a 15 percent increase in atmospheric ozone; obviously, Storm had lived up to her name.

But how often could she pull off that EMP trick? Iron Man decided not to take any chances. The swirling mists at the base of the Horseshoe Falls hid his return for at least a second or two; Iron Man used that momentary surprise to fix Storm within his targeting display, then unleashed a barrage of tight-beam sonics to rattle her nerves and break her concentration.

It worked. The soaring mutant threw her hands over her ears and grimaced in discomfort.

Kind of like what your buddy Banshee did to Nick Fury and his people, Iron Man thought, appreciating the poetic justice of his ploy. He kept up his sonic assault as he flew toward the airborne heroine.

Afflicted by the relentless sound waves, Storm lashed out instinctively, not with a calculated pulse, but with a raw and elemental thunderbolt that lit up the entire sky before exploding in a shower of sparks against Iron Man's armor. Hundreds of gigawatts crackled noisily, but this time the golden Avenger was ready. The energy conversion system of his armor, running several layers below the enamel and iron plating, absorbed the massive electrical charge and channeled it into the suit's overall power supply. Energy reserves, which had been depleted during his battles with both Storm and Hulk, filled to capacity, leaving him with power to spare.

Feeling more than a little like a latter-day Benjamin Franklin, Iron Man fired Storm's own lightning back at her, in the form of blazing repulsor rays.

Displaced by the Hulk's resounding return to the river, a tremendous wave of cold water washed over the tip of Goat Island. The miniature tsunami knocked both Captain America and Cyclops off their feet, breaking off the tense stand-off that had endured since the star-spangled Avenger landed on the island, surprising Cyclops. Breathless and out of control, both heroes were sent tumbling across the ravaged landscape, ending up sprawled in the mud after the great splash spent itself.

The force of the wave left Cyclops's visor slightly ajar, and his uncontrollable eyebeams escaped through the gap, blasting the ground near Captain America, who had to roll quickly across the wasteland to avoid being struck by the destructive rays, which sent shattered chunks of rock flying into the air. Cyclops hastily adjusted his visor, cutting off the beam, but feared the damage had already been done. Did Captain America think he had been fired upon on purpose?

I may have just made a volatile situation worse, Cyclops thought. He didn't know what the Avengers wanted here, but he doubted it was to invite the X-Men to a friendly inter-team softball game. Slipping and sliding in the now-muddy soil, he scrambled to get back on his feet before Captain America could seize a strategic advantage; even though the legendary hero was only human, with no special powers or abilities, Cyclops knew from experience what a resourceful opponent he could be. He still remembered the way Captain America had led the battle against Exodus during that bloodbath in Genosha a few years back. *I can't let him stop me from escaping with the Hulk,* he thought fervently. *Rogue's life may depend on it.* Whatever the Avengers wanted, with either the X-Men or the Hulk, would have to wait.

Unfortunately, the Captain's reflexes were even faster than Cyclops's. The patriotic colors of his uniform obscured by a clinging layer of slick brown mud, he rose upward from the slippery muck; somehow, despite the power of the unexpected deluge, he had managed to hang onto his shield throughout their headlong tumble. The sturdy metal disk, Cyclops knew, was both a weapon as well as a defense; more than once, he had seen Captain America hurl his shield with devastating effect.

Perhaps the Avenger intended the shield only for his own protection, but Cyclops couldn't take that chance. He could too easily imagine himself succumbing to a single blow from the Captain's shield, leaving him helpless in the mud, no good to Rogue or anyone else.

That's not going to happen, Cyclops vowed. Cool water dripped from his hair, leaking past the top of his visor, only to be reduced to atoms the instant the droplets fell in front of his volcanic eyes. Failing his fellow X-Men was the one thing that Scott Summer had always feared more than anything else, ever since Professor X first entrusted him with leadership of the team. His mission, and his responsibility to the team, took priority over everything else.

"Sorry, Captain," he murmured. Cybernetic controls within his visor allowed him to raise the quartz lens without lifting a hand, even as he clambered upright. He winced inwardly as his forcebeam sped toward the other hero; firing at Captain America felt, in a very real way, like spitting at the flag. Cyclops was grateful for the mud covering the red, white, and blue emblems on the Avenger's celebrated uniform, which Scott suddenly remembered seeing on a *LIFE* magazine cover when he was only seven years old, back when he was just another lonely kid in that orphanage, looking for heroes wherever he could find them.

Shooting Captain America... well, there goes my chance of ever running for President, he thought, indulging in a rare moment of black humor. *Not that I really expect to see a mutant in the White House anytime soon.*

The crimson beam was fast, but Captain America's shield was faster. The convex surface of the shield leapt between the beam and its target, deflecting the ray back at Cyclops, who barely ducked in time to escape being lambasted by his own mutant power. Cyclops was impressed by the speed with which the Avenger had blocked his eyebeams; he would have thought that only Wolverine could react with such split-second timing.

Guess that's why they call him a living legend, Cyclops thought. Clearly, neutralizing Captain America's unwanted interference was not going to be easy.

Then again, he reflected, where the X-Men were concerned, nothing ever was. That's why the Professor had always trained them to be ready for anything—and never to surrender. Not even to the Avengers.

The Vision, Iron Man, Captain America. Cyclops wondered just how many Avengers they were up against. *Last I heard, Firestar and Justice had joined the team.*

A clap of thunder reverberated above him and a shadow fell over the island; Cyclops recognized the early warning signs of Storm in high dudgeon. Keeping one eye on Captain America, he glanced upward in time to see Storm flying overhead, lighting streaming from her fingertips. A moment later, one of Ororo's patented windstorms blew none other than Iron Man himself across the sky. Fiery rockets flared from the armored Avenger's boots as he fought back against the gale. Repulsor rays issued from his metal gloves, only to falter and fade before striking Storm.

Looks like the battle has well and truly been joined, Cyclops concluded soberly, his mouth a fixed, unsmiling line beneath his gleaming visor. Watching Captain America's piercing blue eyes, he saw that the aerial contest above them had not escaped the Avenger's notice. He eyed Cyclops warily, keeping his shield raised in front of him. If nothing else, Cyclops's eyebeams had dispersed the mud that had been smeared over the shield. Now the famous shield could be seen in all its celebrated glory: concentric red and white stripes surrounded a single white star shining brightly against a navy blue background.

Seen through Cyclops's visor, of course, both stars and stripes had a ruby tinge, like most everything else in his world. The driven, young X-Man gave the shield his full attention while he calculated the best way to get his eyebeams past it.

"I hope you understand I don't want to do this," he said to the other hero. Between Storm's thunder and the roaring falls, however, there was little chance that the Captain could hear his apology. Without further warning, he aimed his visor at Captain America's knees, exposed beneath the lower rim of his shield. Extradimensional energy, strong enough to halt a charging rhino, leapt downward like a striking cobra.

Captain America had anticipated the move, though. He

leapt high into the air, so that the beam whizzed by underneath him, and flung his shield straight at Cyclops. Like a star-spangled Frisbee, the shield whistled through the empty air, only to be knocked from its path by Cyclops's eyebeams as they swept upward to meet the spinning shield in mid-flight. Deflected from its course, the shield flew off toward the nearby woods.

Now, Cyclops thought. Keenly aware that his foe was disarmed, if only for the moment, he adjusted his visor to produce a wider beam that spread out like a crimson wedge from where he was standing. *Maximum dispersal,* he thought. *There's no way he can get out of the way this time.*

That might have been true, had Captain America remained deprived of his shield. As if he planned for every alternative, however, the diverted shield bounced off the bark of a standing maple tree and returned to his waiting hand like a boomerang. Ducking his head below the rim of the shield, the Captain dug his heels into the soppy soil, bracing himself against the force of Cyclops's unfettered eyebeams.

The lambent red radiance, which had battered foes as diverse and dangerous as Mr. Sinister and the Living Monolith, left not so much as a nick on the decades-old shield.

What on earth is that thing made of? Cyclops marveled, pouring on the power. *Adamantium? Vibranium? Or something else entirely?*

Whatever it was composed of, the metallic disk repelled his eyebeams better than anything that old and outdated should have been able to. Nor was Captain America kept on the defensive; pushing against the unrelenting pressure of the crimson ray, the Avenger advanced toward

Cyclops, marching slowly but inexorably across the slimy, battle-scarred terrain. Cyclops couldn't see Captain America's face, but he could imagine the look of stubborn determination that surely waited behind the oncoming shield.

Another tactic was clearly called for. Spotting a puddle of filmy water behind and slightly to one side of Captain America, he narrowed his beam to a thin red streak and fired at the puddle instead. The beam ricocheted off the reflective surface of the muddy water toward the Avenger's undefended back. But Captain America must have seen the beam coming, perhaps in the polished underside of his shield, and he leapt into the air again, executing a perfect split over five feet above the ground. He brought his shield down between his outstretched legs, catching the brunt of the beam and reflecting it back at the ground, using its propulsive effect to carry him forward. Cyclops saw Captain America flying toward him, surfing the rechanneled force of the X-Man's own eyebeams!

Cyclops snapped his visor shut, cutting off the beam, but it was too late; Captain America had already acquired too much momentum. His legs swung together and the soles of two bright red boots hit Cyclops squarely in the chest, knocking him onto his back, which splashed down onto the mud and rocks. Cyclops's head snapped backwards, hitting the ground so hard his ears rang. He gasped once, the air hammered out of him, and blinked in surprise. For an instant, he saw Storm high above, silhouetted against a white-hot burst of lightning, her hands cupped over her ears. Then a pair of heavy knees landed heavily on his chest and a painted white star descended toward his face, blotting out everything else.

His visor slammed into the bridge of his nose, and he realized that Captain America was pressing his shield down on top of the visor, effectively blinding the supine X-Man. Cyclops couldn't see a thing! No slouch at hand-to-hand combat, especially after sparring with Wolverine in the Danger Room, he tried to throw Captain America off him, but the veteran super hero countered his every move and kept him pinned to the ground. Strong fingers seized hold of his right wrist while the immovable knees pressed down on his ribs. The unbending metal shield pushed firmly against the visor, keeping up the pressure.

If he thinks he can cap my eyebeams with his shield, Cyclops thought defiantly, *he's got another think coming.*

Abandoning his jujitsu moves, he raised his ruby quartz lens all the way, opening up the floodgates in front of his eyes. The forcebeam erupted like a geyser, tearing Captain America's shield from his clenched fist and carrying it over fifty feet in the air, where it hovered atop a luminous pillar of unearthly energy.

Caught by surprise, Captain America nonetheless delivered a right cross to Cyclops's chin, which left the young mutant seeing stars *and* stripes. His eyebeams required no act of concentration on his part, however; they flowed freely whether he willed it or not. Lifting his head from the mud, he turned his explosive gaze on the hero astride him. Captain America yanked his head out of the way just in time, although the beam tore off one of the miniature eagle wings adorning his cowl. As the beam swept downward, it hit Captain America below the neck like the spray from a high-intensity fire hose, tossing him backwards for several yards, until he ducked behind a ridge of land, left behind by the Hulk's earth-shaking depredations.

We're right back where we started, Cyclops realized as he found himself scrambling up from the mud for the second time in less than ten minutes, watching his renowned opponent do the same despite the scintillating forcebeam strafing the air above his head.

The famous shield, no longer held aloft by Cyclops's unharnessed power, fell from the sky between them, blocking the beam long enough for Captain America to lunge forward and grab the shield before it hit the ground. Once more, Cyclops was forced to dodge his own eyebeams as they bounced off the shield, racing back at him. The rerouted beam dug a deep trench through the dirt he had just climbed out of, and he aimed for the ground at the Captain's feet, hoping to dislodge him, but that maddening shield darted down to meet the beam, right on schedule. For several minutes they battled thus, the shield parrying Cyclops's every move, until the empty space between them was filled with a tangled lattice of intersecting red beams, culminating when the beleaguered mutant ended up firing fresh beams to block returning rays, which, striking once more against the shield, then doubled back on him again.

This isn't good, Cyclops concluded, coolly assessing his ongoing duel with the indefatigable Avenger. From a tactical standpoint, their respective abilities complemented each other much too well. Captain America employed his ubiquitous shield with as much skill and precision as Cyclops had learned to direct his unique eyebeams. *No surprise there,* he acknowledged. *We could be at this all day, before one of us makes a crucial error.*

Risking a peek at the sky, he saw lightning bolts colliding with repulsor rays amidst dark, tempestuous clouds. Meanwhile, the Beast remained out for the count beneath that fallen tree. And where had the Vision disappeared to anyway? Why wasn't the android Avenger coming to aid of his comrades? Had something happened to him?

The habitual scowl below his visor deepened. This entire melee with the Avengers was taking too long, costing them far too much valuable time. Cyclops made a mental note to add holographic Avengers to the Danger Room, so they'd be better prepared for such a clash in the future, but that wasn't going to do them any good here and now. He had to do something—*anything!*—to break the stalemate.

Right after he blocked the beam ricocheting back toward his head . . .

A rusty metal man took potshots at a self-styled goddess way up high in the sky. On a big rock in the middle of the river, a red-eyed geek of a mutant played catch-the-bouncing-stun-beam with a true blue national mascot. The furry blue guy was down and out and that miserable robot was resting in a couple of pieces at the bottom of the Falls. Standing upon the brink of the biggest waterfall in sight, knee-deep in the impatient torrent, the irascible Hulk found himself without anyone to fight.

Sure, there were always those armies lined up on either shore, but they hardly counted. The Hulk sneered at the tanks and soldiers with contempt; he could wallop the American troops, and the Canadians, too, without working up a sweat. And he'd do it, too, if he had to, but right now he was a lot more interested in the grudge match that had broken out between the X-Men and the Avengers. Not that he was rooting for either team; from where he was standing, they deserved each other. They were both a bunch of yappy, self-righteous pains-in-the-butt, always try to rope him into one of their do-gooder crusades. To heck with all of them! A plague on both their houses, as that overeducated wimp Banner might say.

He was mightily tempted, in fact, to just let them fight it out among themselves, but where was the fun in that? His knuckles itched to crack some super hero skulls. That dust-up with the robot had wrapped up too soon, and Ol' Shellhead had found another target for his wimpy repulsor rays. The Hulk felt his adrenaline flowing, feeding his perpetual pugnacity. Where did these costumed clowns get the nerve to cut him out of the action? Just thinking about it made him mad, and the madder he got . . .

"Hey, X-Vengers!" he bellowed, pounding his fists against his lime-green chest like a bellicose gorilla and raising a racket that could be heard over the Falls themselves. "Save a little stompin' for me!"

He crouched in the river, tearing out the knees of his tattered purple jeans, then used his impossibly over-muscled legs to break every single Olympic jumping record. He left the Falls far below him and catapulted into the clouds, forcibly inserting himself into the pitched battle between Iron Man and Storm. Repulsor rays tapped feebly against his ribcage while thunderbolts tickled the base of his spine.

"You call this firepower?" the Hulk called mockingly, his upward trajectory finally reaching its peak within spitting distance of both the mutant and the mechanic, who reacted to his abrupt arrival with expressions of utter surprise. Both of them looked like they'd seen better days; Storm's exposed flesh was nicked and scraped in places, while Iron Man had picked up a couple of nasty dents in his once snazzy chassis. These were the best the super hero world had to offer? Hah! The Hulk glanced down for just a second; the armed forces down below looked like toy soldiers from this height. Then he sneered at the airborne Avenger and X-Man, treating them to equal helpings of his colossal disdain. "Try a load of this on for size!"

As he had on the island, the Hulk clapped his gargantuan hands together with unfathomable force. The resulting shock wave momentarily cleared the brooding storm clouds, permitting a shaft of sunlight to shine through, and sent both Storm and Iron Man tumbling head over heels away from each other. The Hulk chortled boisterously at the sight of the two flying heroes twirling helplessly through the skies they'd thought they owned.

"Just call me Hurricane Bruce!" he hollered.

Too bad Wolverine's still AWOL, he grumbled silently. *Where in blazes is that scrappy little Canuck, anyway?*

Gravity belatedly called the Hulk back to earth, and he accelerated downward at roughly ten meters per seconds squared, arcing through the sky toward the wooded island where Captain America and Cyclops fought on behalf of their respective teams. Rebounding crimson beams formed a glowing cat's cradle between them. His emerald eyes alight with barbaric glee, the Hulk waited impatiently to touch down between the unsuspecting combatants.

Boy, were they in for a rude surprise!

A tremor shook the island. At first, Captain America thought that an earthquake had hit Niagara. Then he saw the colossal green figure at the center of a newly-formed crater at the tip of the small isle.

I should have guessed where that quake came from, he chided himself. Who needed earthquakes when the Hulk was around? The ill-tempered behemoth was a walking disaster area.

Cap stepped backward, giving the Hulk a wide berth while he waited to see what the Hulk would do next. So did Cyclops, who reined in his eyebeams, taken aback by this earth-shaking new development. The Hulk's cataclysmic arrival reminded Cap of a joke that had been old even when a young Steve Rogers had been growing up in Brooklyn during the Great Depression:

Where do you seat an eight-hundred-pound gorilla?

Anywhere he wants.

Like that hypothetical gorilla, the Hulk presented a vastly intimidating appearance. Contemplating Hulk's bestial visage, Cap found it hard to remember that he and the other Avengers had come to the Hulk in search of advice and information. There seemed to be nothing inside that grotesque green frame but unending hostility and paranoia.

If the Hulk is the best lead we have, then Wanda may have to rescue herself.

"Hulk!" he shouted, unwilling to give up while there was the slimmest chance for success. Perhaps, against all odds, the Hulk could be made to see reason. "We just want to ask you some questions. It may be a matter of life or death!"

Either the Hulk couldn't hear him or didn't care. Climbing out of the crater, he stomped toward Cyclops and Cap, his enormous fists swinging at his side. His bare feet left deep footprints in the muddy soil; the immense tracks made it look like Goat Island had hosted Bigfoot. The Hulk's baleful gaze swung back and forth between the two smaller heroes, his misshapen head turning slowly atop a neck that looked thicker than any tree trunk on the isle.

"Eeny-meeny-meiny-moe," he rumbled, louder than the Falls or Storm's deafening thunder, reaching the last syllable at the same time that his malignant gaze settled on Cyclops. "You lose, Cyke," he announced, then lunged at the mutant leader.

Cyclops fought back with his eyebeams, which shot from his visor before the Hulk took one step toward him. The beams barely slowed the Hulk, who waded through the coruscating red energy like it was nothing more than a stiff breeze. A backhanded slap sent Cyclops flying through the air, his crimson eyebeams trailing behind him like the tail of a comet. Looking on, Cap feared that Cyclops would be flung off the small island entirely, ending up in the raging river, but instead he smashed into the side of a tree with considerable force. His eyebeams shut off abruptly as his body crumpled onto the ground.

Is he out cold? Cap wondered. The sudden cessation of the crimson beams suggested that the X-Man couldn't keep his eyes open.

But the Hulk wasn't through with Cyclops yet. He stalked toward the downed mutant, smacking one of his huge fists into the palm of his other hand. From the look of him, Cap doubted that the Hulk intended to administer first aid to his vanquished foe; the Hulk's idea of CPR probably involved pounding the victim's ribs to powder, and then smashing what was left.

Not if I have anything to say about it, Cap resolved. It did not strike him as at all odd, or even ironic, to go to the aid of a man he had just fought to a standstill. No matter what the X-Man's motives were, however misguided they might be, nobody deserved to be beaten while they were down.

And the sooner the Hulk learned that, the better.

"Leave that man alone!" Cap yelled. He hurled his shield with all his strength and it flew like a discus at the back of the Hulk's head, bouncing off his thick skull. Cap reached out with a gloved hand and the shield slid back into his grip, a move that felt as natural to him as breathing. After fifty years of hard-fought combat, during which he had consistently refused to carry a gun, the shield had become more than just a tool; it was a part of him.

He never expected the shield to hurt the Hulk—a cruise missile couldn't do that—but he did hope to get the brute's attention, distracting him from Cyclops's fallen form. After that . . . well, Cap figured he'd cross that bridge when he came to it. Taking on an outraged Hulk was just a chance he'd have to take; after all, he hadn't gotten through World War II by playing it safe.

Bouncing the metal disk off the Hulk's cranium had the desired result. The Hulk looked back over his shoulder, glowering at Captain America, who pointed an accusing finger at the monstrous green giant.

"I always knew you were a savage, Hulk, but I never thought you were a bully. If you're so eager to smash someone, why don't you try someone who can fight back." Looking past the Hulk, Cap saw Cyclops stirring upon the mucky ground. Since he couldn't let the Hulk harm Cyclops before the X-Man had a chance to recover, Cap decided to throw his shield once more for good measure. The weapon sped through the air, on course to hit the Hulk right between the eyes.

Moving with surprising speed, however, the Hulk spun

around and caught the shield with both hands, his awe-some strength easily overcoming the projectile's momentum.

"Hah!" he chortled maliciously. "Lose your little toy, didya?" He held up the brightly-colored shield, inspecting it, then twirled it atop a salami-sized forefinger. "This antique belongs in the Smithsonian. Too bad it will never get there—in one piece, that is!"

The historic shield looked alarmingly small in the Hulk's ample hands. He grabbed the rim on both sides, clearly intending to bend the metal shield in two.

"Say good-bye to your Yankee Doodle Dandy," he taunted Captain America, who looked on silently, betraying not a sign of anxiety except for the narrowing of his eyes. Cap held his breath, crossing his arms atop his chest as he watched the Hulk test his matchless brawn against the ancient shield.

You may be surprised, he thought confidently.

As Cap expected, bending the shield, let alone breaking it, proved more difficult than the Hulk must have anticipated. Muscles that could easily tear apart an armored truck strained against the lightweight metal disk. Distended veins and tendons protruded beneath taut green skin. A painful grimace contorted the Hulk's face as he exerted ever more of his renowned super-strength, his face darkening to a deeper shade of green, with no discernible results.

Irresistible force that he was, the Hulk had finally met a genuinely immovable object. As far as Cap knew, no power on earth (or elsewhere) could damage his shield, which was composed of a unique experimental alloy whose exact composition had been lost for decades. S.H.I.E.L.D. had tried for years to duplicate the one-of-a-kind shield, but their best scientists had never succeeded at the task. Neither had Hydra, A.I.M., Zodiac, or any other terrorist group with access to too many brilliant minds and too much advanced equipment. Like the legendary Super-Soldier Formula that had first endowed Captain America with his extraordinary vigor and agility, the secret of his shield had disappeared into the hazy recesses of history. But the shield's phenomenal durability remained, as the Hulk was now founding out.

Huffing breathlessly, the tip of an emerald tongue protruding from the corner of his mouth, the Hulk slammed the shield down onto his knee, trying strenuously to break it over his leg. Overlapping layers of muscles rippled along his arms and across his shoulders as he hunched over the indestructible shield, refusing to accept defeat.

"This is impossible!" he snarled. "There's nothing I can't smash. Nothing!"

That's what the Axis powers thought, too, Captain America recalled, *but American ingenuity and perseverance proved them wrong.* If there was one thing he had learned over the years, it was something that tyrants and bullies almost never seemed to understand: that there was more to life than raw, naked power. *Maybe the Hulk will figure that out . . . someday.*

At the moment, the Hulk was just growing madder, and stronger, by the minute, but still the shield would not yield. Radioactive perspiration drenched his verdant flesh, and his mighty arms quivered with the unimaginable strain, yet the circular shield kept its shape. His huge knuckles turned greenish white where they pressed against the edge of the shield, until, releasing an enormous gasp, the Hulk abandoned his struggle, the shield looking just as pristine and undamaged as it had been when he first snatched out of the air.

"Get this miserable thing out of my sight!" he bellowed, his chest heaving, and cast the invincible shield into the sky. Cap's heart fell as he watched his trusty weapon fly out of reach, becoming nothing more than a faint red-white-and-blue speck against the dark gray storm clouds.

Tracking the shield's rapid ascent, he let his attention momentarily shift away from the frustrated Hulk. A potentially fatal mistake. Before he realized what was happening, a gigantic green hand came rushing at his face.

Careless! the Star-Spangled Avenger castigated himself a heartbeat before the hand hit him like a chartreuse meteor.

His boots lost all contact with the earth as the blow propelled him across the island, leaving him stunned and blurry-eyed. Even after he hit the ground, he kept moving at a bobsled clip, skidding on his back through the mud and the rocks, only his blue chain mail tunic keeping his flesh from being flayed to the bone. Finally, he slowed to a stop, his head still ringing from the blow. His jaw ached and a tooth felt cracked. He tried to focus, but dark spots encroached on his vision, nibbling away at the sky above him. He felt his consciousness slipping away . . . so that he was barely aware of the two vicious hands that roughly lifted his battered body from the mud and raised it high into the air.

As though from very far away, he heard the endless waters of Niagara crashing over the Falls.

"Good Lord," Colonel Lopez whispered, peering through his binoculars at the scene upon the island. He couldn't believe what he was seeing.

LOST AND FOUND

Captain America, the very embodiment of the American spirit, was clutched in the grip of the monstrous Hulk, who held the defeated hero high above his head, roaring in triumph. The Star-Spangled Avenger, who had defended liberty for as long as the veteran military man could remember, was stretched lifelessly between the Hulk's unnaturally enlarged fists. The colonel couldn't even tell if Cap was still alive.

He has to be! Lopez thought. *Captain America can't be dead. It's unthinkable!*

"Colonel," Lieutenant Russo said, equally transfixed by the heart-stopping drama unfolding before them. He lowered his own binoculars. "Isn't there anything we can do?"

I'm open to suggestions, the colonel thought. He started to open his mouth to reply, only to see something that stole his voice away.

All hope evaporated as the murderous Hulk, not content to brandish the fallen Avenger like a grotesque trophy, pitched Captain America off the island with the same force that he had hurled massive boulders less than half an hour ago. Lopez stared in utter horror as Captain America tumbled through the air toward the American Falls—and a gruesome death upon the rocks below!

Chapter Eleven

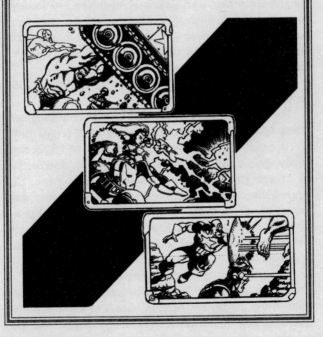

S nikt!

The sound of Logan's claws escaping their sheathes was the first indication Rogue had that her stricken teammate might be awaking from the coma her own powers had induced in him.

Thank goodness! she thought. Wolverine had been out cold for at least an hour or two, long enough for the heightened senses and healing abilities she had leeched from him to fade away. She'd been afraid that their faceless tormentor had done something terrible to Logan while he was in a weakened state, deprived of his special recuperative powers.

"Wolvie?" she called out, watching his lifeless face in the mirror. "Are you all right?"

For a long moment, he showed no sign of hearing her. Then his eyes snapped open, blazing with primal fury. Teeth bared, saliva streaming from his lips, he fought savagely against his bonds, with no better results than before. A savage growl sent shivers down Rogue's spine. His crazed appearance shocked her; even for Wolverine, who usually lived up to his fierce namesake, he looked positively loco, like a wild animal poked and prodded into a rabid frenzy. Rogue had seen hungry 'gators that looked more civilized.

"Logan!" she hollered, hoping to snap him out of it. "Can you hear me?" She tried to make eye contact with him in the mirror, but he didn't seem to know her. His claws sprang in and out of his clenched fists over and over again, like some sort of involuntary spasm. His fangs snapped at invisible foes. "Talk to me, Logan!"

"Wha—?" Finally, she seemed to get through to him. A hint of sanity returned to his bloodshot brown eyes. He stopped fighting against his restraints. "Rogue . . . is that you?"

His claws retracted into his hands and stayed there. Rogue breathed a sigh of relief. Logan was coming back to normal; she wasn't alone anymore. "Ah'm here," she assured him. "How you doin', Wolvie? You okay?"

The metal band across his throat kept him from nodding, but he managed to meet her eyes at last. "I think so," he said slowly, still a trace of a growl in his voice. "Sorry to give you a fright, kid. Nothin' personal. I was just . . . someplace else."

"The vat?" she guessed. Hellish memories of floating helplessly in that tank full of liquid, breathing through a respirator while molten adamantium poured into her bones, lingered in her mind. It seemed like a bizarre nightmare now. Had Wolverine actually endured that ghastly experience for real?

Judging from the somber look on his face, apparently so. "Picked up on that, didya?" he said gruffly. "My apologies, kid. That's nothing I'd want anybody else to go through." He glared angrily at the sterile test chamber surrounding them; Rogue decided she wouldn't want to be the guilty party behind these experiments when Wolverine got his claws into him or her. "This whole screwy setup reminds me too much of that other place—that's gotta be why you got hit with those particular memories. I keep having flashbacks to the bad old days." He gave himself a searching look in the mirror, perhaps taking note of his red-streaked eyes or the flecks of foam still clinging to his chin. "Can't say it's helping my self-control any."

Rogue couldn't blame him, not if he'd really suffered through the nightmare of the tank. She felt awful for invading his privacy, like she'd accidentally stumbled onto one of his most intimate and traumatic secrets. "Logan," she whispered sheepishly, "you know ah didn't want to do that to ya."

"We can spend the whole day apologizin' to each other, Rogue, and it won't get us any closer to findin' a way out here. From where I'm sittin', you got nothin' to be sorry for." A bushy black eyebrow lifted as another thought occurred to him. "Tell me the truth, kid. Did they test you the same way they tested me?"

"Uh-huh," Rogue admitted. How could she forget the blades slicing into her flesh, the red-hot laser stripping away her skin? The torture instruments had been powerful enough to overcome even her own natural invulnerability. Thanks to Logan's amazing healing powers, no scars or burns remained on her much-abused body, but the whole grisly exercise had been one of the most sadistic ordeals she'd ever had to endure. "It was pretty bad, as I guess you know, but it stopped when your healing factor went away."

"Sounds like we've both got some debts to settle," Logan said darkly. He looked past her to the sarcophagus to her right. "What about the Witch?" he asked. "How's she holding up?"

"Ah'm not sure," Rogue confessed. "They're doin' somethin' to her, ah think, but ah'm not sure what." The blindfolded Avenger had seemed caught up in her own private struggle ever since Rogue managed to shake off the last vestiges of Wolverine's personality and powers. "She just keeps whisperin' the same thing over and over.

Something 'bout keepin' away the black, whatever that means.''

Even now, Rogue heard the other woman chanting hoarsely, ''Not the black, not the black, not the black . . .'' The Scarlet Witch was obviously being subjected to some sort of ordeal. She was breathing hard, her chest heaving like she was running the last leg of a marathon. Her voice sounded exhausted. Rogue could smell her sweat and fatigue. ''Not the black, not the black . . .''

A momentary flash of resentment surged through Rogue. How come the Witch was getting off easy, with some sort of fancy psychological torture, while she and Logan got literally cut up and burned? Why did that snooty Avenger rate special treatment? The anger passed as Rogue realized she was reacting irrationally. It wasn't Wanda's fault that their unknown captors had reserved a different torment for her. Besides, whatever the Witch was going through right now, it was no picnic, that was for sure.

''See what you mean,'' Logan muttered, his ears lifting a tad. Recalling the extraordinary senses she had so recently borrowed, Rogue figured that Wolverine could smell and hear the Avenger's distress better than she could. ''Hey, Witch . . . Wanda!'' he shouted. ''You still with us?'' When she didn't answer, he called out again. ''Pagin' the Scarlet Witch. Sound off if you can.''

''Be quiet!'' Wanda yelled vehemently, acknowledging her fellow prisoners for the first time in hours. There was an unmistakable edge of desperation in her voice. ''Don't distract me!''

It was too late, however. The damage had been done. Wanda let out an agonized scream as her body convulsed; it looked to Rogue like the other woman was being electrocuted. The Witch's back arched as much as her restraints allowed, then she sagged limply within the wired sarcophagus.

"She's out cold," Logan pronounced. "I can tell by her heartbeat." Rogue figured that the electrifying shock, combined with exhaustion, had caused the mutant Avenger to pass out.

Even in her unconscious state, however, Wanda could not escape her trials. Her lips kept murmuring the same pitiful refrain, "Not the black, not the black . . ."

What did they do to her? Rogue wondered. *Whoever* they *are.*

She had only a few seconds to sympathize with the Scarlet Witch's cryptic plight before her own steel casket began moving again, this time toward the Witch instead of Wolverine. Rogue's sudden fears were confirmed when the right wall of the sarcophagus slid downward in tandem with the left wall of Wanda's coffin.

"No!" she protested loudly. "Not again! Not with her!" Not content to have forced Rogue to steal Logan's mind and powers, if only temporarily, their unknown jailers clearly now intended to have her absorb the Scarlet Witch's essence as well. Rogue flinched inwardly at the prospect. *Wanda already hates me for what I did to Carol Danvers,* she despaired. *Now I have to do the same thing to her!* She could only pray that the transference would not prove as permanent as it had in Ms. Marvel's case, but how could she prevent that when she didn't have any control over what was going to happen—and for how long?

Rogue had often wished for a mutant power she could turn on and off at will, like Storm or Iceman had. Hopelessly, she yearned for that impossible blessing again as concealed mechanisms carried her ungloved hand closer to the Scarlet Witch. The curved metal shell enclosing the Witch's left hand rolled to one side, revealing Wanda's five fingers resting within a hand-shaped depression; with the Avenger unconscious and unable to employ her mutant sorcery, the unseen experimenter had obviously judged it safe to partially liberate her hand, although a metal band still stretched across her slender wrist. Rogue knew too well the danger of exposing the Witch's warm skin to her own thirsty touch.

"Please forgive me," she pleaded as her hand brushed against Wanda's.

Their minds and memories merged, proving strangely compatible. Rogue found herself experiencing a sort of inward double vision, with faces and feelings from Wanda's past superimposed upon her own remembrances, two different lives intersecting and amplifying each other, like synchronized waves that meld together to create a single wave greater than the sum of its parts. . . .

Her name is Rogue/Wanda, and she still pines for the lost days of her idyllic childhood in the backwoods of Mississippi/the countryside of far-off Transia. Tragedy consumes that childhood one sunny afternoon/smoke-filled night, and she finds herself homeless and on the run, until Mystique/Magneto offers her refuge within the Brotherhood of Evil Mutants. The Avengers/X-Men become her enemies, which feels wrong somehow, even as she tests her newfound mutant powers in battle after pointless battle. The life of a super-villain unsettles her conscience, and in time she rebels against her ruthless mother/father, finding a new life with the X-Men/Avengers. A different kind of loneliness awaits her, though, as she loses her

*heart to an enigmatic thief/android whose flesh/soul she
can never truly touch.*

*Then the puppets/garments attack, pecking at her face
and suffocating her, and she wakes to find herself here,
entombed in a mechanized sarcophagus and subjected to
cruel and seemingly senseless experiments. Knives cut
her, lasers burn her, and a clicking white ball bounces
endlessly around a spinning disk divided into equal slices
of red and black. . . .*

"Not the black!" Rogue shouted as, in reality, a metal
visor slid into place above her eyes. Metal shells enclosed
her hands, immobilizing her fingers. In the darkness into
which she had been abruptly thrown, a virtual roulette
wheel began spinning before her eyes. A sibilant voice
whispered in her ears, but Rogue required no explanation
of the test ahead, all she needed to know had already been
extracted unwillingly from Wanda's recent memories. She
recalled the pain in store if she failed as vividly as if she
already experienced it many times before.

"Not the black," she repeated, unsure where Wanda's
memories ended and her own ordeal began. They all
blurred into a single continuous struggle to keep that accursed ball from landing in the wrong place. "Not the
black. . . ."

"Stop it!" Somewhere in the background, Wolverine
howled in rage, growling every syllable. "What you doing to her? Stop it, you heartless sleazes!" His words
sounded more like snarls with every moment, until she
could barely make out what he was saying. "Stop it—or
I'll tear your heart out!"

Who is he roaring at? she couldn't help wondering.
Who is on the other side of that mirror?

"Interesting," the Leader declared. "Very interesting."

Once, a lifetime and an identity ago, he had been merely Samuel Sterns, a common laborer making his way through a mediocre and uneventful life with only the limited intelligence and perceptions of any other human drone. Then a fortuitous accident exposed him to the transforming power of gamma radiation, expanding his brain and intellectual capacity until it became increasingly obvious, at least to his superlative awareness and understanding, that he had evolved into the destined master of the earth. On that day, Samuel Sterns had died, shed as readily as a monarch butterfly discards its humble chrysalis, and the Leader was born.

Now the mutated mastermind sat behind the one-way mirror, thoughtfully contemplating the unfortunate subjects of his current experiment. His enlarged cranium, swelling above his brow like an overinflated beachball, rested against the padded back of a futuristic metal chair. The bulbous lobes of his mega-brain were riddled with pulsating convolutions. Pale green skin, the sickly shade of some nocturnal fungus, marked him as a product of gamma radiation. Thin, bony fingers were tented above his lap as he watched the experiment progress, clad in a seamless orange labsuit not much different than those worn by his unwilling specimens. The control room was dimly lit, the better to provide an unencumbered view of the highly informative proceedings in the test chamber. The only illumination came from a lighted control panel that stretched before him like the keys of a grand piano. An elegant experiment such as this was like any great musical masterpiece, he reflected; both required a genius composer adept at both conception and execution.

Beethoven would be proud, he decided, as a recording of the German composer's Piano Concerto No. 5 played softly in the background. On the other side of the glass, three captured mutants displayed any number of intriguing behaviors and characteristics. *Yes, this is a true scientific symphony.*

"Note," he pointed out, with the slightly pedantic air of one who preferred delivering lectures to exchanging dialogue, "how the stress of his captivity is triggering an atavistic regression in the subject called Wolverine. The physical and/or psychological trauma appears to be inducing a marked devolution in the subject's personality, as the facade of civilization gives way to the barely-sentient animal at the core of his identity . . . not unlike a certain muscle-bound green primitive of my acquaintance." He stroked the thick black mustache above his lip, his sole concession to mundane vanity; in fact, it was the only body hair that still sprouted upon his body. "Interesting indeed."

"So you say," his partner said gruffly, standing in the shadows behind the Leader's chair. His voice was deeper and more guttural than the Leader's epicene tones. "For myself, I needed no further evidence that these primates are little more than beasts."

As though you are significantly more evolved, the Leader thought sarcastically. He did not bother looking at his belligerent and impatient ally, whom he privately considered his intellectual inferior. But, then again, who wasn't? As long as his new associate contributed resources that were useful to their cooperative enterprise, the Leader was willing to maintain the polite fiction of an equal partnership.

"In any event," the Leader stated, "our plans are developing precisely as I predicted.'' He consulted his wrist-watch, easily adjusting for the time difference between his present location and the probable whereabouts of his various pawns. *Ah, yes. Exactly time for the inevitable altercation.*

''Observe,'' he instructed.

A greenish-white finger pressed a touch-sensitive pad on the control panel. The transparent window before them turned into a large television screen, their view of the three prisoners hidden behind pirated satellite feed from CNN. The Leader nodded smugly, totally unsurprised by the live footage depicting a three-way battle between the Avengers, the X-Men, and his longtime nemesis, the Hulk.

''You see,'' he boasted. ''Right on schedule. As I calculated, the clues we left behind when your operatives appropriated our three subjects have drawn their various heroic peers into a pointless contest of arms, while simultaneously inconveniencing the Hulk as well.''

''You worry too much about that brute,'' his partner scolded. ''He is even less intelligent than the average human.''

''Never underestimate the disruptive efficacy of naked force and aggression,'' the Leader replied. His mood darkened as he recalled the innumerable instances when Banner and his monstrous counterpart had interfered with the Leader's plans for world domination; if not for the untamed violence of the Hulk, he would have long ago achieved all his grandest ambitions.

True visionaries have always been opposed by the mindless vandalism of the barbarian, he consoled himself. *The Hulk's persistent obstruction of my plans only con-*

firms my ultimate destiny as the precursor of a new age of enlightenment.

"I have learned through hard experience that the Hulk must always be factored into my computations." He gestured toward the screen. "This prearranged imbroglio will serve to keep the infernal creature busy while we continue with our preparations."

Besides, he admitted silently, *beyond all valid logistical concerns, there is an undeniable satisfaction to be found in making that misanthropic monster's life even more tumultuous and tormented than it is ordinarily.* Thankfully, the Leader was not so highly evolved that he couldn't appreciate the simple pleasure of revenge. *All the world is against you again, Banner. How delectable.*

The Leader savored the sight of the assorted heroes pitted against each other in a contest he provoked. Niagara, he decided, provided an attractive and enjoyably hazardous setting for such a diverting spectacle. "There's something to be said for gladiatorial entertainments," he commented, "especially when conducted amidst scenes of breathtaking natural splendor. I must remember to include a few such coliseums in any world of my devising."

On the screen, the Hulk tore the Vision asunder, then consigned his separate parts to the less-than-tender mercies of the plunging cataract.

Behind the Leader, his hard-to-please partner grunted in approval. "Good," he declared bluntly. "Not so long ago, that android came between me and an enemy of my people. I was unable to punish him for his impertinence then. It is well that he suffers now."

"Yes," the Leader agreed, glad that something had met with his surly confederate's approval; he was getting weary of hearing the other constantly complain. "It's a shame we can't count on them destroying each other completely, but the odds are dramatically against such a delightful resolution. Their innate heroism and foolish reverence for human life will doubtless prevent them from inflicting mortal injuries on each other, although, where the Hulk is concerned, you never can tell. He can be surprisingly ruthless when he wants to be, which is usually at the worst possible moment."

As if to prove the latter point, the camera zoomed in on the top of the Falls, where the Hulk appeared seconds away from hurling Captain America to his death. The Leader leaned forward in his chair, a malicious smile revealing his eager anticipation. Captain America was a relic of a bygone past; he had no place in the brave new world the Leader intended to create.

"Hmm," he said, "this looks like an unexpected bonus. Still, regardless of the final body count, all of Earth's super-powered defenders are living on borrowed time. Once our plans reach fruition, we will eliminate every one of our enemies from the face of the planet!"

He did not need to look behind him to know that his dour partner shared the same glorious vision. "But what if all these warriors join forces?" the other asked, his metaphorical cup half empty as usual.

"Not if, *when*," the Leader conceded. That, too, was inevitable; super heroes had a regrettable tendency to put aside their differences in the end. "Have no fear. That is where *you* assume a personal role in the saga I have scripted, one that will strike at the very heart of our mutual foes. . . ."

To be continued . . .

Greg Cox is the author of the Iron Man novels *The Armor Trap* and *Operation A.I.M.* In addition, he was the author of *Star Trek: The Q Continuum* trilogy as well as the coauthor of two *Star Trek* novels (the *Deep Space Nine* novel *Devil in the Sky* with John Gregory Betancourt and the *Next Generation* novel *Dragon's Honor* with Kij Johnson). Greg served as coeditor of two science fiction/horror anthologies (*Tomorrow Sucks* and *Tomorrow Bites* with T.K.F. Weisskopf), and he has also published many short stories, in anthologies ranging from *Alien Pregnant by Elvis* to *100 Vicious Little Vampire Stories* to *The Ultimate Super-Villains* to *OtherWere*. Greg lives in New York City.

George Pérez, one of the most renowned artists in comics, is best known for his stints on *The Avengers, Fantastic Four, Justice League of America,* and *The New Teen Titans* (which he also cowrote and coedited). Other noteworthy efforts include his work on *UltraForce, The Silver Surfer* (as writer), *Isaac Asimov's I-Bots, Sachs & Violens,* and *The Incredible Hulk: Future Imperfect.* He coplotted and drew *Crisis on Infinite Earths,* and wrote and drew the revamp of *Wonder Woman* (both for DC). Recently, George returned to the series that made his career, Marvel's *The Avengers,* where he collaborates with writer Kurt Busiek. George lives in Florida.

CHRONOLOGY TO THE MARVEL NOVELS AND ANTHOLOGIES

What follows is a guide to the order in which the Marvel novels and short stories published by Byron Preiss Multimedia Company and Berkley Boulevard Books take place in relation to each other. Please note that this is not a hard and fast chronology, but a guideline that is subject to change at authorial or editorial whim. This list covers all the novels and anthologies published from October 1994–January 2000.

The short stories are each given an abbreviation to indicate which anthology the story appeared in. USM=*The Ultimate Spider-Man*, USS=*The Ultimate Silver Surfer*, USV=*The Ultimate Super-Villains*, UXM=*The Ultimate X-Men*, UTS=*Untold Tales of Spider-Man*, UH=*The Ultimate Hulk*, and *XML=X-Men: Legends*.

If you have any questions or comments regarding this chronology, please write us.

Snail mail: Keith R.A. DeCandido
                 Marvel Novels
                 24 West 25th Street
                 New York, NY 10010-2710

E-mail: KRAD@IX.NETCOM.COM
                                —Keith R.A. DeCandido

X-Men & Spider-Man: Time's Arrow Book 1: **The Past [portions]**
by Tom DeFalco & Jason Henderson
   Parts of this novel take place in prehistoric times, the sixth century, 1867, and 1944.

CHRONOLOGY

"The Silver Surfer" [flashback]
by Tom DeFalco & Stan Lee [USS]
   The Silver Surfer's origin. The early parts of this flashback start several decades, possibly several centuries, ago, and continue to a point just prior to "To See Heaven in a Wild Flower."

"In the Line of Banner"
by Danny Fingeroth [UH]
   This takes place over several years, ending approximately nine months before the birth of Robert Bruce Banner.

X-Men: Codename Wolverine ["then" portions]
by Christopher Golden
"Every Time a Bell Rings"
by Brian K. Vaughan [XML]
   These take place while Team X was still in operation, while the Black Widow was still a Russian spy, while Banshee was still with Interpol, and a couple of years before the X-Men were formed.

"Spider-Man"
by Stan Lee & Peter David [USM]
   A retelling of Spider-Man's origin.

"Transformations"
by Will Murray [UH]
"Side by Side with the Astonishing Ant-Man!"
by Will Murray [UTS]
"Assault on Avengers Mansion"
by Richard C. White & Steven A. Roman [UH]
"Suits"
by Tom De Haven & Dean Wesley Smith [USM]

CHRONOLOGY

"After the First Death . . ."
by Tom DeFalco [UTS]
"Celebrity"
by Christopher Golden & José R. Nieto [UTS]
"Pitfall"
by Pierce Askegren [UH]
"Better Looting Through Modern Chemistry"
by John Garcia & Pierce Askegren [UTS]
  *These stories take place very early in the careers of
Spider-Man and the Hulk.*

"To the Victor"
by Richard Lee Byers [USV]
  *Most of this story takes place in an alternate timeline,
but the jumping-off point is here.*

"To See Heaven in a Wild Flower"
by Ann Tonsor Zeddies [USS]
"Point of View"
by Len Wein [USS]
  *These stories take place shortly after the end of the
flashback portion of "The Silver Surfer."*

"Identity Crisis"
by Michael Jan Friedman [UTS]
"The Doctor's Dilemma"
by Danny Fingeroth [UTS]
"Moving Day"
by John S. Drew [UTS]
"Out of the Darkness"
by Glenn Greenberg [UH]
"The Liar"
by Ann Nocenti [UTS]
"Diary of a False Man"
by Keith R.A. DeCandido [XML]

CHRONOLOGY

"Deadly Force"
by Richard Lee Byers [UTS]
"Truck Stop"
by Jo Duffy [UH]
"Hiding"
by Nancy Holder & Christopher Golden [UH]
"Improper Procedure"
by Keith R.A. DeCandido [USS]
"The Ballad of Fancy Dan"
by Ken Grobe & Steven A. Roman [UTS]
"Welcome to the X-Men, Madrox . . ."
by Steve Lyons [XML]

These stories take place early in the careers of Spider-Man, the Silver Surfer, the Hulk, and the X-Men, after their origins and before the formation of the "new" X-Men.

"Here There Be Dragons"
by Sholly Fisch [UH]
"Peace Offering"
by Michael Stewart [XML]
"The Worst Prison of All"
by C.J. Henderson [XML]
"Poison in the Soul"
by Glenn Greenberg [UTS]
"Do You Dream in Silver?"
by James Dawson [USS]
"A Quiet, Normal Life"
by Thomas Deja [UH]
"Livewires"
by Steve Lyons [UTS]
"Arms and the Man"
by Keith R.A. DeCandido [UTS]
"Incident on a Skyscraper"
by Dave Smeds [USS]

"One Night Only"
by Sholly Fisch [XML]
"A Green Snake in Paradise"
by Steve Lyons [UH]
   These all take place after the formation of the "new" X-Men and before Spider-Man got married, the Silver Surfer ended his exile on Earth, and the reemergence of the gray Hulk.

"Cool"
by Lawrence Watt-Evans [USM]
"Blindspot"
by Ann Nocenti [USM]
"Tinker, Tailor, Soldier, Courier"
by Robert L. Washington III [USM]
"Thunder on the Mountain"
by Richard Lee Byers [USM]
"The Stalking of John Doe"
by Adam-Troy Castro [UTS]
"On the Beach"
by John J. Ordover [USS]
   These all take place just prior to Peter Parker's marriage to Mary Jane Watson and the Silver Surfer's release from imprisonment on Earth.

Daredevil: Predator's Smile
by Christopher Golden
"Disturb Not Her Dream"
by Steve Rasnic Tem [USS]
"My Enemy, My Savior"
by Eric Fein [UTS]
"Kraven the Hunter Is Dead, Alas"
by Craig Shaw Gardner [USM]
"The Broken Land"
by Pierce Askegren [USS]

"Radically Both"
by Christopher Golden [USM]
"Godhood's End"
by Sharman DiVono [USS]
"Scoop!"
by David Michelinie [USM]
"The Beast with Nine Bands"
by James A. Wolf [UH]
"Sambatyon"
by David M. Honigsberg [USS]
"A Fine Line"
by Don Koogler [XML]
"Cold Blood"
by Greg Cox [USM]
"The Tarnished Soul"
by Katherine Lawrence [USS]
"Leveling Las Vegas"
by Stan Timmons [UH]
"Steel Dogs and Englishmen"
by Thomas Deja [XML]
"If Wishes Were Horses"
by Tony Isabella & Bob Ingersoll [USV]
"The Stranger Inside"
by Jennifer Heddle [XML]
"The Silver Surfer" [framing sequence]
by Tom DeFalco & Stan Lee [USS]
"The Samson Journals"
by Ken Grobe [UH]

These all take place after Peter Parker's marriage to Mary Jane Watson, after the Silver Surfer attained freedom from imprisonment on Earth, before the Hulk's personalities were merged, and before the foundation of the X-Men "blue" and "gold" teams.

CHRONOLOGY

"The Deviant Ones"
by Glenn Greenberg [USV]
"An Evening in the Bronx with Venom"
by John Gregory Betancourt & Keith R.A. DeCandido
[USM]
   These two stories take place one after the other, and a few months prior to The Venom Factor.

The Incredible Hulk: What Savage Beast
by Peter David
   This novel takes place over a one-year period, starting here and ending just prior to Rampage.

"Once a Thief"
by Ashley McConnell [XML]
"On the Air"
by Glenn Hauman [UXM]
"Connect the Dots"
by Adam-Troy Castro [USV]
"Ice Prince"
by K.A. Kindya [XML]
"Summer Breeze"
by Jenn Saint-John & Tammy Lynne Dunn [UXM]
"Out of Place"
by Dave Smeds [UXM]
   These stories all take place prior to the Mutant Empire *trilogy.*

X-Men: Mutant Empire Book 1: **Siege**
by Christopher Golden
X-Men: Mutant Empire Book 2: **Sanctuary**
by Christopher Golden
X-Men: Mutant Empire Book 3: **Salvation**
by Christopher Golden
   These three novels take place within a three-day period.

Fantastic Four: To Free Atlantis
by Nancy A. Collins
"The Love of Death or the Death of Love"
by Craig Shaw Gardner [USS]
"Firetrap"
by Michael Jan Friedman [USV]
"What's Yer Poison?"
by Christopher Golden & José R. Nieto [USS]
"Sins of the Flesh"
by Steve Lyons [USV]
"Doom²"
by Joey Cavalieri [USV]
"Child's Play"
by Robert L. Washington III [USV]
"A Game of the Apocalypse"
by Dan Persons [USS]
"All Creatures Great and Skrull"
by Greg Cox [USV]
"Ripples"
by José R. Nieto [USV]
"Who Do You Want Me to Be?"
by Ann Nocenti [USV]
"One for the Road"
by James Dawson [USV]

These are more or less simultaneous, with "Doom²" taking place after To Free Atlantis, *"Child's Play" taking place shortly after "What's Yer Poison?" and "A Game of the Apocalypse" taking place shortly after "The Love of Death or the Death of Love."*

"Five Minutes"
by Peter David [USM]

This takes place on Peter Parker and Mary Jane Watson-Parker's first anniversary.

CHRONOLOGY

Spider-Man: The Venom Factor
by Diane Duane
Spider-Man: The Lizard Sanction
by Diane Duane
Spider-Man: The Octopus Agenda
by Diane Duane
These three novels take place within a six-week period.

"The Night I Almost Saved Silver Sable"
by Tom DeFalco [USV]
"Traps"
by Ken Grobe [USV]
These stories take place one right after the other.

Iron Man: The Armor Trap
by Greg Cox
Iron Man: Operation A.I.M.
by Greg Cox
"Private Exhibition"
by Pierce Askegren [USV]
Fantastic Four: Redemption of the Silver Surfer
by Michael Jan Friedman
Spider-Man & The Incredible Hulk: Rampage (Doom's Day Book 1)
by Danny Fingeroth & Eric Fein
Spider-Man & Iron Man: Sabotage (Doom's Day Book 2)
by Pierce Askegren & Danny Fingeroth
Spider-Man & Fantastic Four: Wreckage (Doom's Day Book 3)
by Eric Fein & Pierce Askegren
Operation A.I.M. *takes place about two weeks after* The Armor Trap. *The Doom's Day trilogy takes place within a three-month period. The events of* Operation A.I.M.,

"Private Exhibition," Redemption of the Silver Surfer, *and* Rampage *happen more or less simultaneously.* Wreckage *is only a few months after* The Octopus Agenda.

"Such Stuff As Dreams Are Made Of"
by Robin Wayne Bailey [XML]
"It's a Wonderful Life"
by eluki bes shahar [UXM]
"Gift of the Silver Fox"
by Ashley McConnell [UXM]
"Stillborn in the Mist"
by Dean Wesley Smith [UXM]
"Order from Chaos"
by Evan Skolnick [UXM]
   These stories take place more or less simultaneously, with "Such Stuff As Dreams Are Made Of" taking place just prior to the others.

"X-Presso"
by Ken Grobe [UXM]
"Life Is But a Dream"
by Stan Timmons [UXM]
"Four Angry Mutants"
by Andy Lane & Rebecca Levene [UXM]
"Hostages"
by J. Steven York [UXM]
   These stories take place one right after the other.

Spider-Man: Carnage in New York
by David Michelinie & Dean Wesley Smith
Spider-Man: Goblin's Revenge
by Dean Wesley Smith
   These novels take place one right after the other.

CHRONOLOGY

X-Men: Smoke and Mirrors
by eluki bes shahar
> *This novel takes place three-and-a-half months after "It's a Wonderful Life."*

Generation X
by Scott Lobdell & Elliot S! Maggin
X-Men: The Jewels of Cyttorak
by Dean Wesley Smith
X-Men: Empire's End
by Diane Duane
X-Men: Law of the Jungle
by Dave Smeds
X-Men: Prisoner X
by Ann Nocenti
> *These novels take place one right after the other.*

The Incredible Hulk: Abominations
by Jason Henderson
Fantastic Four: Countdown to Chaos
by Pierce Askegren
"Playing It SAFE"
by Keith R.A. DeCandido [UH]
> *These take place one right after the other, with* Abominations *taking place a couple of weeks after* Wreckage.

"Mayhem Party"
by Robert Sheckley [USV]
> *This story takes place after* Goblin's Revenge.

X-Men & Spider-Man: Time's Arrow Book 1: **The Past**
by Tom DeFalco & Jason Henderson

X-Men & Spider-Man: Time's Arrow Book 2: **The Present**
by Tom DeFalco & Adam-Troy Castro
X-Men & Spider-Man: Time's Arrow Book 3: **The Future**
by Tom DeFalco & eluki bes shahar
These novels take place within a twenty-four-hour period in the present, though it also involves traveling to four points in the past, to an alternate present, and to five different alternate futures.

X-Men: Soul Killer
by Richard Lee Byers
Spider-Man: Valley of the Lizard
by John Vornholt
Spider-Man: Venom's Wrath
by Keith R.A. DeCandido & José R. Nieto
Spider-Man: Wanted Dead or Alive
by Craig Shaw Gardner
"Sidekick"
by Dennis Brabham [UH]
Captain America: Liberty's Torch
by Tony Isabella & Bob Ingersoll
These take place one right after the other, with Soul Killer *taking place right after the* Time's Arrow *trilogy,* Venom's Wrath *taking place a month after* Valley of the Lizard, *and* Wanted Dead or Alive *a couple of months after* Venom's Wrath.

Spider-Man: The Gathering of the Sinister Six
by Adam-Troy Castro
Generation X: Crossroads
by J. Steven York

X-Men: Codename Wolverine ["now" portions]
by Christopher Golden
  These novels take place one right after the other, with the "now" portions of Codename Wolverine *taking place less than a week after* Crossroads.

The Avengers & the Thunderbolts
by Pierce Askegren
Spider-Man: Goblin Moon
by Kurt Busiek & Nathan Archer
Nick Fury, Agent of S.H.I.E.L.D.: Empyre
by Will Murray
Generation X: Genogoths
by J. Steven York
  These novels take place at approximately the same time and several months after "Playing It SAFE."

Spider-Man and the Silver Surfer: Skrull War
by Steven A. Roman & Ken Grobe
X-Men and the Avengers: Gamma Quest Book 1: **Lost and Found**
by Greg Cox
X-Men and the Avengers: Gamma Quest Book 2: **Search and Rescue**
by Greg Cox
X-Men and the Avengers: Gamma Quest Book 3: **Friend or Foe?**
by Greg Cox
  These books take place one right after the other.

X-Men & Spider-Man: Time's Arrow Book 3: **The Future [portions]**
by Tom DeFalco & eluki bes shahar

CHRONOLOGY

Parts of this novel take place in five different alternate futures in 2020, 2035, 2099, 3000, and the fortieth century.

"The Last Titan"
by Peter David [UH]
This takes place in a possible future.